John Rawlings

# A History of the Origin of the Mysteries and Doctrines of Baptism

and the eucharist as introduced into the Church of Rome and the Church of

England

John Rawlings

**A History of the Origin of the Mysteries and Doctrines of Baptism**
*and the eucharist as introduced into the Church of Rome and the Church of England*

ISBN/EAN: 9783337382315

Printed in Europe, USA, Canada, Australia, Japan

Cover: Foto ©Andreas Hilbeck / pixelio.de

More available books at **www.hansebooks.com**

A

# History of the Origin of the Mysteries and Doctrines

OF

# BAPTISM AND THE EUCHARIST,

AS INTRODUCED INTO

THE CHURCH OF ROME AND THE CHURCH OF ENGLAND;

AND THEIR

## JEWISH AND HEATHEN ORIGIN

DELINEATED IN

PROFANE AND ECCLESIASTICAL HISTORY, GENERAL COUNCILS, CANON LAWS, AND
ECCLESIASTICAL CONSTITUTIONS, FROM THE DAYS OF THE APOSTLES TO THE
PRESENT TIME; AND COMPARED WITH THE SACRED SCRIPTURES
AS THE STANDARD OF TRUTH.

By JOHN RAWLINGS.

"Had I ten thousand gifts beside,
I'd cleave to Jesus crucified,
And build on Him alone;
For no foundation is there given
On which I'd place my hope of heaven,
But Christ the corner-stone."

LONDON:
ALFRED W. BENNETT, 5, BISHOPSGATE STREET WITHOUT.

1863.

# PREFACE.

THE accompanying work has been the labour of a life, the product of much thought and of forty years' patient and unwearying research. It has been also a labour of love, inasmuch as it is the object of the writer, at the close of a long and useful life, to present to others the arguments, unanswerable to his own mind, which have led him to see the unsoundness of a belief in the sacramental efficacy of Water Baptism and the Eucharist. In this belief he was himself brought up, and it is a portion of the creed of the Roman and Anglican Churches, and to a greater or smaller extent, of most forms of Protestant Dissent. He was thus led to the conviction of the scriptural soundness of the entire disuse of these ceremonies as taught by the Society of Friends, and by some obscure and so-called "heretical" sects of Early Christendom.

The writer does not lay claim to a favourable consideration of his labours on the ground of their originality. Although his own views and reflections are necessarily often expressed, he has been largely indebted for the facts on which these views are based, to others who have preceded him in the same field, and to the most trustworthy compilers of ecclesiastical history. It must be understood, also, that this remark does not apply merely to those passages which are placed in the text between marks of quotation as being given in the *ipsissima verba* of previous writers; but that in other portions of his work also, the conclusions of others are frequently merely connected together by the writer. The works of which most copious use has been made, are given in the accompanying list; but in all cases, where practicable, their quotations from still earlier

A 2

sources have been verified by going to the fountain-head itself, the writings of the "Fathers" of the Christian Church. The author does not hope for a reception of his work on any other ground than as presenting in a compendious form, which he believes has never been done before, a history of the gradual manner in which the doctrines referred to have crept into the Christian Church, and have exercised their baneful influence over the writings and teachings of even its most renowned and orthodox champions.

In conclusion, the writer would commit his labours to the careful attention of his readers, in the hope that they will find the tendency of the views he would wish to inculcate, is to " build up " the truth rather than to pull down and destroy it ; that as they throw off the shackles of a dependence on any mere outward forms and ceremonies, they will unite with his experience that they can lay hold with the more certain grasp on those great spiritual truths, in which consist the life and efficacy of the New Dispensation.

A. W. B.

# INTRODUCTION.

CHRIST appeared: He and his Apostles introduced the Gospel in its purity; and one of the very first attempts to corrupt it was made by Judaizing teachers, who were continually endeavouring to bring the Gentile believers under the yoke of the Jewish law of ceremonies. The principal teachers of this doctrine were Cerinthus and Carpocrates, who professed to interpret the Scriptures by the aid of philosophy, agreeable to Pythagoras and Plato. Thus the system of Judaized and philosophic Christianity gradually ripened into Gnosticism. A desire arose at this time on the part of many, to introduce something in the New Dispensation which might give occupation and profit to a numerous priesthood; this appears from history to have operated soon after the days of the Apostles in the rise of Cerinthianism and Clementinism.

Worldly policy in the priests was evidently one of the chief causes which in the outset, as well as ever since, acted as a hindrance to the reception of Christianity in its purity. It is plain from the very nature of the case, that the desires of worldly profit, or advantage of any kind—all considerations of supposed political expediency, must have been at first arrayed in opposition to the pure Gospel:—every part of the sacred narratives confirms this. The causes which began to operate in the days of the Apostles had much of this corrupting influence in later times: which it will be our task as historians to prove.

The one great object sought to be attained in the following pages, is to show the rise and continuous history of these errors; for if they are seen in their unfolding form of development, they immediately supply their own refutation. The antecedents of each error show the motives, not only of that error as it stands alone; but also the reason of other errors which become necessary to support those of hierarchism, baptismal regeneration, and the supposed Christian virtues derived from the eucharist.

The history is also designed to exhibit the phases through which Christianity has passed since the days of the Apostles, as to the doctrine of Baptism, the Eucharist, and other things most intimately connected with them; and to supply the reader with indisputable data, from which he may deduce such conclusions as shall appear to his own mind to harmonize with Scripture revelations, or otherwise. To contemplate these things, in connexion with their antecedents, is the only way of truthfully treating the subject. It is incumbent that we should mark the rise of the essential elements of the Grecian, Roman, and English hierarchy and their dogmas, as well as their combination. To omit a notice of these events, which exerted a plastic power on the ecclesiastical fabrics in all times, were as serious an error as the concealment of their character and results. Had these things been different, the Church of Rome and the Church of England, as they at present exist, would never have been. Under this conviction, our present course has been determined, and pursued; but throughout, we have desired that truth should be our polar-star; not only in an unobtrusive tract, if such a thing can be found, amid the violent contentions of party feeling, in the first, second, third, and fourth centuries; the time of Constantine; and in the Catholic Church before it became decidedly Romish; but also in the times of the Ancient Britons; the Anglo-Saxons; the Normans; the Plantagenets; the Tudors; the Stuarts; and the House of Hanover. This will portray personages and events most conspicuous in the corruptions of the Church; and the times and manners of their introduction. Truth, without sectarianism, we wish to be our motto; as our object is the exposition of error, and the establishment of Gospel truth, and to all who love it in sincerity, we respectfully commend our labours.

The greater portion of mankind take their prevailing notions of religion from existing laws and traditions, of the origin of which they know nothing; and of practices, of the foundation of which they are equally ignorant. These are the media through which they obtain their knowledge, if they have any. By these they estimate their obligations, and govern their conclusions; no matter how absurd, presumptuous, or contrary to Scripture; there are also some who will justify and maintain them, and aid in persecuting those who differ from them, even if it be the Hindu Trinity of Brahma, Vishnu, and Shiva, or Judaism, Paganism, or Mahomedanism.

Some of the following pages will be found to contain a concise compilation of the declarations of various Christians, as well as Heathens; and especially of those faithful reformers, who yielded up their lives in support of their conscientious convictions; and whose clear, but neglected testimonies, are adduced to confirm what we believe to be evangelical truth. Hence it requires a frequent and anxious recurrence to the pure principles of the religion of Christ, as set forth in the New Testament.

It is very possible, that in treating on so unpopular a subject as the one before us, some sentiments may be found to be inadvertently expressed in terms that are equivocal, or open to objection, to a traditional Christian; should such be the case, we must request from the reader a favourable construction of one part, by the general bearing of the whole; at the same time, always bearing in mind the doctrines and principles of Christianity, as laid down in the New Testament; where the Divinity, Sovereignty, and Priesthood of Christ, are set forth and defined.

If what we have written shall lead any to think, and to examine for themselves—to take their views not from tradition, but from Scripture,—we shall feel that we have not written in vain. There are within the limits of Christendom, more than twenty different views of those who participate in the " Lord's Supper," either in the meaning of the rite itself, the manner of its administration, or to whom, and by whose hands, it ought to be administered. A similar remark applies to the rites of " Baptism." If these discordant views were to be exemplified and placed side by side, they would present such a mass of error and contradiction, as is not often to be met with. In these days of Puseyite pretensions, when the obsolete dogma of sacramental efficacy is so extensively revived, the author feels assured that many Christians will feel an anxious desire to know what can be said against the perpetual obligation of ordinances, which have been, and are now, so extensively abused; and they will find this desire gratified, in the perusal of this history; where it is clearly and distinctly shown, that all ceremonies, or sacraments, under the Christian dispensation, are alien from its spirit. The history of those called sacraments, shows them to be partly Jewish, and partly Heathen, and not Christian ordinances appointed by Christ, to be observed in His Church. The author, therefore, submits the doctrinal points set forth in this history, in opposition to the traditions of various sects of religion, to the test of the Sacred Scriptures; and to the honest, unprejudiced inquirer after the mind of Christ and his Apostles, as unfolded therein.

What, then, is the course, we, as historians, should pursue, who believe the Bible, and disbelieve the legends and dogmas of the Catholic Church? Surely we should labour to detach the legend from the Bible; to sever the pseudo-sacred from that which is indeed sacred; and persuade men everywhere to turn away the ear from seducers, and listen to Him " who speaketh from heaven." This is the Author's purpose; to endeavour to induce his readers not to blend fables with sacred truth, and a blind credulity with intelligent conviction. An agreeable task—and a useful one!

It might seem as if there were already Church History enough in existence; and yet it may be asked, where is the one which gives contentment to a truly Christian mind, if well informed in this department of history? Where is the work that comes near the mark of excellence in the several points of fidelity, exactness, Christian feeling, and Christian truth? What seems to be needed is, not a continuous narrative of apostolical succession, and of a course of events which has so often been presented to the world; but a series of disquisitions on subjects, the most important in establishing Christian truth, and in reference to the faith and present position of the Christian community, and to its yet undetermined controversies, which exhibit a very dim reflection of evangelic truth.

Ought we not, then, to acknowledge the spirit and presence of the Lord, as set forth in the calm consistency of the Apostolic Writings? For the moment we step off from this sacred ground, what is it that meets us? We suppose it will be granted by all persons of intelligence and candour, that the writings of the " Nicene fathers," and the practices of the " Romish Church," are strikingly deficient in that practical discretion which distinguishes the Epistles of the canonical Scriptures and the doctrines therein contained. The early Nicene bishops did not enjoy that supernatural guidance which preserved the Apostles from falling into absurdities, or wandering into extravagances. On the contrary, at that critical era, the Nicene bishops lent their utmost endeavours to the work of urging forward what they should have checked and repressed. Paganism and Christianity had, in fact, become so intimately blended by the very means adopted for spreading the latter; that it was hard to draw the line of demarcation between the two in the Nicene age, as we shall endeavour to show. Well had it been for the Church in all ages, if the sacramental notions of Tertullian, Elxai, Clement, Victor, Cyprian, Chrysostom, Ambrose, and Augustine, embodied in their writings, had entered less into the formularies of the Church, to the total neglect of all the Christian principles laid down in the New Testament.

# LIST OF WORKS

PRINCIPALLY REFERRED TO AND QUOTED FROM.

THE FAITHS OF THE WORLD. By James Gardner. 2 vols.

BINGHAM'S ANTIQUITIES OF THE CHRISTIAN CHURCH.

COOPER'S FREE CHURCH OF ANCIENT CHRISTENDOM.

ALTAR SINS. By Edward Muscutt.

A TREATISE CONCERNING BAPTISM AND THE COMMUNION. By Thomas Lawson. 1703.

THE DOCTRINES OF HEATHEN PHILOSOPHY COMPARED WITH THOSE OF REVELATION. By Joseph Priestly.

CHRISTIAN BAPTISM, SPIRITUAL, NOT RITUAL. By R. Macnair.

SCHLIEMANN'S DIE CLEMENTINEN.

NEANDER'S CHURCH HISTORY AND PLANTING OF CHRISTIANITY.

EUSEBIUS'S CHURCH HISTORY AND LIFE OF CONSTANTINE.

DUPIN'S ECCLESIASTICAL HISTORY OF THE FIRST SIXTEEN CENTURIES.

AND MANY OTHERS.

# CONTENTS.

## CHAPTER THE FIRST.

### BAPTISMS AND LUSTRATIONS OF JEWISH AND HEATHEN ORIGIN.

PAGE

SECTION I.—The Jewish or Heathen lustrations or baptisms as practised at the Advent of Christ, in the Oriental nations as well as the Jewish, and by the authority of the State—The followers of Christ held in contempt by the Jews and Pagans—The Christians put to death by them for refusing to conform to their worship—Religious ablutions or baptisms general among Jews and Heathens—Their gods not to be approached without sprinkling—The order of the priesthood and their traditions treated with great respect—Children dedicated to God by lustration or baptism all over the Grecian and Roman empires—The rise of the hierarchy of priests—The Gnostic heresy—Their separation from the Nazarenes—Their attempt to model Christianity according to their own ideas and tendencies, all proceeding from Heathen philosophy .............................. 1-13

### INTRODUCTION OF HIERARCHICAL DOCTRINES INTO THE CHRISTIAN CHURCH.

SECTION II.—The Christian Church had a separate existence from philosophy—The rise of the Catechetical School of Alexandria—The origin of the Monarchian Controversy—The proceedings of Victor, Callistus, and Cœcilius Natalis—The rise of the Hellenists—The source from whence the hierarchical ideas of the Catholics were derived—This the source from whence the Church of Rome received her hierarchical ideas and sacramental dogmas—And hence brought Christendom into bondage to the prelates ................................................. 13-21

THE ESTABLISHMENT OF THE "CATHOLIC CHURCH" BY CONSTANTINE
AND THE COUNCIL OF NICE.

PAGE

SECTION III. — The Catholic Church as it was established by
Constantine—Its dogmas—The Nazarenes and Novatians separated from them—Their persecutions—All other sects tolerated
—The precedence given to the Catholic Church—Penal laws
enacted against others—The Church of Christ not identical
with any society of men united together with outward symbols
—But united by the Spirit of God—Christ the only Mediator... 21-35

## CHAPTER THE SECOND.

### INTRODUCTION OF BAPTISMAL AND EUCHARISTIC RITES INTO THE RELIGION OF CHRIST ;—INTO THE BRITISH CHURCH.

Baptism put on an equal footing in point of dignity to that of
the Pagans—Origen and Cyprian—Christianity transformed
into a mixture of philosophic Paganism and Judaism in the
"Catholic Church"—The emperor of the world called a
Christian—Popery introduced into England by Austin—Two
synods summoned there — Obedience to the Roman See
required—The same rejected—Conflicts between Rome and
British Christians ensue—Rome rules supreme—The ancient
Christianity annulled—The dogmas now first introduced into
the English Church—The first English law on baptism—
Fines imposed—Baptism performed according to Roman canon
law—These laws confirmed by King Alfred—The different
kingdoms of the Heptarchy all embrace the views of Austin
and the pope—Consecration of water in baptism—Special
reasons set apart for baptism—The manner of preparation
for it—The white garment after baptism—Fines to enforce
baptism—Fires burn heretics who refuse the eucharist—
Christianity crippled and its purity corrupted .................. 36-53

## CHAPTER THE THIRD.

### THE SEVEN SACRAMENTS OF THE ROMISH CHURCH.—BAPTISMAL REGENERATION A DOCTRINE OF THE ENGLISH CHURCH.

Religion deemed to consist in outward acts and ceremonies—
Two Sacraments allowed to remain at the Reformation—
Fatal delusions connected therewith — The human mind

PAGE

naturally superstitious—Great diversity of opinions on the Sacraments and their effects—The Scripture definition of baptism—Baptismal regeneration maintained by the Church of Rome and the Church of England—The Scriptures furnish no ground for such a belief—The doctrine finally settled in England by the Common Prayer Book of Charles II. and the Act of Uniformity—The doctrine founded on tradition—Received from the Alexandrian School, &c.—The necessity for the baptism of infants not an early doctrine of the Church—Man fallen—Redeemed through Christ alone ...... 54-77

## CHAPTER THE FOURTH.

### THE DOCTRINES OF WATER BAPTISM INVESTIGATED.

Conflicting opinions respecting water baptism—Baptism not a substitute for circumcision—Forms and ceremonies sanctioned under the Levitical law—Not so under the Gospel—Gospel baptism spiritual—Misapprehensions concerning it—These considerations deeply momentous to Christians— John the Baptist the last prophet of the legal dispensation—His baptism a figure of the baptism of Christ with the Holy Ghost —No mortal ever regenerated by "christening" with water — This the opinion of various sects of the early Christians, and others since—The Apostles sent out into the world to teach Christ crucified and the resurrection—Paul went out to convert the Gentiles, not to baptize with water, but into the name (power) of the Father, Son, and Holy Ghost—True faith is baptism into God's name—Saul of Tarsus, Lydia of Thyatira, and the day of Pentecost, are instances of this—To be baptized into Christ is to have Christ spiritually living in us—Paul's epistles written purposely to dissuade from ritualism—True Protestantism the renouncing of all human ceremonies—The English Church does not resemble primitive Christianity .................................................................... 78-121

## CHAPTER THE FIFTH.

### WHAT IS MEANT BY BAPTISM IN THE NEW TESTAMENT?

Conflicting views thereon—The subject far from being settled— Before they are ended a deeper question must be investigated—Is it a Christian institution ? Christ's baptism is in

PAGE

all cases the baptism of the Spirit—A new dispensation
called the kingdom of heaven—This the exaltation of his
power and glory—Paul under the influence of the Spirit of
Christ preached Christ crucified, unto the Jews a stumbling-
block, and to the Greeks foolishness—Things which are
despised hath God chosen—Jewish, rites and heathen philosophy were mixed up with Christian realities—A distinction
between the baptism of John and the baptism of Jesus—
Water baptism in condescension to the prejudices of the Jews
and Greeks—Cannot claim a Divine sanction.................... 122-130

## CHAPTER THE SIXTH.

### CANON AND STATUTE LAWS CONCERNING THE EUCHARIST.

Religious rites clothed with a secret grandeur and mystery —
Strong prejudices in favour of Water Baptism and the Eucharist—Regarded as a sacrifice—Cyril, Ambrose, and Chrysostom teach baptismal regeneration and the real presence in
the eucharist—This traced to a desire to accommodate themselves to the converts from heathenism—This the grand
doctrine of Gregory and Austin which they brought into
England—Ine's sacramental test the first in England—the
communion imparts a higher sanction to an oath—Eucharistic
errors receive consolidation from Ecbriht's and Cuthbert's
laws—Laymen to purge themselves twelve days before they
partake of the eucharist—Giving the eucharist at Easter—
This borrowed from paganism—King Alfred's curious Law
concerning the eucharist—Elfric's laws broached in canonical
form respecting transubstantiation—The edict of Ethelred—
The laws of William the Conqueror respecting the eucharist
—The host obtains a pre-eminence above other sacraments—
The eucharist the Lord's body, a sacrament, the sacrifice of
a sacrament—Non-communicants not to enter the Church or
have Christian burial—The burning of heretics—None allowed
to dispute the things determined on by the Church—All to
assist in destroying heretics—The Constitutions of Arundel
—The Six Article Act................................................. 140-178

## CHAPTER THE SEVENTH.

### THE TRUE LORD'S SUPPER.

PAGE

The commencement of the new life is regeneration with the Holy
Ghost—Sometimes expressed in figurative language—Words
only useful as conveyors of meanings—The Jewish passover
commemorative of a great deliverance—Christ associated
it with the sacrifice of Himself on the cross—With the idea
of the nourishment of his body spiritually—The Levitical
ceremonial law imposed till Christ came—Transubstantiation
a prominent doctrine of the Church of Rome and the Church
of England—This has no other origin than the Pagan superstitions of Greece and Rome at the advent of Christ............ 179-196

## CHAPTER THE EIGHTH.

### CHRISTIAN COMMUNION SPIRITUAL NOT SACRAMENTAL.

A proneness to sin in all men, and yet a divine principle in all
men—A State-church not conducive to Christianity—Hierarchism, Rationalism, Christianity, the three religions of the
day—The doctrine of apostolical succession—Not sustainable
from Scripture—The conversion of Paul a proof of direct
divine revelation—The modern sacramental doctrines analogous to paganism—Salvation depends, not on eating and
drinking, but on faith in Christ—True communion as set
forth in the Scriptures—Conclusion .............................. 197-217

# THE

# ORIGIN OF THE MYSTERIES AND DOCTRINES

## OF

# BAPTISM AND THE EUCHARIST.

## CHAPTER I.

### SECTION I.

#### BAPTISM AND LUSTRATIONS OF JEWISH AND HEATHEN ORIGIN.

In writing a history of Baptism and the Eucharist, the query naturally arises, do the Christian churches generally entertain sound Scriptural views respecting them? Such an inquiry is forcibly suggested by the controversies which arose in the time of the Apostles, and have been carried on ever since; controversies by which many are confirmed in the belief that neither the Church of Rome nor the Church of England, nor many others, take a sound Scriptural view of the subject.

At the time of our blessed Lord's advent, the Jews and heathens were very strict in their observance of lustrations and ablutions as a purification from all defilements. This was the custom from very early times. Among the ancient pagan Greeks and Romans, their sacrifices were generally accompanied by lustrations, which were performed by sprinkling water with branches of laurel and olive. Many ceremonies were used at this time to initiate the people into the Jewish and pagan mysteries; and ablution, lustration, and sprinkling among the rest.

There was an ordinance of the law of Moses, an abuse of which seems clearly to have given rise to the washings and purifyings of the Jews, which were called baptisms: this connexion became familiar to Jewish minds, being a connexion between the washing with water of Jewish converts, and a separation from everything unclean to the peculiar service of God.   (See Numbers xix.)   Hence we perceive the close analogy between the washings of the Mosaic law, and the traditional washings of the Jews in case of proselytism.

From the remotest periods among the Jews, as well as among other oriental nations, divers washings were practised as symbols of inward purification; some of them being expressly enjoined by the law of Moses, and others sanctioned by the traditions of the elders.   We are not left to mere inferential reasoning on the point of Jewish baptism of proselytes.   The ancient Jewish writers explicitly affirm, that every convert to their faith was received by baptism.   The Babylonian Talmud, indeed, declares that " a person is not a proselyte until he is both circumcised and baptized."   The same doctrine is taught by the Jerusalem Talmud.

Under the law of Moses, washing was a judaical ceremony as well as circumcision ; for, according to the account of Maimonides (Vide John Luesden, Philo. Hebre Dissertat. 21 de Proselyt., sec. 1, p. 144) " A Gentile who would be received into outward covenant with the Jews, must be washed or baptized as well as circumcised, whereby he became a proselyte."   Whence it evidently appears that baptism did not come either into the Jewish or into the Christian Church to answer the purposes of circumcision, as hath been often urged to persuade the ignorant.

Under the dispensation of the Levitical law, outward modes of purifying were sanctioned by Divine authority; various sacrifices, washings, sprinklings, separations, and anointings, were used for legal purgations : and were, with other ceremonies of that typical system, tokens, signs, and symbols of corresponding spiritual operations in these Gospel days.

The various pagan religions of Greece and Rome at the advent of Christ were all ceremonial, as well as that of the Jews, and all connected with the State, and endowed by the State, and patronized by the philosophers. The Athenians, as well as other nations, adopted the ceremonies and the worship of other gods than Jupiter; but this worship must be sanctioned by the authority of the State; and at Athens it was done by the authority of the court of Areopagus. Nor can we wonder at this, since it was considered in all heathen countries that the prosperity of the State depended upon the observance of the religious rites sanctioned by the founder of the respective States. (See Priestley on Heathen Philosophy, p. 13.)

It was the opinion of the heathens, as well as the Jews, from the earliest to the latest times, that it was right, and even necessary, to adhere to the religion of their ancestors, since the prosperity of the State was thought to depend upon it. On this principle, absurd and groundless as it was, the wisest of the heathens acted. It was on this principle that Marcus Antoninus, Trajan, and other Roman emperors, wished to exterminate the Christians, in order that the rites of the ancient religion might not grow into disuse, to the endangering of the State. "It is every man's duty," says Epictetus (sec. 31), "to make libations, to offer sacrifices, and firstfruits, according to the custom of his country, not sordidly or negligently." (See Priestley, p. 195.)

The probability is, that Marcus Antoninus, Trajan, and other heathen emperors, held the Christians in too great contempt to make any proper inquiry into their religion, or to read their writings. Marcus Antoninus "had learned," he said (Lib. i. sec. 6), "of Diognetus, not to spend his time about trifles, nor to give credit to those who deal in enchantments, and exorcisms, and other impostures of that nature." And being under the influence of the Greek philosophers, and taking all his lessons from them, he was taught to believe that all the miracles the Christians pretended to as the foundation of their religion, were no better founded than the enchantments and exorcisms to which many of the heathens pretended. So educated and instructed, he could have no proper idea of the faith and hope of the Christians ; with this excellent religion he was unacquainted ; and from his pride as a philosopher and emperor, which is evidenced in his writings, it is sufficiently conspicuous that his contempt of the new doctrine of the Christians, who made no account of his philosophy or imperial power, and his zeal for the welfare of the empire, at the head of which he was placed, and on which his glory depended, and in which the Christians refused to join, were very great.

Had Marcus Antoninus, Trajan, and other heathen emperors, been acquainted with the Christian religion, they would not have called their non-conformity to heathenism *obstinacy*, because it had a natural and real foundation under the New Dispensation. But they, like Plato, had their dread of innovations in matters of religion, as we learn from Plato's *Epinomis*, where he says, " A legislator of the least understanding will make no innovations, and take care not to turn his State to any other mode of worship, or dare to remove what his country has established by law or custom concerning sacrifices, &c., for he knows that no mortal can come at any certainty with respect to these matters." Here we see in Plato, as well as Socrates, and the people of Athens, the strong attachment the heathens had to the rites of their ancient religions : to disregard them and adopt others was punishable with death, even if it was only a refusal to worship their god Jupiter, or adopt their ablutions. No Jew or Christian could appeal with more confidence to the justice and equity of the True God, than the heathens did to their Jupiter and their ablutions.

From the earliest time ablution (or lustration) has been practised as a religious ceremony, intended to denote inward purity. The Egyptians, as we are informed by Herodotus 450 years before Christ, made use of ablution as a sacred rite from the most remote antiquity. It formed a part of the religion of the Syrians also.

It is allowed on all hands that there is, and always has been, a similarity of religious rites among heathens and Jews; and that the temples of idols have had some ceremonies resembling those of the Jews. Some authors think that the founders of the pagan religion incorporated into their superstitious ceremonies some rites borrowed from the Jews. Others suppose that Moses took some pagan ceremonies, and incorporated them into the service of the Jews.

Of all the religious ceremonies among Jews and Pagans, that of ablution, or washing with water immediately before worship, is the most general, and its performance the most obvious. The Egyptians, the Greeks, the Romans, and all Pagans, had divers washings; hence Homer (Iliad), in the ninth century before Christ, represents Hector as afraid to offer a libation to Jove before he had washed his hands. He makes Telemachus wash his hands, and Penelope her clothes, before they prayed to the gods. (Homer, in Odyss.)

In after times, when superstition had multiplied gods, so that in Greece alone there were 30,000 (Hesiod, Op. et Dier., Lib. i. 250); when the superior gods were approached, the worshippers washed themselves all over; when sacred rites were performed to the inferior gods, a sprinkling sufficed. (Virgil, Æn. ii., 719.) None of the gods were approached without sprinkling, washing the hands, or the whole body. For these purposes, a vessel of clean water was placed at the entrance of the pagan temples. A priest in waiting sprinkled those who went to worship three times with boughs. (Plin. Nat. Hist. v. 30; Sozom. Hist. Eccl. vi. 6; Æn. vi. 229; Ovid. Metam. vii. 2.) And a written order was fixed to the porch of the temple, that no man should proceed further without washing. (See Potter's Greek Antiquity.)

The heathens, at length, not content with this simple expressive rite, multiplied religious ablutions to excess. The Egyptian priests washed themselves four times a-day. (Herodotus ii. 37.) Egypt for ages before Christ was the land of symbols. What country then bids so fair for the union of Paganism and Christianity as Egypt? and what place in Egypt so likely as the catechetical school of Alexandria the capital? Here, catechumens trained for baptism are supposed to be an order of Christians coeval with the Apostles. But, be it remembered, that even professed Christians had no schools of philosophic science before that at Alexandria, established by the heathen philosophy of its priests; and no order of catechumens before that school transformed baptism into a mystery.

The whole order of this priesthood, and their traditions, were treated in Egypt with the greatest respect, and they were thus enabled to exercise great influence over the people. The chief cause of this ascendancy is to be attributed to the mysteries of their religion, which were carefully concealed from the great mass of the community, and revealed only to the favoured few, in order to throw a halo of glory around them. These mysteries of the Egyptians, like the Eleusinian mysteries among the Greeks, consisted of two degrees, usually termed the greater and the lesser. The privilege of institution into the greater mystery was reserved for the priest alone. (See Faiths of the World, by James Gardner, M.D. and A.M.; Fullarton's ed., vol. i., p. 801.)

Other heathen nations went into greater extremes: they washed or sprinkled not only men, but all utensils of worship, sometimes their fields, often their houses, and annually their gods. (See Ovid. Fast. iv.; Tert. De Bapt., cap. v.) The Romans, also, had a general lustration every five years, when they lustrated, baptized, or sprinkled all the Roman people. (Varro, De Re Rust., Lib. ii. c. i.; Tacit., Lib. iv.)

It is a fact, that the dedicating children to God by lustration, or baptism, was first heard of in Africa. There were no schools of catechumens or infant baptisms before the school of Alexandria transformed what they called Christianity into a mystery consonant to Paganism, which grew in the third century into creeds, establishing the clergy, their dogmas, and the lay and catechumen state of the people; and so went on in the following century, till it ripened into a systematic divinity, of which the matter was furnished by Plato, and the manner was taken from Aristotle. (See Budei Isagog., tom. i., Lib. Pastor, cap. i.)

This tended to defeat the great end for which Christ came into the world.

From the effects ordinarily ascribed to baptism in the " Catholic Church," established at Carthage and its vicinity in the second and third centuries, through the influence of the Alexandrian school, it would seem that the ceremony is as much of heathen as Jewish origin. And no remark is more common among Catholic writers, than that there is a striking resemblance between baptism as it is administered by the " Catholic Church," and the lustration of infants as it was practised by Pagans. (See Ludovici Pratei natæ in Persii; Satir. 2, ver. 3 ; Rodolphi Hospiniani de Templis, Lib. ii., cap. 25.) Hence they very often call baptism lustration. In general, pagan lustrations were an initiation into mysteries. (Jo. Laur. Moshemi Hist. Tartaror. Eccles., p. 194.) In Greece, infants were lustrated on the fifth day after their birth. (Plauti Truculent., Act. ii. Scen. 4.) The Romans performed the ceremony on female children on the eighth day, and on males on the ninth. (See Pompeii Testi. et M. Verii Flacci, Macrobii, Saturn. Lib. i., cap. 16 ; Plutarchi Quæst. Rom. cii.) The primitive Christians, that is, the followers of Christ and his apostles, looked on lustration or baptism with abhorrence, and deemed it a sort of magic, and preached and wrote against it ; but a habit so ancient and inveterate was not easy to be eradicated. (See Lomiier, cap. xxxix. ; Theodosiano, Lib. xvi. Tit. 2.)

The sprinkling of infants was an article of pagan mythology in Africa long before the Christian era ; and it is traced by antiquarians, from monument to monument, on Roman and Etruscan remains, till it hides itself in the depths of the most remote antiquity. (See Gorii Museum Florentiæ, 1737, tom. ii., tab. clxxii. ; and Grævii Thesaur. Antiq. Romanor., tom. v.)

It is also certain that this notion of dedicating children to God by baptism, or lustration, is found all over the Roman empire in the second and third centuries in the " Catholic Church." Fidus, a bishop full of judaism and heathenism, applied the doctrine of circumcision to the case of baptism, or lustration, at eight days.

Cyprian thought that if it was necessary at eight days, it was so as soon as an infant was born. In perfect agreement with every circumstance of *this* time, the Alexandrian tutors are to be accounted the true parents of the custom of infant baptism in the " Catholic Church," as a symbol of that mystical birth, into which converts by baptism or lustration had been born again, as Clement explains at large in his Pædagogue, and as Jerome, African councils, and others of later date, expressly affirm. (See Pædagogue, Lib. i. cap. vi.; Hierom in Esai., iv. 1; Lac. significat: Conc. Carthage, 3, Can. xxiv.; Tertul. cont. Marcion, Lib. i. cap. xiv.)

Origen about this time came in from the philosophical school of his master Ammonius, and endeavoured to form a coalition of all sects, pagan and Christian, out of which proceeded a multitude of evils, and among the rest the seeds of Egyptian symbols; and the Spartan education grew and ripened into an hierarchical aristocracy, (see Mosh. Eccl. Hist., vol. i., cent. 2, part 2, chap. 1, s. 12,) and the natural effect followed; the pupil became a Pedagogue, the Pedagogue a bishop, the bishop an archbishop, the archbishop a patriarch, the patriarch a general, able at the head of an army of monks to resist the governor of Alexandria, to destroy the synagogue of the Jews, dethrone true Christianity, and dispute empire with Roman emperors themselves. (See Du Pin, Bibliot. Sièc. v. St. Cyrille d' Alexandrie.) Such were the fruits of transforming Christianity into philosophy, and of converting the Pedagogue into a Pædo-baptist, in order to wash away original sin.

The Brahmins are said still to baptize with this view at certain seasons in the Ganges, to the water of which they ascribe a cleansing and sanctifying quality: and hence it is that people flock from all parts, even of Tartary, in expectation of being thus eased of their sins. On this point many professed Christians seem to have gone beyond the folly of the heathens. The doctrine of the total remission of sins, and regeneration by baptism, could not fail, therefore, to scandalize many among the heathens, and to furnish the apostate Julian with an occasion of ridiculing Christianity; "who," says he, "is guilty of rapes, murder, sacrilege, or any abominable crime, let him be washed with water, and he will become pure and holy." (See Encyclop. Brit., vol. iv., p. 425, 8th edit.)

The different opinions which have been entertained concerning baptism and its effects would be endless to enumerate. The early Gnostics exalt the power of baptism, holding that by it sin is entirely taken away—that it absolutely confers grace *ex opere operato*. Some also speak of an indelible character impressed in the soul by it, called *character dominicus*, and *character regius*. But from whom did they receive this idea?

This Gnostic heresy arose among a sect of the Jewish Christians who existed in Palestine and other parts of the East in the first century. Cerinthus,* and Carpocrates,† an Alexandrian by birth, are said to have founded the sect of the Gnostics,‡ in the forming of which a prominent part was taken about A.D. 105, by Elxai, who founded a sect in Palestine by adulterating Christianity with the principles of the Essenes, who regarded

* Cerinthus, who received his training in the school of Alexandria, was the first who taught the system of Judaizing Christianity in Asia Minor, which gradually ripened into Gnosticism. He was, in fact, one of the first who taught a regular system of heresy after the Apostles' times, and paved the way for Elxai the Ebionite. (See Faiths of the World, vol. i., pp. 489, 490.) He is supposed to have been a disciple of Simon Magus. He was a man of loose and pernicious principles, endeavouring to corrupt Christianity by many damnable errors. (See Epiphan. Hæres. 28, p. 53 ; Caius apud Euseb., L. iii., c. 28, p. 100.)

† Carpocrates formed an ascetic sect similar to the Essenes among the Alexandrian Jews, who exercised a servile attachment to ceremonies.

‡ The rise of the Gnostic sects is to be traced to the prevalence of a theoretical spirit, which sought to solve all the great problems of religion by mere human speculation. The systems of thought which were thus to account for all difficulties, and to explain all mysteries, were themselves complicated in their nature, being composed of elements drawn from the Platonic philosophy, Jewish theology, and old Oriental theosophy. It is impossible, even cursorily, to examine Gnosticism in the diversified aspects it assumed, without being at almost every point reminded of the old pagan religious systems of Asia, Parsism, Brahmanism, and Budhism. (See Faiths of the World, vol. i.. p. 977, Gnostics.)

ceremonies, and exercised a servile attachment to them.
Epiphanius (Hær. 19, s. 1) "assigns the reign of Trajan as the
period when Elxai founded a sect in Palestine by adulterating
Christianity with the principles of the Essenes, when an
organized society of godless error began to be formed in opposition to the hitherto virgin church of Jerusalem; when the
heretical spirit which till then had lurked in secret began to
show itself in open front." (See also Euseb. H. E. iii., 32.) Elxai
(as well as the Gnostics) laid great stress upon baptism, to
which he attached, *ex opere operato*, the forgiveness of sins. (See
Schliemann, p. 226; and the Free Church of Ancient Christendom, pp. 148—151.) This paved the way for Victor, the first
bishop of Rome.

The Gnostics were a sect which separated themselves, or were
separated, from that branch of the Nazarenes mentioned in Acts
xxiv. 6, who remained faithful to the apostolic doctrine. They
differed from the Nazarenes in this also; they denied the Divinity
of Christ, and rejected many parts of the Scripture, and asserted
the permanent obligation of the whole Mosaic law; and on this
account they retained circumcision, baptism, and the passover
supper. This, with the mixture of philosophy with the Scriptures of Truth, laid the foundation for Clementinism. (See
Epiphanius Adv. Hær. 30, s. 3; Schliemann, p. 226 seq.)

They were now tempted to model Christianity according to
their own ideas and tendencies, and to cast it in a theosophic
form of their own, from which, in the following century, manifold
branches of Gnostics proceeded. They boasted of a mixture
of Oriental and Grecian philosophic ideas, transmitted by
tradition among the initiated. They pretended to a higher
knowledge than that contained in the Gospel, and that they
could communicate it to others who were disposed to be initiated
into the mysteries. Such allusions deceived them, by the
dazzling appearance of something higher than what was offered
them in the simple and ever practical doctrines of the Gospel.
This Paul appears to describe (Col. ii. 8) as the higher philosophy
of religion, of which these people boasted as the followers of

human traditions—as cleaving to the elements—both in the Judaism and heathenism of the world, and not proceeding from Christ, being raised above the revelation of the Mediator, and thus above Christianity. This idea was always to be found among the different sects of the Gnostics, the disciples of the Clementines and Elxai, styled by Schliemann "the Gnostic or Elxaite Ebionites," as distinguished from those whom he calls "the vulgar Ebionites," as the followers of Symmachus. (See Neander's Planting of Christianity, vol. i., pp. 319—324.)

The origin of the Gnostic system has been traced to various sources. Some have derived their doctrine from the Alexandrian school of philosophy; others from the Jewish Cabala; others from the school of Ammonius Saccas, a pagan Christian, and his disciple Origen, who, of all men, has been suspected as deficient in point of orthodoxy. Many parts of the Gnostic system may be alleged in favour of each of these.

The followers of Ammonius Saccas, who taught in the school of Alexandria towards the close of the second century, strove to combine into one consistent set of opinions the Egyptian and Platonic systems of philosophy. They were called the Eclectic sect, or Eclectic Ebionites, because they selected and picked up the choicest parts of philosophy out of all sects: this apparently laudable attempt was undertaken by men accounted eminent, *i.e.*, Polomon, Plutarch, Ammonius, and other philosophers of the same stamp. The school of Ammonius embraced those among the Alexandrians who were desirous to unite the profession of the Gospel with the name and worldly prestige of philosophers, and it rapidly extended itself from Egypt over the whole Roman Empire. Ammonius laid the foundation of the sect of philosophers distinguished by the name of Neo-Platonists (see Alexandrian School, in Faiths of the World, vol. ii., p. 666), who endeavoured to reconcile the discrepancies between the Aristotelian and Platonic systems. Porphyry, in his work against Christianity, calls Origen a disciple of Ammonius, by way of disparagement. And, indeed, there is every reason to believe, that though born of Christian parents, and educated in a knowledge of Christian truth, this philosopher became afterwards an apostate from the Christian faith. Milner calls him "a pagan Christian, who imagined that all religions meant the same thing at bottom." Mosheim thinks it probable that he did not openly renounce Christianity, but endeavoured to accommodate himself to the feelings of all parties; and therefore he was claimed by both Pagans and Christians. The grand idea which he seems to have had in view, was to bring all sects and religions into harmony, by converting Paganism into an allegory, conveying under its mythology important truths; and then, on the other hand, by robbing Christianity of all its high and holy principles, he endeavoured to make the two extremes meet, and to amalgamate Christianity and Paganism into one system. This he effectually accomplished in what was called the "Catholic Church" in his time. And immense harm was done to Christianity, when plain Scripture truth began to be wrapped up in obscure philosophic language, and the way was thus opened for the rushing in of that flood of erroneous doctrines and useless ceremonies which have to this day overwhelmed the Church of Christ. (See Faiths of the World, vol. i., p. 81, Ammonians; and p. 58, Alexandrian school.)

We learn from Job. Pic. Mirand "that all the disorders of divines have proceeded from philosophers; forasmuch as divines have mixed philosophy with the Scriptures of Truth." "If the pattern of the primitive church had been observed," (saith Theophilus Gale,) "neither Origen, Arius, Pelagius, Socinus, nor the schoolmen, had been overwhelmed in so many monstrous errors." Where, we now ask, did Paul of Samosata, who denied the Divinity of Christ, derive his venomous errors against the Son of God, but from Plotinus the Egyptian, and his philosophic disputations in the school of Alexandria? Did not Arius, too, a presbyter of the Church of Alexandria, imbibe or drink in his blasphemies against the Divinity of Christ from the same source? Origen, also, and Pelagius, derived their pestilent errors against the grace of God out of the same school. "We that have obtained the knowledge of God, by and through grace," said Piscat, (on 1 Cor. i.,) "are far more wise and blessed than Plato, Aristotle," &c., &c.

Tertullian, also, about the beginning of the third century, said "that errors were propagated by the Platonists, by the Stoics, by Epicurus, by Heraclitus, by Zeno, by Aristotle." And he also adds, "from the philosophy of Plato and Aristotle, pestilent errors first invaded, and have long possessed, and at this day do waste, the Christian Church. Hereby they brought it to pass, that the faith of Christ had no residence in the hearts of many who professed him. Where Aristotle reigns, there ungodliness hath great dominion." (De Oratione.)

---

## SECTION II.

### INTRODUCTION OF HIERARCHICAL DOCTRINES INTO THE CHRISTIAN CHURCH.

THE Christian Church at first had a separate existence from philosophy and prelacy; she had a development of her own, and was comparatively pure. But scarcely was John cold in his grave at Ephesus, when a society or societies, which had held out against the preaching of Christ and his apostles, found in Cerinthus, Carpocrates, Clement, and Elxai, a basis on which they could capitulate. They assumed the Christian name, but without the cross: and with the rejection besides of nearly every distinctive truth of the New Testament. Thus the Gnostic and Ebionite churches were formed, which afterwards ramified themselves throughout Perea, Nabathea, Paneas, Moabitis, Batanea, and even spread to Asia Minor, Cyprus, and particularly to Rome. (See Schliemann, Die Clementinen, p. 480.)

It was about this time that the catechetical school of Alexandria was established. This is the school which produced Clement, the founder of what is called Christian philosophy; but in so far as he introduced the philosophy of the eclectic sect, so far he tarnished Christianity. The mystic philosophy to which he was so much addicted, naturally darkened his views of some of the most precious truths of the Gospel. Therefore, Clement is, as is well known, a great favourite with Catholic theologians; but this is, perhaps, in a great degree accounted for by their studying him backwards, from Augustine, Chrysostom, Cyprian, Callistus, and Victor; instead of forwards from Mark, John, and Paul. And it was through the same channel, that Cerinthus, Carpocrates, Elxai, the Gnostics, Victor, Callistus, Cyprian, and Chrysostom, acquired their knowledge of what they held to be Christianity, as distinguished from that of Christ, and the virgin Church of Jerusalem. This Church already conceived an ecclesiastical unity, i.e., the unity of the episcopate as exhibiting itself in concert, and realizing itself in a single person. It placed, as we learn from the Clementines, at the head of the college of bishops, a supreme bishop, in Victor, bishop of Rome, A.D. 200, who was a man capable of giving a tone to all future times.

The origin of the Monarchian* controversy, which broke out at Rome, in the reign of its first prelate, Victor, is another case in point. Just as the outbreak of Gnosticism in Palestine, and of Montanism in Asia, were the bitter fruits of a too great backwardness shown in the churches in these countries to keep to the New Testament dispensation; so the rise of the Theodotian heresy at Rome, tends to show, that since the time of Clement, A. D. 94, the church of that city must have experienced a

---

* This Monarchian party appeared in Rome, headed by Theodotus, from Byzantium, who, on account of his heretical opinions, was excommunicated by Victor, the Roman bishop. The party continued to propagate their opinions independently of the dominant church. Another Monarchian party was founded in Rome, by Artemon; and hence they received the name of Artemonites. They seem to have disclaimed all connexion with Theodotus and his followers. They both continued to diffuse their opinions in Rome, till far into the third century. (See Faiths of the World, vol. ii., p. 477.)

marked relapse into a Judaizing and heathen spirit. The Theodotian system is repeatedly compared by Hippolytus (Philosop., Lib. vii., cap. 9. 35; Lib. x., cap. 23) with Cerinthianism and Gnosticism. It was under Victor that this Gnostic faction, for such it really was, was excluded from the Apostolic Church (see Euseb. H. E., v. 28). Here we recognize, at once, the obvious features of the Gnostic system, causing a separation from that branch of the Nazarenes who remained faithful to the apostolic doctrine of the Gospel. Whence, doubtless, they thought they must have a prelate at their head, to bestow regeneration and the forgiveness of sins; and give the saving body and blood of Christ in the eucharist. And, accordingly, they won over a confessor, Cæcilius Natalis, a Carthaginian presbyter, to fill this office, while the Theodotian separatists were wont to allege, that all the primitive men, and the Apostles themselves, taught as they did. In this statement there is much falsehood; but when a man entrenches himself in some particular dogmatic interest, and makes that his central position, he can easily explain everything in conformity with his own views. This has been the case in all heresies from Gospel Truth. We discover that it was not here, as among the heathens, scepticism, which stifled religion in an atmosphere of doubt; but superstition, which overlaid and smothered it, among a load of Jewish, philosophic, and heathen traditions. This marks a sad evidence of the decay of that joyous confidence of redemption through Jesus Christ which had been so deeply felt in the Apostles' days—the unchristian principle of a vicarious priesthood and their dogmas being once admitted, there is no check against that evil. The application of the theory of a representative action in the church, is but the political side of sinking the redeeming principle in man—the sacred birthright of every believer in Jesus Christ—to nullity.

In all the proceedings of Victor, the first prelate of Rome, A. D. 190, and of Callistus, an African, a member also of the Church of Rome, we may mark the inter-penetration of both the heterogeneous elements of Clementinism* and Hierarchism :† if it, however, be asked which of the two interests was the soul of their souls, the answer must be the Hierarchical. They clearly saw, that a church at all dependent upon the synagogue, can be no " Catholic Church." And there floated before their minds the idea of an organized Christian community, co-extensive with the world, and the prelate the organ of its intercourse with Christendom, and the bestower of its graces in baptism, and the medium of its fellowship with God in the eucharist.

After the accession of Victor, the churches of the Capital of the world almost uniformly indicated a predominance of the Jewish and heathen elements. In the early years of Victor's sway, Blastus, a Hellenist‡ (a name applied to the Grecian Jews, probably from Asia), became a presbyter of the Roman church ; and, by the influence of the language and literature of Greece, which at this time began to be largely felt, ended in establishing the Hellenist party ; which, by combining the

* Neander considers the so-called 'Clementines,' as a sort of romance, partly philosophical, and partly religious ; and though he admits it to be a fiction, it appears to him to be clearly a fiction from real life. They were received from a few persons in Rome and Cyprus, in the second century. The author of them seems to have adopted the doctrine of the Elxaites, and he sets himself to combat the Gnostics in the person of Simon Magus. (See Faiths of the World, vol. i., p. 547, " Clementines.")

† The word Hierarchy is used to denote a Church, when viewed in its ecclesiastical constitution, as having a regular gradation of orders among its ministers. But there is no evidence of any difference of rank in the age of the Apostles, or of their immediate successors.

‡ The name Hellenists was applied to the Grecian Jews who lived in Egypt and other countries where the Greek language was spoken. In the time of Alexander the Great, the Jews began to divide themselves into Hebrews and Hellenists ; and, by the influence of the language and literature of Greece, which, at this period, began to be largely felt, the foundation was laid of a new epoch in Jewish literature, which received the name of Hellenistic. Thus arose (that source of evil) the Alexandrian school of philosophy, which, by combining the Grecian with the Oriental mode of thinking, led to the diversified forms of Gnosticism, which formed so characteristic a feature in the second and third centuries. (See Faiths of the World, vol. ii., p. 18, " Hellenists.")

Grecian with the Oriental mode of thinking, helped to form a characteristic feature in the aspect of Christianity in the third century of the Christian era. In this way sacerdotalism first insinuated itself into the "Catholic Church;" and the hierarchy thus early developed itself into the hands of a single human guide in each church, who began to be regarded as the exclusive organ in the communication of the Holy Ghost.

After Victor's death, Zephyrinus, his successor, took Callistus entirely into his confidence in the management of the Roman clergy. Hippolytus testifies, that besides these flagrant abuses, Callistus, taking advantage of the superstitious views with which men were beginning to regard the outward ceremony of baptism, indulged those who had sullied the purity of the water (in heretical baptism), with a repetition of the rite (in the Catholic Church), and thus prepared the way for the decision of the Council of Carthage, A. D. 258. This goes far to show how sweeping a revolution had been made in the church by Victor, Zephyrinus, and Callistus; and, at the same time, to confirm the impression of its remarkable character. It also affords a very interesting indication of the source from whence the Catholic hierarchical ideas were derived. It is first found in the Clementines, and from them traced to Victor, Zephyrinus, Callistus, Cyprian, and the Council of Carthage. In all these we discern nothing but the carrying out, to the most extraordinary length, of Victor's principles. For it is plainly, he, by whom the original *momentum* was first furnished in its fulness. In all his vigorous proceedings in the "Catholic Church," we may mark the inter-penetration of the heterogeneous elements of the hierarchical innovator. (See Cooper's Free Church of Ancient Christendom, pp. 249, 257, &c.)

The churches of Asia at first refused to acknowledge this false principle: they were summoned in the persons of their bishops, who, here, are the entire entities recognised to desist from countenancing rebellion against lawful authority: they are ensnared into meeting in synods about A. D. 209. In the following years synods were statedly convened in Greece. (See Neander

c

Ch. Hist., vol. i., p. 287— Bohn's translation.) These councils were held in certain places throughout the Grecian provinces, in which all grave matters were debated in common ; and an actual representation of the whole of those (*falsely*) bearing the Christian name took place with great éclat. Of these synods, Neander, after duly noticing the evils which were so irreparably and continuously connected with them, rightly remarks:—" they must have operated as a check on the development of the Church (of Christ), if, instead of providing for the interests of the communities, according to the various wants of each period, they should attempt to bind changeable things to unchangeable laws. Finally, it seems to us an evil, that the people were excluded from all participation in these assemblies." (See Neander, vol. i., p. 288.) They met with opposition at first, as they had done in Asia, as an innovation, but the prevailing spirit of the prelates in council decided in their favour ; and being pushed to a pagan extreme, they resulted in forming,' what is called in history, thus early, " the Catholic Church," founded on Cerinthianism, Carpocratenism, Gnosticism, and Cyprianism. (See the Free Church of Ancient Christendom, pp. 248-261.)

About sixty years elapsed between the opening of Victor's eventful career, and Cyprian's elevation to the prelacy. During this time, the synodical organization unfolded the *germ* of the prelatical system, and that of the ripe development of the hierarchical system ; when presbyters are spoken of as invested by the prelates with the power of baptizing, confirming, and ordaining. Of course these dignitaries would not be inclined to look too morosely upon a system which tended so greatly to magnify their office. During this hierarchical period, just as baptism came to be confounded with regeneration, of which it was only the symbol, so the (outward) Church became identified with the Church of Christ. This could not but tend grievously to lead men to mistake the Church's baptism for true holiness, and Divine forgiveness. A black day this in the annals of Christianity ! There is no fact in the whole history of the Church which gives rise to more painful reflections, than the frequency with which literary frauds were perpetrated at this time. (See Free Church of Ancient Christendom, p. 290, &c.)

The catholic hierarchy was formed long before Constantine established it by law, and the forty-four city congregations described by Cyprian sixty years before, were all in union with one high priest, and subject to as much control as the pagan government would permit. (Mabillonii Mus. Ital., tom. ii. In Ord. Rom. Comment., cap. 3.)

Their ecclesiastical polity had divided the city into regions. Their titular churches had been instituted for baptism and the burial of the dead. (Anastatius in Marcello.) But it must be observed here, that there were real Christian churches in the city, with whom "the Catholic Church" had no communion, and whom it persecuted as far as it could; and Constantine only brought the great faction—the Catholic Church—more prominently into view, and established it by law. And so it was that baptistries grew by donations into baptismal churches, with numerous appendages of schools, monasteries, and nunneries; hospitals and chapels grew into cathedrals and episcopal palaces, where splendour and wealth, patronage and power, united to form a strong temptation to avarice.

This is the source from whence the Roman and English churches received their hierarchical ideas, and sacramental dogmas, and which led to the substitution in the place of Christ in his Church, of the prelate in the Church of Rome, as the organ in the communication of the Holy Ghost, and to the supplanting the Holy Spirit altogether. Out of this system sprang the constitution of the church which hailed Constantine as its head, instead of spurning him as a seducer, and an establisher of antichrist, by whom Christendom was organized politically into Rome ecclesiastical, and impressed with an orthodox stamp, and catholicised; under circumstances somewhat analogous to those in which the empire was afterwards ecclesiasticised; when communion with the hierarchy became more and more the essential thing, and union and communion with Christ more and more an accident. The consequence was that the priesthood waxed great, and the spiritual life of Christendom ebbed away.

The strong hierarchical character of Judaism, heathenism, and Clementinism— setting up their notions of sacraments, the virtues of which are conveyed through the prelate as the immediate organ of the Holy Ghost—is the fibre and sinew of the absolute authority of the prelate. (See Dr. Lechler's prize works, published at Haarlem, and entitled "Das Apostolische und das Nach-Apostolische Zeitalter, p. 335.) Now there are three very prominent characters, viz., Victor, Blastus, Callistus, as well as some others belonging to the age which gave birth to the so-called Ignatian Epistles, clearly the forgery of a later period, setting up their hierarchical notions of sacraments, and denying the indwelling of the essence of Christ in man, except as conveyed through the prelate in such language as the following :—"That we ought to look unto the bishop as unto the Lord Jesus Christ himself." (Ephes., cap. 6.) "Inasmuch as ye are subject to the bishop as to Jesus Christ." (Trall., cap. 2.) "Let all reverence the deacons as the commandment of Jesus Christ, and the bishop as Jesus Christ, and the presbyters as the sanhedrim of God, and college of the Apostles ; without these it is not called a church." (Trall., cap. 3.) "All of you follow the bishop as Jesus Christ . . . . Let that eucharist be considered valid which is celebrated by the bishop. It is not lawful without the bishop either to baptize or celebrate the eucharist. What the bishop approves of, that is pleasing to God." (Smyrn., cap. 8.) "He who honours the bishop is honoured of God : he who does anything without the privity of the bishop worships the devil." (Smyrn., cap. 9.) These are the men who first suggested the plan of calling synods of priests to establish the prelacy, its baptisms and sacraments : thus they heathenised and catholicised the church, and impressed it with an orthodox stamp. (See Neander's Gen. Ch. Hist., vol. ii., p. 411 ; and the Free Church of Ancient Christendom, pp. 267-269.) The remark of Ambrose, "that almost every heresy has sprung from the clergy," certainly holds good here.

This outline of the political and hierarchical SCENERY is given with a view to render intelligible the ecclesiastical occurrences of these momentous ages. And the œcumenical council of Nice, convened by Constantine's authority in A.D. 325, set the seal to the sacrilegious bargain ; and presented the " Catholic Church " to Christendom in bondage to the prelates and their dogmas ; and through them to the Imperial throne, to bring into play all the machinery of the State for the suppression of the true Christian religion—the barbarian religion, as the philosophers scornfully term it.

## SECTION IIL

### THE ESTABLISHMENT OF THE "CATHOLIC CHURCH" BY CONSTANTINE, AND THE COUNCIL OF NICE.

Now let us see further what were the dogmas of the " Catholic Church," established by Constantine and his 250 prelates from Europe, Asia, and Africa, in the Council of Nice, A.D. 325, and by what means they arrived at these conclusions. This church considered "the totality of baptized persons throughout the world, organized by the sacerdotal college of prelates into a unity," as the true church. (See Hieronymus de Viris Illust., cap. 67.) A heretic was one professing to be a Christian, and not in communion with the prelatical college ; and deemed to be worse than a heathen. This is the Clementine, Cæcilian, and Cyprian doctrine ; while before their time a man—a heretic— would have been a contradiction in terms ; nevertheless, they boldly aver, again and again, this revolting conclusion, which indeed follows logically enough from their fundamental maxim, "that the Church consists only in the prelates and the priests.

The prelates they regarded as the exclusive organs in the communication of the Holy Ghost." (See Clem. Const., Lib. vi., cap. 14; Lib. ii., cap. 26, 32, 33; and Schliemann, p. 248.) "In the sacraments the priests, and they alone, by themselves impart and sustain spiritual life; they assure men of the forgiveness of sins, and regenerate them in baptism, and feed them with the body and blood of Christ in the eucharist." (See Clem. Const. Apost., Lib. ii., cap. 32, 33.)    It is but fair now to state that Constantine and his 250 prelates, as well as the eighty-seven bishops of the Council of Carthage, forty years before, all regarded the prelate and the priests of the Church as the proper and qualified men on whom they made the eternal life of the laity absolutely to depend. It was this party whom they favoured, and this corrupt religion which they took under their protection, and endeavoured to uproot all dissident Christians, however pure their doctrines and practices might be. This was remarkably the case with the Nazarenes, the Novatians, and the Waldenses, who separated themselves from the "Catholic or Nicene Church." NAZARENE, especially, was a name of reproach applicable to the early Christians by the Jews, as we find in Acts xxiv. 5. The Jews we are told, by early Christian writers, were wont to curse and anathematize this sect of the Nazarenes (not the sect which Jerome and Epiphanius call by this name, who taught the obligations of the Jewish law) three times a day, morning, noon, and night, using this imprecation in their prayers in the synagogue: "Send thy curse, O God, upon the Nazarenes." And why did they curse the Nazarenes? "Because they rejected the Jewish and heathen dogmas of the Carthaginian Council, and called Christ the first-born of the Holy Spirit, and described how the Holy Ghost descended upon him at his baptism, and abode permanently with him, and called him their resting-place who remaineth for ever."

Notwithstanding all that has been, or can be, written and said in favour of Constantine, and the edicts of the Council of Nice, over which he presided as the head of the church, and judge of heresy, it is impossible to speak with any degree of satisfaction respecting the religion he endeavoured to establish. In whatever light the subject is examined, the verdict of the unbiassed mind goes against him—it will confirm the opinion expressed by Niebuhr, in the following words:—"The religion which he had in his head must have been a strange compound indeed. The man who had on his coins the inscription 'Sol invictus,' who worshipped pagan deities, consulted the auspices, (soothsayers and diviners,) and indulged in a number of pagan superstitions, and interfered in the Council of Nice, must have been a repulsive phenomenon, and was certainly not a Christian. He was a superstitious man, and mixed up his Christian religion with all kinds of absurd superstitions and opinions; when, therefore, certain Oriental writers call him equal to an Apostle, they know not what they are saying; and to speak of him as a Saint is a profanation of the word." (See Niebuhr's 79th Lecture on the History of Rome.) That he established Christianity, none who know what Christianity is will admit for a single moment; that he established a mixture of Polytheism, Judaism, Heathenism, and Christianity, and called it the "Catholic Church," and gave consolidation, influence, and vast augmentation to the corruptions that followed, and exist at the present day, cannot be denied.

The predecessors of Constantine, with a very few exceptions, had regarded the Christians with an hostility as fierce as it was singular. It was a proscribed and persecuted religion, its professors were treated as Atheists, and pronounced as heretics. Its fellowship was branded as ignominious; to patronize it never entered their thoughts. To exterminate it, if that could be accomplished, was their sole aim; therefore, the names of the apostolic men who succeeded the Apostles have nearly faded from the pages of history; although, doubtless, the most radiant in the Book of Life. The following striking passage in Eusebius (H. E. 3, 37), relating to the missionaries of this age, must be accepted for want of more detailed information:—"Among those who flourished in this age (the reign of Trajan) besides Ignatius, Papias, and Polycarp, was Quadratus, who, as well as the daughters of Philip, are reported to have been eminent in the gift of prophecy. Many others, no doubt, whose names are lost to us, became distinguished at this time, who, like the disciples of Christ, built on the foundation of the church, laid by Christ and his apostles, scattering over all the world the seeds of the kingdom of God." The Jews and heathens beheld this strange religion, without temples, altars, images, consecrated priests, with amazement and dismay ; the temper of the heathen masses being hostile to the Christians, and being imperfectly held in check, indeed rather encouraged by the government, who insisted upon being recognized as the exclusive organs of the persecuting spirit, which began in Cyrenaica ; and spread to Lybia, Egypt, Cyprus, Palestine, Mesopotamia, Bithynia, Antioch, Athens, Philippi, Rome, and Jerusalem, some of which were well-nigh depopulated ; they committed great havoc in Egypt ; put 200,000 to death in Cyrenaica ; in Cyprus, also, they massacred nearly a quarter of a million of the inhabitants. In the dreadful massacre of the Christians, Judea was reduced to a wilderness, and 500,000 were massacred, besides a vast multitude who perished by famine, pestilence, and the burning of more than 900 towns and villages over the heads of the inhabitants. (See Dio. Cass., l. c.) Perhaps it is not too much to assume that in the persecutions under Trajan and Hadrian alone, no fewer than 4,000,000 of human beings were sacrificed. The sufferings of the Christians, chiefly of course those of Palestine, in the persecution of Hadrian, are not mere matters of inference, but are expressly attested by Justin Martyr, (Longer Apology, cap. 31,) who lived at the time when the Christians were led away to the slaughter, to be executed with dreadful torture, unless they denied Jesus to be the Messiah, and blasphemed him. This completed the work of prelacy, and the heathen government, all over Christendom. A criminal aversion to that which is Divine, is the enormous error lying at the root of Hierarchism and Heathenism.

Here we see that the "Catholic or Nicene Church" had slid from the true foundation. These dissensions arose by means of false doctrines leading to corrupt practices.  Wherefore, in order to prevent divisions, the arm of ecclesiastical authority, backed by heathen potentates, was resorted to, in order to coerce a conformity with the corrupt doctrines sacrilegiously brought in by the Catholic Church and the State, whereby they were enabled to force men into a kind of unity, in conformity with their will and pleasure, and bind the body fast to their decrees. But, alas! what was the worth of that unity, which was through the most subtile contrivance forced upon the church?  Nothing at all; nay, a thousand times worse than nothing; because the greater the number that are brought to join in wrong things, the greater the evil, and the more injurious and lamentable are the consequences.  But this is the way in which the church, in its lapsed condition from the truth, has *ever* been found to be at work all the world over, exercising every possible means within its reach at all times to gather the multitude to itself, and reconcile them to its own ways, and persecute all dissent.  For instance, the Catholic Church, when it had become apostate, which it did in the second century, from true Christianity, declaimed against the followers of Christ and his Apostles, who protested against their degenerate doctrine, and avowed those of the Gospel.  History informs us how exceedingly that degenerate body strove against those better Christians because they testified against them, and separated from them.  And it has been so ever since.  But it was, and is, the prominent characteristic of Christianity, to do that which the Lord and his Truth requires, a prominent part of which is not to persecute, without regarding those consequences which the wisdom and fear of man might suggest.

All other religions, however gross, were tolerated; all the varieties of pagan superstitions received the formal sanction of Rome; but the followers of Jesus of Nazareth were persecuted to death in the ten general persecutions of the three first centuries, as the most pernicious of heretics.  Yes! they were the heretics of those days, and they remained the same under the reign of Constantine, after the Council of Nice, when the

church was established by law, which had existed for nearly
two centuries, under the appellation of the "Catholic Church."
This is a point of primary importance for all to know who would
form a correct opinion as to the religion established by
Constantine.

Constantine, having been educated in Paganism, and having
observed the pomp of pagan worship, connected with the ex-
cessive honours paid to the pontiff, thought it fit to raise Christianity (so called) into an imitation of them, to soften down the
prejudices of the pagans against it. Yes! the ministers of this
church succeeded to the character, rites, and privileges of the
Jewish and heathen priesthood, at the same time (falsely) professing it to be the pure religion of Jesus Christ.

Constantine found the Church of Christ an independent and
persecuted body. He nominally received its name into alliance
with the State, only with a view to corrupt it. He constituted
himself its director and guardian, in order to enslave it to the
trammels of Paganism; combining in himself the highest ecclesiastical, with the highest civil authority. As the head of the
church, he became the judge of heresy—of which vital Christianity was the greatest. He issued edicts, and published
rescripts. In his letters to the churches he declares:—" that
every question had received due and full examination, so that no
room was left for any further discussion or controversy relating
to the faith." The religion of the " Nicene Catholic Church "
now differed very little from the heathen Greeks and Romans;
and was established on the opinions of Cerinthus, Carpocrates,
Clement, Victor, Callistus, Fidus, and Cyprian; and Augustine,
bishop of Hippo, in the latter part of this century, declared
that " the yoke of religious rites under which the Jews formerly groaned, was more tolerable than those imposed on
many Christians." Can we marvel at this when the sixth Canon
of the Council of Nice ran in these words:—" Let the ancient
custom which has prevailed in Egypt, Libya, and Pentapolis,
that the bishop of Alexandria shall have authority over all these
places be still maintained, since this is the custom also with the

Roman bishop ; in like manner, at Antioch, and in the other provinces, the churches shall retain their ancient prerogatives." (See Faiths of the World, vol. ii., p. 445.)

Thus we see that the Roman emperors went so far as to decide questions of faith in opposition to the Gospel, under the Christian name, as they had done in a state of semi-paganism, by edicts, and to convoke synods almost entirely for the purpose of adopting Imperial articles of faith, and exterminating the followers of Christ from the earth, if that were possible.

It remains now to be seen how the precedence given to this body was followed by the continued persecution of those who differed from them in doctrine, and adhered to the earlier practices of the Christian Church. It was at the council of Nice that severe laws were enacted against heretics, as the true followers of Christ were called ; and who were persecuted with a personal rancour and malice that afford an edifying proof of the paternal government of Constantine, and his council of prelates :—" Understand, now," said they, in addressing them in one of their edicts, " by this present statute, that all ye who have devised and supported heresy by means of your private assemblies, with what a tissue of falsehood and vanity—with what destructive venomous errors, your doctrines are inseparably interwoven : in league with destruction ! Why do we bear with such abounding evils ? Why not at once strike at the root of so great a mischief by a public manifestation of our displeasure ?" Such was the haughty and bitter language in which the Council addressed some of the purest Christians of the day. But words would have fallen harmless upon them as the Council well knew ; therefore the edict proceeds to forbid their assembling together, in the following terms :—" We give warning, by this present statute, that none of you, henceforth, presume to assemble yourselves together. We have directed, accordingly, that you be deprived of all the houses in which ye are accustomed to hold your assemblies ; and our care in this respect extends so far as to forbid the holding of your superstitious and senseless meetings, not in public merely, but in any private house, or place whatever.

Let those of you, therefore, who are desirous of embracing the true and pure religion, take the far better course of entering the ' Catholic Church,' and unite with it in holy fellowship, whereby you will be able to arrive at the knowledge of the truth. In any case, the delusions of your perverted understandings must entirely cease to mingle with, and mar, the felicity of the present times : we mean the impious and wretched double-mindedness of heretics and schismatics . . . . . And in order that this remedy may be applied with effectual power, we have commanded that ye be positively deprived of every gathering point for your superstitious meetings, and that these be made over without delay to the ' Catholic Church ;' that every other place be confiscated to the public service, and no facility whatever be left to any future gathering." (See Eusebius's Life of Constantine, Book iii., cap. 64, 65.)

It is not to be supposed, however, that there were no dissentients who rejected the dogmas, and refused to acknowledge the authority, of that body, and Constantine's right to establish it by law ; there were many who maintained the headship, and the priesthood, of Christ, by which perfection was to be established ; and that in such God put his law, writing it in their hearts, to guide them into all truth.

But from the time of Constantine to that of Theodosius the younger, and Valentinian III., various penal laws were enacted by the so-called Christian emperors, against those called heretics, as being guilty of crime against the welfare of the State. Thus, both in the Theodosian and Justinian codes, they were styled " infamous persons ;" all intercourse was forbidden to be held with them ; they were deprived of all offices of profit and dignity in the civil administration, while all burdensome offices were imposed on them ; they were disqualified from disposing of their own estates by will, or of accepting estates bequeathed to them by others ; they were deprived of the right of giving or receiving donations ; of contracting, buying, and selling ; pecuniary fines were imposed on them ; and they were often proscribed and banished, and in many cases scourged before they were sent into exile. In some particular cases sentence of death was pronounced upon the heretics. Theodosius is said to have been the first who pronounced heresy a capital crime. This sanguinary law was passed A.D. 382, fifty-seven years after the Council of Nice against the Encratites,* the Saccophori, the Hydroparastatæ, and the Manicheans. (See Faiths of the World, vol. ii. p. 37.) What an evidence is this that the tender mercies of the wicked are cruel at all times, and of the truth of the Apostles' doctrine, that he that is born after the flesh, persecuteth him that is born after the Spirit. This truth has held good through all ages of the church.

The Church of Christ at this time was very weak and very poor, almost afraid to show her face, because of the oppression of the enemy. The heathen Roman rulers, under the name of Christians, drove their haughty chariots over her like the mire in the streets. And political power put its heel upon her neck; yet, she prayed in lonely rooms in Jerusalem, lurked in the back streets in Alexandria and Antioch, and hid herself in the dark catacombs of Rome. What was she like then? She was like the woman who said to Christ, "Thou seest the multitude throng thee, and sayest thou, Who touched me?" Yes, the true church was trodden in the crowd of nations, hidden in the press of the heathens, but close to Jesus, and drawing precious virtue out of him.

Here we perceive that the Church of Christ is not identical with any determinate society of men, united together by outward symbols, such as baptisms, the eucharist; and a prelate, any more than a baptized person is necessarily a perfect Christian, which has never yet been proved to be so. But during the rise of

---

* The Encratites were a sect which arose in the second century. It owed its origin to Tatian of Assyria. He taught that it was necessary to abstain from wine, and that water ought to be used instead of wine in the eucharist. Hence they were sometimes called Hydroparastatæ, or waterdrinkers; and Apotactatæ, or renouncers. The name Encratites was often used in general terms, and applied to all sects practising austerities. The Manicheans in the fourth century assumed to themselves the name of Encratites. The Saccophori seem to be heretics of the same stamp.

the hierarchical period in the second and third centuries, just as the Jewish baptism came to be confounded with pagan regeneration, of which it was only a symbol, so the (Imperial) church became identified with the two, and a connection with the church and the hierarchy, by baptism and the eucharist, became more and more the essential thing; and anon, union and communion with Christ an accident. The consequence was, that as the priesthood waxed great, the spiritual life of Christendom ebbed away into Cerinthianism, Gnosticism, and Cyprianism, and ultimately into Roman Catholicism. But this is not the way God hath chosen.

Spiritual despotism has always laid its foundation upon the priests, and a religion of rites; our Lord then, in assailing as he did, and even with unwonted vehemence, and high indignation, the formalism of his times, has prejudged and condemned the Carthaginian, the Nicene, and the Roman churches in their very characteristics. The terrible rebuke, "Fools and blind hypocrites," if deserved by the sanctimonious and profligate pharisees and lawyers, must be held to come home to them, with not less force, in every age, who have flattered the human mind into its fatal aptitude, to continue for itself, or accept when contrived, a religion of sacraments, as a substitute for the religion of the heart. Has, then, the Church of Rome favoured this common delusion? Yes! but not more so than it had been taught to do by Cerinthus, Elxai, the Gnostics, Cyprian, and the Nicene doctors.

No one but a Romanist would be tempted to undertake the task of proving that the pharisaic pietism of our Lord's time, was more formal, and more trivial, and more dangerous than were the sacraments and pietism of the Carthaginian and Nicene ages. But Cyprian's doctrine of baptism, and the doctrine of Ambrose concerning the eucharist, compromise truths far more serious than "the washing of cups and platters," and the tithing "of mint and anise" of the rabbis; and if they stand condemned in loud terms of displeasure, those by necessary implication are denounced in thunder.

A good part of our Lord's discourses bears more or less directly upon the very point of announcing a spiritual system, as opposed to a system of ceremonial sanctity. The principle upon which these rebukes are given, is uniformly of a kind that, by necessary implication, condemns a servile or anxious regard to what is ritual and external.

The Scriptures say that Jesus Christ himself is king to rule and reign in our hearts, and to send the gifts and graces of the Holy Spirit to redeem us from all sin. Yes! and he is the Apostle and High-priest of the Christian's profession. "Him hath God exalted to be a Prince and a Saviour, to give repentance to Israel, and the forgiveness of sins. Neither is there salvation in any other, for there is none other name under heaven given among men whereby we must be saved." God sent his Son to bless us, in turning away every one of us from our iniquities. For it is he who saveth his people from their sins; He came to save the world.

The danger attendant on the introduction of unscriptural and unwarranted ceremonies into the church, is strikingly seen in the history of the Church of Rome from the Apostles' days, and which has originated many innovations, not only different in themselves, but very absurd and injurious to religion itself. Dr. Middleton, in his " Letters from Rome," has very strikingly pointed out the conformity between the Pagan and Roman ceremonies, exemplifying it in the use of incense, holy water, and other similar ceremonies. (See his Free Enquiry, A.D. 1646.) A history of the ancient ceremonies was also published by M. Ponce, tracing the rise, growth, and introduction of each rite into the church, and their general abuses as they appeared. Many of them, too numerous to be stated here, he traces to Judaism, but still more to heathenism. We refer our readers to the works themselves for further information.

But the Gospel having for its end the glory of God and the salvation of men, Jesus Christ dethroned the idols of the nations —the hierarchy and the sacraments; and took from men what they had taken from God and his Christ: and brought the soul

again into immediate communion with himself the Divine source
of truth. Jesus proclaimed himself sole master and mediator :
"One is your master, even Christ," said he, "and all ye are
brethren." This is the true communion—the true church-fellow-
ship—not limited by sects, or name, or profession, but to be found
wherever communion with, and faith in, Jesus is to be found.

It is the sinner's duty to come to Christ who gave himself for
him. By coming to Christ, we mean believing on him as the
sinner's only hope of salvation. It is the sinner's interest to come
to Christ as his Saviour and his God, instead of to the priests and
their traditions. It is remarkable how beautifully and closely
duty and interest are linked together in the sacred volume. We
are commanded to do nothing whatever which is not promotive
of our interest ; well, then, we are commanded not to be conformed to this world, nor the way of the heathens, nor the
traditions of men. But if it be the sinner's duty to come to
Christ, it is equally his interest and duty to forsake what the
Scripture warns us against ; for there is not a want in the sinner
but there is a corresponding fulness in the Saviour. "Of his
fulness have we all received, and grace for grace." We repeat
it, there is not a want in the sinner, but there is a corresponding
fulness in the spiritual baptism, and communion of our blessed
Redeemer. Is the sinner hungering after righteousness? Let
him come to Christ and he shall be filled! Is the sinner thirsty ?
Let him come to Christ, and he shall be permitted to drink of
the well of salvation. Is the sinner blind ? Let him come to
Christ, and he shall have his eyes opened to see wondrous things
out of God's law. Is he deaf? Let him come to Christ, and his
ears shall be unstopped to hear the voice of harmony in the
Gospel speaking peace to his soul, in the rejection of all traditional religion. Is the sinner burdened under the guilt of sin ?
Let him come to Christ and fulfil his righteous law, and his
burden shall be taken away. Is he trembling under an appre-
hension of wrath ? Let him come to Christ, believing that man
is not appointed to wrath, but to obtain salvation through Jesus
Christ our Lord.

Although it is the sinner's interest and duty to come to Christ, yet such is the ruling power of sin, and such the depravity of the sinner's heart, and such the dominion of the world, and the power of traditional religion, that no man can come to Christ as a true believer except he be divinely drawn. "No man," said Christ the Saviour, "can come unto me, except the Father which hath sent me draw him." This language clearly implies that there is such a thing as a Divine drawing. "I," says the Saviour, "if I be lifted up from the earth, will draw all men unto me." The doctrine of a Divine drawing, baptism, eating, drinking, and communion, is as clearly revealed in Scripture, as man's helplessness and ruined condition by nature—they are linked together—and what God hath joined let no man put asunder by tradition.

Faith or belief is a fundamental principle of the redeemed heart; yet, no object of faith can be admitted as at all effective in purifying the heart, or in rectifying the conduct, which is not fitted to awaken men's moral emotions and feelings, and create them new in Christ Jesus unto good works. Faith without regard to its object—Jesus Christ and good works—is not productive of good.

The followers of Christ have been like himself--anointed ones. They are anointed through faith in their Saviour, by the unction of the Holy One. The Christian in reality is anointed with the Holy Ghost in its fulness—it is the Holy Spirit who sets his soul apart for the service of God—brings the soul by faith into the presence of God—enjoins him to walk continually as in the presence of God. Such as these God admits to his baptism and communion with the Father, Son, and Holy Ghost; and enables them to live under an habitual feeling of the gracious privileges conferred on them thereby. It also renews their minds after the image of Christ, and causes them to rejoice in the holy and righteous will of Jehovah, and inspires in them a gracious longing and waiting for the purity, as well as the peace, of the kingdom of glory.

"There is one God, and one mediator between God and men,

the man Christ Jesus, who gave himself a ransom for all; who will have all men to be saved, and to come to the knowledge of the truth, for this is good and acceptable in the sight of God our Saviour, who, because he continueth an high priest for ever, hath an unchangeable priesthood. Wherefore, he is able to save them to the uttermost that come unto God by him, seeing he ever liveth to make intercession for them. For such an high priest became us, who is holy, harmless, undefiled, and separate from sinners, and made higher than the heavens." The law made men high priests which had infirmities, and so did the " Catholic Church ;" but the word of the oath which was since the law (mark! since the law!), maketh the Son, Jesus Christ, who is consecrated or perfected for evermore. And being made perfect, he became the author of eternal salvation to all them that obey him ; who hath saved us, and called us with an holy calling, not according to our works, but according to his own purpose and grace, which was given us in him before the world began. He is a faithful and merciful high priest in things pertaining to God and godliness, to make reconciliation for the sins of the people. Seeing, then, that we have a great and everlasting high priest that is passed into the heavens, let us hold fast our profession of faith in him. For he can have compassion on the ignorant, and on them that are out of the way; bringing many sons unto glory.

As it was in the times of the advent of Christ and his Apostles, so it is now : there are thousands who profess to call themselves Christians, who would be highly offended were any individual to question the reality of their religion. But, alas! their religion, if religion it may be called, has little or nothing to do with Jesus Christ. It is not founded on faith in him. It is not connected with exclusive dependence on the sacrifice and righteousness of Christ. It does not lead them to a constant application to him for mercy, grace, and salvation. No! but to the priests and their dogmas. It does not constrain them supremely to love the Saviour, habitually to delight in him, gratefully to praise him, willingly to serve him, and universally to obey him. No! their application to, and love of, grateful praise, and filial obedience—as well as their faith and dependence, is exclusively placed on a human priesthood, and their traditions: as baptisms, confirmations, the eucharist, and priestly absolutions: or, it may be, confessions, indulgences to sin, and purgatorial fire to consume them. Is not this the case with multitudes? Is not this the case with nearly all who profess the Christian name? What, then, is the nature of their religion? Is it experimental? Is it genuine? Is it saving? No! It is traditional! It is a religion without Christ! And will such a traditional religion save them from the guilt of transgression, the dominion of sin, and the wrath of God? No! That religion that does not begin by looking to Christ as the Saviour, Sanctifier, and Redeemer, and place dependence upon him for all its supplies of grace to keep the soul within the attractions of the cross, and secure obedience to the Divine commands, is not acceptable in the sight of God now, and will not stand the test of a judgment day. Now, my readers, what is your creed? Is it founded on the opinions of Corinthus, Carpocrates, Elxai, Victor, Callistus, Cyprian, and Constantine? Examine yourselves! What is the nature of your religion? On what is it founded? the traditions of men, or salvation by, and through, Jesus Christ? What are its principles? What are its effects? Is it connected with repentance towards God, and faith in our Lord Jesus Christ, as being made of God unto us, wisdom and righteousness, sanctification and redemption? Does it constrain you to love, serve, and obey him, as God over all? O! remember! it is only by exercising faith in him as a Saviour, and seeking the influence of his Spirit, and the blessing of his salvation, that you can live and die in the practice, possession, and enjoyment of experimental, vital, and saving religion. " This is a faithful saying, and worthy of all acceptation, that Jesus Christ came into the world to save sinners."

# CHAPTER II.

THE rites and ceremonies introduced into the " Catholic Church," in the second, third, and fourth centuries, from Africa, Greece, and Rome, destroyed the beauty and simplicity of the Gospel plan of man's redemption from sin, and superseded the spirituality thereof, setting up in baptism a magical lustration, which they said could at once render those subjected to it entirely pure. Cyprian, bishop of Carthage, asserts in the most express language, that " remission of sin is granted to every man in baptism." To establish this idea, the church gave the name of " mystery" to baptism, in order to put it upon an equal footing in point of dignity with that of the pagans; and proceeded so far as to adopt some of the rites and ceremonies of the renowned pagan mysteries—hence the idea of lustrations and " baptismal regeneration." Thus there occurred what the apostle designated "a falling away," when the spirit of formality began to take the place of faith, love, and obedience to the law of Christ. Step by step the evil advanced, until in the end the original institutions of Christianity were supplanted by the inventions of Tertullian, Irenæus, Cyprian, Origen, Constantine, Augustine, Ambrose, Gregory Nazianzen, Basil, Jerome, Cyril of Alexandria, Chrysostom, and Gregory Nyssen.

In exact accordance with this idea are the following quotations from some of these fathers, who say, " It is the food which is sanctified by the word of prayer, which is no longer common bread, or common drink, but the flesh and blood of the incarnate Jesus." (Just. Mart. Apol. i., 66.) It is when " the bread from the earth receives the invocation of God, that it is no longer common bread, but eucharist, consisting of two things, an earthly and a heavenly." (Iren. iv., 18, 5.) Augustine says, "Our bread and our cup is not any one," *i.e.*, any species of food partaken; "but it is a mystical one, which is produced by a fixed consecration. That which is not produced in this way, though it may be bread and a cup, is only the means of bodily refreshment, not a sacrament of religion." (Aug. Con. Faus. xx., 13.) "Before the blessing of the sacred words another species is named; after consecration the body is signified. Before consecration it is called a different thing; after consecration it is called blood." (Amb. de Myst. ix., 54.) This evidently shows that the fathers of the early "Catholic Church" did not believe in the effects of consecration in the eucharist, as at all different from those produced by prayers of consecration when used in baptism, the priesthood, or any other religious rites.

The invocation or consecration of the baptismal water by prayer is mentioned by Tertullian: he says, "The waters are made the sacrament of sanctification by invocation of God. The Spirit immediately descends from heaven, and rests upon them, and sanctifies them by himself; and they, being so sanctified, imbibe the power of sanctifying." (Tertul. de Bap., cap. 4.) Cyprian, also, declares, "that the water must be sanctified by the priest, that it may have power by baptism to wash away the sins of men." (Cyp. Ep. lxx.) And so the whole Council of Carthage, in the time of Cyprian, says, "The water is sanctified by the prayer of the priest to wash away sin." (Conc. Carth. ap. Cypr., p. 233.) Augustine often mentions this invocation in his books of baptism. (Aug. de Bapt., Lib. ii., cap. 10; and Lib. v., cap. 20.)

Here, we observe, concerning the effects of this consecration, that the very same change was supposed to be wrought by it as in the water of baptism, the chrism, and the priest, as by the consecration of the bread and wine in the eucharist. For they suppose not only the presence of the Spirit, but also the mystical presence of Christ's blood to be there after consecration. Julius Firmicus, speaking of baptism, bids men "seek for the pure water, the undefiled fountain, where the blood of Christ would whiten them by the Holy Ghost." (Firm. de Error. Profan. Relig., c. 28.)   Gregory Nazianzen and Basil say, "upon this account, a greater than the Temple, a greater than Solomon, a greater than Jonas, is here," meaning Christ, by his mystical presence, and the power of his blood.   (Naz. Orat. xl., de Bap., p. 657; Basil de Bapt., Lib. i., c. 2, t. i., p. 558.) Augustine says, "Baptism, or the baptismal water, is red, when once it is consecrated by the blood of Christ."   (Aug. Tract xi., in Joh., p. 41.)   Prosper is bold to say, "that in baptism we are dipped in the blood of Christ."   (Prosp. de Promissis, Lib. ii., cap. 2.)   Jerome (Hieron. in Esai. i., 16) uses the same bold metaphor.   And Cyril of Alexandria, says, "We are partakers of the spiritual Lamb in baptism."   (Cyril in Exod. xii., Lib. ii., t. i., p. 270.)   And Chrysostom, "that we thereby put on Christ, not only his Divinity, or only his humanity—that is, his flesh, but both together."   (Chrys. Serm. xxvii. de Cruce, t. vi., p. 293.)   And Nazianzen, "that in baptism we are anointed and protected by the precious blood of Christ, as Israel was by the blood upon the door-posts in the night."   (Naz. Orat. xl., de Bapt., p. 646.)   Philo-Caparthius (in Cantic. iv. 12) says, "the spouse of Christ, his church, receives in baptism the seal of Christ, being washed in the fountain of His most precious blood."   Other fathers tell us, "that the water is transmuted or changed in its nature by the Holy Ghost, to a sort of Divine and ineffable power."   Cyril of Alexandria frequently uses the word "transelementation," both when he speaks of the "water in baptism," and "the bread and wine in the eucharist," or any other changes which are said to be wrought in the "mysteries" of the Christian religion.   (Cyril Catech. Myst. iii., n. 3.)

Gregory Nyssen (de Baptismo Christ. t. iii., p. 369) makes the same change to be in the mystical oil (chrism), and in the altar, and in the ministers, and in the water of baptism, as in the bread and wine in the eucharist, after consecration.   The bread is at first common bread, but when it is once sanctified by the

holy mystery—consecration—it is made, and called, the body of
Christ. So the mystical oil, and so the wine; though they be
things of little value before the benediction, yet after they are
sanctified they all work wonders. The same power of the
word—consecration—makes the priest become honourable, and
venerable, when he is separated from the community of the
vulgar by a new benediction. "For he who was before only
one of the common people, is now immediately made a ruler
and president, a teacher of piety, and a minister of the secret
mysteries."

Pope Leo (Serm. xiv. de Passione, p. 62) goes one step
further, and tells us, "that baptism makes a change not only in
the water but in the man that receives it: for hereby he receives
Christ, and Christ receives him, and he is not the same after
baptism as before, but the body of him that is regenerated is
made the flesh of Him that was crucified." (See Bingham on
Consec. in Bapt., Book xi., c. 10, s. 1-4.)

The grand apostasy into which nearly the whole of Christendom fell, was not brought about by believing the monstrous
fables of those called heretics without the church, but by listening
too uninquiringly to what was taught within what was called the
"Catholic Church,"—by renouncing private judgment, and by
trusting implicitly to official decisions; in one word, by over-
valuing the effect of the outward ceremonies of ordination or
consecration, sanctification of priests, baptism by water, and the
eucharistic bread and wine. So rapid had been the progress of
superstition, that in the third and fourth centuries these ceremonies had established for themselves a belief in their necessary
efficacy, such as inevitably drew in afterwards that mass of false
religion which overspread Christendom.

Nominal Christianity now shakes off the honourable responsibility of all its members being equal organs in the church, and
begins to concentrate their accountability upon the head of the
consecrated priests in every church, whom they invest with a
false nimbus of spiritual glory. Hence the church confirmed the
hierarchical dogma, and a decisive impulse was given to the

prelatical organization of Christendom, and the new regimen almost everywhere supplanted the primitive and apostolical institution.

Porphyry, who studied under Origen, takes notice of his allegorical mode of interpreting Scripture, when he writes against the Christians, and acknowledges that he continually perused Plato, and the rest of the Pythagoreans; that he was well versed in Chæremon the Stoic, and in Cornutus; and that from all these masters he borrowed the Grecian manner of allegorical interpretation, and applied it to the Scriptures. Origen, as well as Porphyry, Jamblichus, Hierocles, and Proclus, by their fondness for Plato, adulterated the Gospel. Are these the genuine Christians of the three first centuries? or were those whom Celsus named the despised Christians, such men as these? The facts presented to the reader forbid the conclusion.

In history, both sacred and ecclesiastical, we find that two things have uniformly taken place—first, that there existed all along a number of persecuted persons bearing the Christian name, whose lives proved them to be "the excellent of the earth;" and, secondly, that as far as appears, the character of genuine virtue belonged exclusively to these men, who espoused the peculiar doctrines of the Gospel, independent of philosophy, baptism, and the eucharist. Yes; from the Apostles down to Ignatius, Polycarp, and Irenæus; and from them to the age of Origen, Cyprian, and Constantine, both of these assertions are demonstrable by the clearest evidence, as well as ever since.

Though the notions of philosophers may vary in different ages, they never fail, in some form or other, to withstand the religion of Jesus. Clemens Alexandrinus was of the Eclectic sect,* and

---

* At the period when this philosophical sect, which has often been termed the Eclectic and Neo-Platonic, arose, the world was distracted into two opposing and mutually repulsive forces,—the Grecian systems of philosophy, and the polytheistic worship of pagans. These two it was thought necessary to unite into one harmonious whole. But Grecian philosophy was divided into hostile systems; polytheistic ritualism into

so far as he mixed his notions with Christianity, so far he tarnished it. The mystic philosophy to which he was much addicted, naturally darkened his views of some of the most precious truths of the Gospel: so it is with all the "fathers," as they are called. Thus the entire aspect of Christianity as a living principle in man, was completely transformed into a mixture of philosophic Paganism and Judaism. Such was the condition of the "Catholic Church" at the time when Constantine began to favour what is falsely called the Christian party.

The Emperor of the world is now said to be a Christian! And *pagan* Christianity comes forth, and suns herself in the warmth of court favour and popular applause; and the word of the mightiest is ready to defend her. She is the religion of the wealthy, the noble, and of the throne. Then it was said much people followed Christ. But ah! no longer was a humble believer allowed to touch the hem of Christ's garment, but a haughty autocrat reigned in his name, who was no stickler for anything except uniformity to the dogmas of the "Catholic Church;" so that Christ's lowly followers are no longer allowed to be his bride—the true church. No! but she becomes the harlot of the nations. But in her weakness she was strong. Power paralyzed her; yet she was lively in the catacombs of Rome, and the lowly rooms of Jerusalem. From this time the Bishop of Rome began to put forth those arrogant claims which terminated in the full development of popery throughout the world, and in England by Austin and the forty monks, A.D. 597.

Having taken a glance at the proceedings of the church in Palestine, Africa, Greece, and Rome, in the second, third and

hostile worships. Ammonius Saccas, who lived about the end of the second century, and who appears to have been an apostate from the Christians, opened an eclectic school for the purpose of blending together Platonism and Aristotelianism. The principal representatives in this school after him were Origen, Porphyry, Jamblichus, Hierocles, and Proclus. (See Faiths: Alexandrian School, vol. i., p. 58.)

fourth centuries, we will now turn our attention to England in the several succeeding ones. Here we shall perceive that the English had received the same superstitious notions from Austin and Theodore, as they had received from Carthage and Rome—namely, that in the sacraments, the priests, and they alone, by themselves, impart and sustain spiritual life, assure men of the forgiveness of sins, and regenerate them in baptism, and feed them with the body and blood of Christ in the eucharist.

We have a memorable instance of this when Austin arrived in England, and directed his way to Ethelbert, the pagan king of Kent, who favourably received him and the monks, and permitted them to take up their permanent abode at Canterbury, and publicly to establish their own religious rites. One year after his arrival, Austin baptized the pagan monarch according to the custom of Carthage and Rome, whereby he was declared to be a Christian; and unadulterated Christianity, which had existed in England for centuries, and which the Romans had attempted to hunt down, and the Anglo-Saxons had despised, now became a proscribed religion. From this period commenced the conflict between the Bishop of Rome and the English churches, both Christian and pagan: he to be supreme; they to retain their self-government, and their Christian or pagan principles, as the case might be. But no! Christian churches and Anglo-Saxon pagan temples were speedily converted into Romanized Christian churches; and the first effort of Austin was to induce the Britons to acknowledge his mission and accept his baptism. For this purpose he sought and obtained a conference with them: seven of them met him once and again. At the first meeting he endeavoured to bring them into conformity, or unity, with the "Catholic Church." Still the Britons delayed, and disbelieved. "We cannot change our customs," said they, "until we have obtained the leave and consent of the people." (Bede, the Saxon Chronicler, p. 69.)

A second synod was summoned. Austin then said,—"You act in many particulars contrary to our custom, and yet, if you will comply with me in these three points—viz., Keep Easter at the due time,* also administer baptism, by which we are born again to God, according to the custom of the holy Roman Catholic Church" (where Jewish baptism came to be confounded with pagan regeneration, see page 18), "and join with us in preaching the Word of God" (as interpreted by heathen tradition), "we will readily tolerate all the other things you do contrary to our customs."

This was the memorable reply: — "The British churches owe the deference of brotherly kindness and charity to the Church of God, to the Pope of Rome, and to all Christians; but other obedience than this we do not know to be due to him whom you call Pope. And besides, we are all under the jurisdiction of the Bishop of Caerleon." (Rapin i. 236.) "To whom," (says Bede, p. 71,) "the man of God (Austin), in a threatening tone, said, that in case they would not join in unity with their brethren, they would be warred upon by their enemies, and should at their hands undergo the vengeance of death." This was the first specimen of a coerced unity in the Church of Rome in Britain, and is nothing more than carrying out the policy of Constantine, Theodosius the younger, and Valentinian III. in Rome.

From this period commenced the conflict between the Bishop of Rome and the ancient British Christian churches, as well as the Anglo-Saxon pagans. This struggle continued till the year 669, when Theodore came under another direct appointment from the Pope of Rome; under him eventually the ancient English churches, as well as the Anglo-Saxon pagans, were brought to submit to Rome. And Theodore administered baptism according to the rules of that church, by which they

---

* The term Easter is said by the Venerable Bede "to have been first used when Christianity was introduced among the Saxons in Britain," and this old historian traces it "to *Eostre*, a Saxon goddess, whose festival was celebrated at the season, annually, in which Easter is now held; and when the worship of the heathen deity was abolished, the name was still retained in connexion with the Christian festival to which it gave place" —the day of the resurrection of Christ.

were said "to be born again to God." Theodore was the first archbishop whom they all obeyed as their head, the delegate of the pope, and the administrator of baptismal regeneration. This led the way to the great apostasies in England in A.D. 597 and 669, when Romanism ruled supreme, and the religion of the Gospel of Jesus Christ was annulled ; when religion, in fact, became a judaized and paganized Christianity, and the universal priestly character of all true believers, grounded on the common and immediate relation of all to Christ, as the source of Divine life, was suppressed: the idea being introduced of a particular mediatory priesthood, attached to a distinct order of men.

What faith Austin brought into England is plain from Bede's Ecclesiastical History. He says, "this apostolical man and his companions taught religious vows, the confession for sins to a priest, with absolution and satisfaction, veneration for relics, invocation of saints, purgatory and prayers for the dead." They used holy water and holy oil, wax tapers and lamps burning day and night at the shrines of the saints, and other holy places. They called the Eucharist the true body of Christ, and termed the Mass a sacrifice. They also taught the supremacy of the pope, whom Bede calls the bishop of the whole world. (See these points shown at large in England's Old Religion, from Bede's own words; also England's Conversion and Reformation Compared.)

The first penal law against religion ever known in England related to baptism, and is contained in the ecclesiastical code of Ina the West Saxon monarch, in whose kingdom Romanism had been introduced about sixty years, when the following law was made by his parliament, A.D. 693:—"Let a child be baptized within thirty nights. If it be otherwise, let the father make satisfaction with thirty shillings. If he then die without baptism, let him make satisfaction with all that he hath." (Wilkin's Concilia, vol. i., p. 58.) Forfeiture of lands, goods or chattels, for neglecting to baptize, preceded confiscation for heresy 715 years.

Fines continued to be imposed for omissions. Among other offenders were the priests, who, "if so drunk," says the canon of A.D. 740, "that they could not baptize," were to be suspended from their office during the pleasure of the bishop. Nor did the parent escape further punishment for allowing his child to remain and die "an heathen." How deeply sunk in immorality must have been the priesthood, and in ignorance the people, ere such a law as this could have passed! The next was as absurd. The canon of Ecbricht, Archbishop of York, A.D. 740, says, "Let the parent, whose child is dead without baptism through his neglect, never live without penance. If the priest, whose duty it was, neglect to come, when asked, let him be chastised by the law of the bishop for the damnation of a soul. Nay, it is commanded that all men should snatch a soul from the devil by baptism."

In the Council of Cealchythe, in A.D. 785, it was decreed that " baptism be performed according to the canons of the Romish Church, and not at any other time, namely, at Easter and Pentecost, and that those who receive children from the font, and answer for those who cannot answer for themselves, for the renouncing of Satan and his works, and for believing of the faith, know that they are their sureties unto the Lord according to their promise." (Wilk. Conc., vol. i., p. 146.)

These outrageous enactments of the churches remained in full force, and the former of them was confirmed by Alfred the Great 184 years afterwards, thus, "that if the mass priest neglect to fetch the chrism, or refuse to baptize, in the case of necessity, let him pay a mulct among the English, and a fine among the Danes of twelve ore." This was in A.D. 950. He then ushered in, among other ecclesiastical laws, the following :—

" I, Alfred the king, made a collection of what our predecessors had observed, and which I approved, to be transcribed, and those which I approved not, altered, with the advice of my councillors, and commanded them to be observed in another manner, for I durst not presume to set down in writing very many of mine own, because I know not what would please those that would come after me. What I found in the days of Inæ, my kinsman, or of Offa, king of the Mercians, or of

Ethelbert, (who first of the English received baptism,) which seemed to me most righteous, I have here collected, and passed over the rest. Then I, Alfred, king of the West Saxons, showed them to my councillors, and they declared that they approved of the observance of them all."

By this we obtain a knowledge of the fact that Saxon monarchs copied from each other's laws, as the "Catholic Church" of the second and third centuries had copied from Judaism and Paganism, and Austin had copied from that church. Here are Alfred, Inæ, Offa, and Ethelbert, who all of them received their code of laws, through Austin, from pagan Romanism. The connecting link between them all was the ecclesiastical law of each. The kingdom of Northumbria adopted laws strongly assimilated to those of the West Saxons.

By this time, three kingdoms, Kent, Wessex, and Northumbria, had embraced the views of Austin and his coadjutors and successors, imported from pagan Rome in full-blown splendour, and thus paved the way for Cuthbert to bring the whole nation under the same government. He, therefore, in a national council, held A.D. 747, enacted that "all priests perform every sacerdotal ministry everywhere in the same way or fashion, in baptizing, teaching, and which is the principal point, that they prepare the creed to infants, and to them who undertake for them in baptism (the sponsors), and teach them the renunciation of diabolical pomps, auguries, and divinations, and afterwards teach them to make the established profession." It was easier for Cuthbert to prescribe than to secure "the same way and fashion of baptizing." For another national council, held A.D. 816, required that—"the priest be taught when he administers baptism, not to pour as they had been accustomed to do, water on the head of infants, but that they be immersed in the font." A conflict ensued, and the priest exclaimed, "We will do nothing of the kind!" when some poured, some sprinkled, some immersed, for two or three centuries.

Consecration of the water of baptism by means of the chrism, and the consecration of the element of bread by means of sacerdotal officers, appear to have run in parallel lines. From the

earliest origin of the "Catholic Church," it was laid down as a
rule, that no valid baptism or eucharist could be had where there
was no priest to consecrate, and this authority was confined to
those who had been admitted to the priesthood.    In the earliest
of uninspired documents, the Epistle of Clement, the office of the
priesthood is described as that of presenting the eucharistic
offering. (See Clem., c. 40 ; and again see Clem., c. 44.)  In the
next writer, Ignatius, the validity of the eucharist and baptism
is expressly limited to those who consecrate by episcopal commission. (Ad Smyrnæos, 8.)    Then comes the Apology of
Justin, (i. 65,) stating that "the principal minister offered the
eucharist."   This is fully confirmed by Tertullian.   "The holy
eucharist," he says, "was not received except from the hands of
the church's public ministers."   (De Corona Mil., s. 3.)

As we advance into a period when writers became more
numerous, the proof that consecration was the specific office of
the priesthood, and confined to them alone, are so numerous,
that selection becomes the only difficulty.  Cyprian speaks of
the offering of the consecrated eucharist, as the appointed act by
which the priests were to imitate their Lord. (Ep. lxiii., p. 104.)
In the Apostolical Constitutions (so called), the thing demanded
of the priest was "to offer the pure consecrated bloodless victim,
the eucharist, as the mystery of the new covenant," (Ap. Con.,
viii. 5,) "because they honour you with the saving body and the
precious blood, and release you from sin, and make you partakers
of the holy eucharist." (Ap. Con., ii. 33.)  "Without the priest,"
says Hilary, "the sacrifice cannot be offered."    (Ex Opere
Hist. Frag. ii. 16, p. 1294.)  But we say, that which produces
in man the Divine likeness, must be his sanctification through
the spirit of Christ, without the intervention of a priest as its
agent, and the mystery of the sacrament.   According to Bishop
Pearson, the use of chrism came into the church soon after the
time of the apostles ; little mention, however, is made of it till
the third century, when it is referred to by Origen and Tertullian, in speaking of confirmation.   And what is remarkable in
the fact is this, that just as these two subjects were placed under

priestly influence and control, so at the same time the people, by an adroit crowning act of spoliation, were deprived of conjoint administration of the affairs of the church. This is carrying out Ignatianism and Cyprianism to the letter. (See first chapter, section 2nd.)

Is there, then, any inherent virtue in baptism? inquired the people in this as well as in later times, "Listen, ye doubters," replied Archbishop Langton in A.D. 1223:—"Baptism should be celebrated with great reverence and caution, and in the prescribed form of words, *wherein the whole virtue of baptism consists,* and likewise the salvation of the children," that is, "I baptize thee, &c." What! Virtue and salvation in words! Where is grace then?

The church at this time set apart special seasons for the celebration of baptism. The people were not satisfied with this arrangement. The inquietude increased among them in this respect, and induced many to call for a special remedy. Cardinal Otho, legate to Pope Gregory IX., supplied a legatine constitution A.D. 1237, when it was decreed that:—"The two sabbaths, viz., before the resurrection of the Lord, and Pentecost, are by the holy canons appointed for the solemn celebration of baptism, on a mysterious account," that is, the mystery as to Easter consisted in the form of baptism, representing the death and resurrection of Christ, administered by the immersion of the child, and its being lifted up out of the water; which notion was of itself a mystification of the words of the Apostle Paul, "buried with him in baptism." The mystery respecting Pentecost consisted in the assumption by the church that it was a second Easter. The Legate goes on to say, "that some in these parts, as we have heard, being imposed upon by a diabolical fraud, suspect danger if children be baptized on those days, which fears are inconsistent with faith; and it is demonstrated to be false, because the chief pontiff does personally solemnize this mystery on the days before named."

Still difficulties prevailed. The people had not the mysteries sufficiently explained. Another legate, Othobon, took up the subject; and in the cathedral church of St. Paul's, London, on the 9th of May, A.D. 1268, declared that "baptism is known to be the first plank which brings those that sail through this dangerous world to the port of salvation, and which is the gate to the other sacraments. Since, then, an *error* in our entrance by the gate 'baptism' is most dangerous, the legate aforesaid (Otho) desired to recall some from their execrable idolatry, who suspected danger to their children if they were baptized on the days, and in the manner, assigned for the celebration of baptism."

An explaining canon was yet required, and it was soon after Othobon's departure supplied by Friar John, Archbishop of Canterbury. He said in A.D. 1279, "We think fit to explain what is provided in this present constitution concerning receiving children to be baptized till the general baptization at Easter and Pentecost, out of regard to the statute (Otho and Othobon's, which seems to have been hitherto neglected). Let children receive baptism within eight days, or let inquiries be made for the children of their sponsors, between the time of their birth and their being perfectly baptized, and that nothing but the immersion remain to be performed on the day of baptism."

Half baptisms were now common, and tended to perplex and mystify baptism itself. This notable friar, therefore, found plenty of work in curing the evils. We will hear him once more. In A.D. 1281 he states:—"We find some have transgressed as to the sacrament of baptism. Let the exorcisms and catechisms be used over children baptized, in reverence to the ordinances of the church. But the form of the sacrament in the vulgar tongue consists not only in the signs, but in the series of the words in which it is instituted, inasmuch as Christ the Lord hath conferred a regenerative power to those words, so arranged as they are in the Latin tongue. Let then the baptizer say thus, *"Ich Christine the in the Fadere's name."* (See Spelman, vol. ii., p. 320.)

The exorcisms here referred to were of ancient date. The first unequivocal trace of exorcism is found in the acts of a council of eighty-seven bishops, which convened at Carthage,

E

A.D. 256. In the early days of the Catholic Church, when many of the converts came over from heathenism, the practice was adopted in baptism; in England, so far back as A.D. 740, the exorcist held a distinct place among the seven orders of the church. The English church then adopted a canon of Carthage, which required that exorcists lay hands on the possessed of evil every day. Giving his hand to the exorcist, he solemnly declared that he renounced the devil and all his pomps, referring to the public shows of the heathens, which Neander conjectures to have been based on the notion that the heathen gods were evil spirits who had seduced mankind. This principle is recognized in the first Book of Common Prayer of Edward VI., A.D. 1549, in which the priest, on taking the child into his arms at the font, was required to use these words:—" I command thee, unclean spirit, in the name of the Father, and of the Son, and of the Holy Ghost, that thou come out and depart from these infants; remember, thou cursed spirit, thy sentence; remember the day to be at hand wherein thou shalt burn in fire everlasting. And presume not hereafter to exercise any tyranny towards these infants whom Christ hath bought with his precious blood." There a mighty stride was made, and a great delusion maintained, against all kinds of demoniacal possessions.

Having already quoted Edward's institutions respecting exorcisms, and shown their origin, let us now trace his laws about baptizing. In his time the very font itself, as well as the water in it, was to be sanctified. His first book of Common Prayer, therefore, required the water in the font to be consecrated in the form prescribed:—" O, most merciful God, our Saviour Jesus Christ, who hast ordained the element of water for the regeneration of thy faithful people; send down, we beseech thee, the Holy Spirit to assist us, and to be present at this our invocation of thy holy name; sanctify this fountain of baptism, thou that art the sanctifier of all things, that by the power of thy word all those that shall be baptized therein may be spiritually regenerated, and made the children of everlasting adoption." The minister was also to put the white vestment, commonly called the chrism, upon the child, saying, "Take this white vesture for a token of the innocence which by God's grace in his holy sacrament of baptism is given unto thee." (See Liturgies of Edward VI., Parker Society, p. 116.)

The white garment put on at, and worn during seven days after, baptism, was a very ancient custom, even before Inæ, A.D. 693. In the second book of Edward VI., "the white vesture ceremony" was dropped, and thus the church was silently freed from a custom ancient in date, and anti-christian in practice and in effect.

Had there been a similar sweeping away of error as to other and more important principles, the result would by this time have proved highly beneficial. But we find that not only did Mary revive the old laws of persecution, and the still older customs pertaining to the baptismal rite; but Elizabeth also gathered up the expiring embers of the once blazing piles where martyrs suffered. In A.D. 1563, Elizabeth threatened a suit in the Ecclesiastical Court, with a view to authorize the civil courts to issue a writ of imprisonment against every person who shall " refuse to have his or their child baptized according to the custom of the Church of England." (5 Eliz., c. 23, sect. 13.) This act was designed to cut two ways,—against papists, and Protestant dissenters. This penalty may not appear so terrific as that of Inæ, in A.D. 693, which threatened the confiscation of " all that he hath" upon the negligent parent, but the principle is as vicious. It forms part of the old Saxon law of compulsory baptism, and goes far to sharpen the edge of that punitive enactment which immediately follows the above sentence, by which similar penalties are incurred by those who do not partake of the eucharist.

It is not hazarding too much to assert that, but for the civil penalties which drove men and women with their children to the font, there never would have been so many and so fierce a set of laws compelling them to approach the altar. Had there never been fines enforcing baptism, there never would have been fires flickering about the eucharist. And it is to the great reproach

of the Elizabethan age, that such a connecting link between the
two things should have been re-established in her day; except,
indeed, it be the greater reproach of the present day, to allow
such a statute to remain unrepealed.   For is it not a scandal to
Elizabeth's Protestant church, to have gone back to the very
worst periods of the papal Anglo-Saxon church for its model
of religious coercion?   It forms one among many other *nuclei*
around which the growing papal church may, at a future day,
rally its forces, and legally prevail once more.

But a still more remarkable statute requires and invites attention.   It is the 12 Charles II., cap. 17, sect. 4., passed in A.D.
1660, which says:—"Every minister formerly ejected and
kept out after lawful presentation to the profit of any ecclesiastical benefice or promotion, which hath not subscribed any
petition to bring the late King Charles, of blessed memory, to
trial; or which hath not by writing, printing, preaching, or
other open acts, procured, endeavoured, or justified the murder
of the said late king; or which hath not by preaching, writing,
or constant refusal to baptize, declared his judgment to be
against infant baptism, shall be restored to the possession of
his ecclesiastical promotions."

The grouping is almost grotesque.   It forms the finale of a
series of canons and statutes in England spreading over a period
of 967 years, during which the church had occupied itself with
the matter of baptism, and is a clear proof that of no one thing
will the human intellect remain so long or so determinedly
enamoured, as when it can lay hold of a religiously manifested
trifle.

Whatever may have been the conscientious opinions now
entertained as to the obligation, the virtues, the mode, or the
subject of baptism, one thing is evident—that the ceremony, by
having had bestowed on it so large an amount of ecclesiastical
legislation, has had an importance attached to it which has
proved highly dangerous.   That danger has arisen from what
it has been made *per se*.   Othobon had, in A.D. 1268, said it
"was the entrance gate to salvation," and in so saying he

embodied a sentiment as old before, as it has become since he spoke. This, the "plank that brings to the port of salvation," is in reality the sunken rock at the mouth of the harbour, and, what is more, with the pilot on board ; for the same doctrines of error which apply to baptism are equally applicable to the eucharist.

The contingency is, however, swallowed down whole. Were it apprehended, it would go far to destroy one of the most fatal and insidious dispositions of the human mind in its appreciation of religion. That mind never luxuriates so complacently as when taught that a form is as effectual as a principle. By all (except those who design to deceive) this is acknowledged to be at one and the same time the weakest and the strongest point : the weakest, because forms alone do not and cannot establish sympathy between the mind and God's character, purposes, or government ; and the strongest, because, when once forms superinduce false reliances, they simultaneously create the mightiest of all resisting powers the human mind can bring against the entrance or indwelling influence of the principles which beget and sustain spiritual life.

Once bring the authority of law to foster and patronize this suicidal religious tendency in the human mind, and formalism is legalized ; and by how much this is encouraged, by so much are the energies of Christianity crippled, its purity corrupted, its progress retarded, and its expulsive power of evil checked. But allow its inherent attractions to become its only law, let it resemble the light of day, and impart beauty, fertility, and order to all, without borrowing from any purely adventitious resources, and you may then watch, and as you watch admire, the outspreading certainty with which it will quicken into life whatever is morally great, noble, free, and benignant, among the endless groups into which the human family is divided. (See Muscutt's Altar Sins, pp. 310–323.)

# CHAPTER III.

THE SEVEN SACRAMENTS OF THE ROMISH CHURCH. BAPTISMAL REGENERATION A DOCTRINE OF THE ENGLISH CHURCH.

During the dark ages of the apostasy, when ignorance and superstition were developed, and debased the minds of men, religion was deemed principally to consist in outward acts and ceremonial observances; spiritual, and even miraculous, effects were attributed to some of these, and many of them were dignified with the title of Mysteries, or Sacraments. In the twelfth century, seven in particular obtained this character. The number of seven sacraments was first devised by Peter Lombard, and first decreed by Pope Eugenius IV., and first confirmed by the provincial council of Senes, afterwards by the council of Trent. (Leigh. Comin. de Sue., Lib iv., cap. 1.)

By the Reformers at the time of Wicliffe, &c., only two of these were allowed to retain their rank as sacraments. According to the Council of Trent, and the creed of the Church of England, a sacrament is the symbol of a " sacred thing, and the outward and visible sign of an inward and spiritual grace." But both churches violate their own definitions. They make baptism and the eucharist not the symbol of invisible grace, but the of means bestowing it, through the medium of their priests.

How often, in the hour of dissolution, has the mind of man been occupied, the conscience soothed, and hope inspired, not by what Christ has done, but by what the priest has performed. He has baptized him, he has confirmed him, he has heard his confession, pronounced his absolution, has given the eucharist, has administered the unction, and, therefore, all is safe. Fatal delusion! produced by rites which possess no more authority or efficacy than can be found in the cabalistic talisman, or in the water of the Ganges.

It is the grand doctrine of the Church of England, that by the administration of Baptism the priests are empowered to plant the seeds of Divine grace even in infants, to take away that original sin which they believe to exist, and to make them, by a spiritual birth in baptism, new creatures—partakers of a fresh life—children of God—and inheritors of the kingdom of heaven.

Through Confirmation, the bishops undertake to confirm this faith and strengthen this life.

By the Eucharist, the priests profess to renew this life in those who receive it; and finally, by Absolution, forgiveness of sins is assumed to be imparted to the dying. This we conceive to be a corruption of gospel truth, as the Scriptures declare that all such power must be of the Lord, and not of man.

We can scarcely conceive such presumption to be exceeded, except by another act of the Romish Church, which claims for itself a power, by a certain process of consecration, to create the Deity himself, under the form of bread and wine, and to present Him to the people for participation and adoration as a seal of their redemption. Yes, redemption itself! (Can this be true? Yes! for. Archdeacon Wilberforce and his church asserted it in A.D. 1854.) Well may Mahommedans and heathens be shocked with such vain pretensions on the part of Christian ministers! Those who have become involved in such flagrant errors, both priests and people, have a strong claim on the compassionate interests of their fellow-Christians, while the errors themselves are judged and condemned.

After the general introduction of infant baptism into the Church at Carthage, confirmation immediately succeeded as the completion of baptism. And in the Oriental churches generally, baptism, confirmation, and the eucharist were soon administered in immediate succession, even in the case of infants; this notion was formed so early as the middle of the third century, since the idea had then sprung up, in imitation of Judaism and paganism, of a spiritual character belonging exclusively to the bishops, on which priestly character the prerogative of the Holy Ghost in the Church was dependent through the sacraments.

Though in the ancient Greek and African churches confirmation immediately followed baptism, seven years are now allowed to pass after infant baptism before a person is confirmed in the Western or Roman Catholic churches, and in the English Church persons are not confirmed till they are fifteen or sixteen years old. Since the year 1660, it has been customary for the English bishops to require before confirmation, in the person to be confirmed, a renewal of the covenant made in baptism by the sponsors, by a repetition of the Church catechism, according to the decree of Pope Eugenius.

The human mind is naturally superstitious. It is soon attracted by external symbols supposed to possess some religious efficacy and charms. People are apt to confound the sign or figure with the thing signified. The generality of men find it easier to prostrate their bodies before a visible shrine, than to humble their souls in the presence of an invisible Jehovah ; and it better accords with the degenerate heart to adore a material cross, a consecrated wafer, bread, wine, and water, in the presence of the priest, than to receive, so as to be influenced by them, the world-denying doctrines of Jesus Christ and his Apostles. This is one aspect of our danger—a fondness for the ceremonial, in preference to the substantialities of religion.

At the time of what is called the Reformation in England, there were many who renounced the propriety of retaining the two sacraments of baptism and the supper. They saw, too, that the reformation that had commenced had to deal with antiquated and deep-rooted errors and prejudices ; that superstition, after so long a reign, could not reasonably be expected to be overthrown at once. Many sincere reformers deeply regretted the human policy and secular authority, which presented itself in hindering the work of a thorough renovation in the Church.

Great were the differences of opinion among the leading reformers as to the effect produced in the recipients of the two sacraments still retained. And, besides the great and fierce contentions in the administration of baptism and the supper, there were also differences of opinion as to those who are the proper recipients of the rite of baptism, whether infants or adults; and of the eucharist, whether it should be received in one or both kinds; and when and by whom;—this was the contention of centuries. It had been the doctrine of the Church of Rome that their due administration conveyed spiritual grace to all who received them, by the very act itself, whatever might be the qualifications either of the minister or receiver, whether converted or unconverted. Few, if any, of the reformers adopted this extreme view.

All true believers in Christ readily admit that the cleansing and purifying of the soul is essential to salvation, and is the great object of Christian baptism and communion; and that without washing, sprinklings, or immersions, or partaking of bread and wine, or the consecrated *host*.

Spiritual grace and a sign do not involve and produce each other: essentially different in nature, as matter and spirit, their properties cannot pass from one to the other, but must subsist separately in each. But water had been so long, and so intimately, associated with the word baptism in the public mind, that it was difficult for them to conceive the idea of a baptism without water; and there was, and is to the present day, a very general opinion in Christendom, which ages have sanctioned without inquiry, that this is true baptism, and that the ministers of each respective congregation are the only authorized ministers of the rite. Some, however, question their right to the prerogative.

Spiritual grace is essential to religion under every dispensation. It is the very life of religion in the soul of man. Shadows and signs have no moral nature or virtue in themselves, nor a natural or necessary connection with the spiritual things they have been employed to represent. Even shadows of material objects, though they indicate the existence of bodies projecting before them, have nothing of their reality, substance, or life; and therefore cannot communicate the properties of those bodies. This alone is sufficient to illustrate the fallacy of water baptismal regeneration, and sacramental union and communion. A man

may be regenerated by the Holy Spirit before he is immersed
or sprinkled, or has partaken of the eucharist, or undergone
either ceremony. And on the other hand he may have been
sprinkled, immersed, or have partaken of the eucharist, and yet
he may never be regenerated. This is the language of common
sense, and the general testimony and evident tenor of Scripture.
Yes! purifying water is but an appropriate emblem of the
sanctifying spirit ; the whole of its significance lies in the figure :
it washes the body as the spirit cleanses the soul.

Baxter (p. 117) calls water baptism " a sign of regeneration ;"
Dr. Taylor calls it "a shadow;" Danvers "a sign or figure of the
mystery of the Gospel." Hammond, in his Paraphrase and
Annotations on Matt. iii. 11, calls John's baptism "a ceremony ;"
saying, "John initiated disciples with water, but Christ by
fire ;" and on Mark i. 5-8, he paraphrases, saying, "Water is
the only sign that John used after the Jewish manner ; but
Christ was to send down the Holy Spirit from heaven, and is not
Christ the end of ceremonies, types, and shadows ? John's water
baptism, as all the shadows of Moses, was but to endure for a
time ; for as all the prophets were until John, so John was until
Christ ; and Christ by his spiritual washing not only fulfilled
and ended Moses, but John also." (See Thomas Lawson's Treatise
on Baptism, pp. 20-22, A.D. 1703.)

That the baptism of Christ is not a washing with water,
appears from 1 Peter iii. 21 : "The like figure whereunto even
baptism ;" or, as it should be translated, " whose model, baptism,
doth also now save us, not the putting away the filth of the flesh,
but the answer of a good conscience toward God by the resurrection of Jesus Christ." So plain a definition of baptism is nowhere
else to be found in the New Testament. And therefore, seeing
that it is so plain, it may well be preferred to all the coined
definitions of the schoolmen, e. g., Cerinthius, Elxai, Victor,
Cyprian, Callistus, or of even a pope, or an archbishop. The
apostle tells us first, negatively, what it is not,—"not the putting
away the filth of the flesh ;" then surely it is not a washing with
water, for that is so. Secondly, he tells us, affirmatively, what it

is—"the answer of a good conscience towards God, by the resurrection of Jesus Christ." Now this answer of "a good conscience" cannot be but where the Spirit of God hath purified the soul. Jesus, as a Saviour, is equal to all the consequences of the fall. In him God can as generally and as necessarily re-create as the lamentable circumstances of the fallen race require; those in whom this work is wrought may truly be said to be baptized with the baptism of Christ. The apostle in this place seems especially to guard against those that might esteem water baptism to be the true baptism of Christ, and to prevent such a mistake, he plainly affirms that it is not that, but another thing. It is also manifest from the epistles of the Apostle Paul, and from the necessary fruits and effects of baptism, which are three times particularly expressed. First, when he saith, "that as many of us as were baptized into Jesus Christ, were baptized into his death, buried with him by baptism into death, that we should walk in newness of life." Secondly, to the Galatians he says positively, "For as many of you as have been baptized into Christ, have put on Christ." And thirdly, to the Colossians he says, "That they are buried with him in baptism, and risen with him through faith of the operation of God." Therefore it is evident that this is not meant of water baptism, but of the baptism of the Spirit. But to return :—

There can be no doubt as to the teaching of the Romish and the episcopal English Church, on baptismal regeneration, from the time of their first establishment to the present day. The well-known Baptist W. Noel, says (p. 418), "I once laboured hard to convince myself that our reformers did not, and could not, mean that infants were regenerated in baptism—but no reasoning avails. This language is too plain." In a footnote, he says, "It seems impossible, in the face of our Church, and of the expressions directed to be used in the catechism, and the service of baptism and confirmation, to deny that the doctrine of baptismal regeneration is, distinctly, the doctrine of the Church."

B. W. Noel further says that, in looking over the writings of Bishop Ridley, we find (p. 240), that "the water in baptism hath grace promised, and by that grace the Holy Ghost is given: not that grace is included in water, but that grace cometh by water."

Again: Cranmer, archbishop of Canterbury, says, in his works (vol. i., p. 25):—" St. Paul says, So many as be baptized into Christ put Christ upon them: nevertheless this is done in diverse respects; for in baptism it is done in respect to regeneration: in confirmation they receive the Holy Ghost to enable them to overcome temptations to sin: and in the holy communion in respect to nourishment and augmentation." Again (p. 176): " What Christian man would say that we be not regenerated body and soul, as well in baptism as in the sacrament of the body and blood of Christ; or that in baptism we be not united to Christ's divinity by his manhood ?" Again (p. 366): " As in baptism we must think that the priest putteth his hand on the child outwardly, and washeth him with water, so must we think that God putteth his hand inwardly and washeth the infant with the Holy Spirit; and, moreover, that Christ himself cometh down upon the child, and appareleth him with his own self." Again: " The second birth is by water of baptism; because our sins be forgiven us in baptism, and the Holy Ghost is poured into us as into God's dear children; and so by baptism we enter into the kingdom of God, and shall be saved for ever." So much for Archbishop Cranmer.

Now let us see what Jewel, bishop of Sarum, says, in his Tracts (vol. i., p. 80):—" Such a change is made in the sacrament of baptism, through the power of God's work, that the water is turned into blood; they that be washed in it receive remission of sins. The grace of God doth always work with his saints: but we are taught not to seek the grace of God in the sign, but to assure ourselves that, by receiving the sign, it is given us by the thing signified. For this cause are infants baptized, because they are born in sin, and cannot become spiritual but by this new baptism of water and the Spirit."

It is evident, from Holy Scripture, that neither our Lord's example nor precepts, nor those of his apostles, furnish any reasonable grounds for such notions as these. Under the pure spiritual dispensation of Christ, holiness is not an attribute of insensible things—as water, bread, and wine,—but of the Divine Being, who cleanseth and sanctifieth the heart by the Holy Ghost, through Christ, and not through water as the sign, or men as the operators.

Mayer, in his explication of the Church Catechism, says, " Outward water makes none partake of such privileges; and the externals of the New Covenant are of no more virtue than the externals of the Old Testament; alleging, that in Christ Jesus neither circumcision availeth any thing, nor uncircumcision, but a new creature, and the keeping of the commandments of God. Baptism," says he, " confers not grace, *ex opere operato,* as the Church of Rome teacheth " (and may we not add, the Church of England too?); " and if not grace, neither those precious effects of grace ; neither is external baptismal water any more effectual than the blood of bulls and goats, to take away sin."

The error, then, of Cyprian, bishop of Carthage, and Ambrose, bishop of Milan, of the Church of Rome, and the episcopal Church of England, in teaching the doctrine of baptismal regeneration, originates in confounding the ritual of the Jewish law, heathen mythology, and a baptism like that of John's, with the baptism of Christ. The grand distinction, even between John's baptism and Christ's, was again and again enforced upon the people, by John himself. " I have baptized you with water, but he shall baptize you with the Holy Ghost." And Jesus himself spoke to his disciples in similar terms :—" John truly baptized with water, but ye shall be baptized with the Holy Spirit." No better proof of the decided superiority held forth in the Scriptures of the inward over the outward, could possibly be adduced than this. And why is this internal cleansing called a baptism, but to indicate that the external washing or baptism is a type or symbol of the inward washing of the Spirit? It is not an outward, but an inward baptism, that regenerates and saves us. Baptismal regeneration, then, in the sense in which it was understood by some of the early fathers, as they are called, and in which it is taught in the Common Prayer-Book, and by the Anglo-Catholics of the present day, is a doctrine which can claim the sanction neither of Scripture nor of reason. It is founded on one of those half-truths in which error so often presents itself,—an assertion of the regenerating power of baptism; while it ignores the grand distinction between the outward baptism with water, and the inward baptism with the Holy Ghost sent down from heaven. Let but this distinction be acknowledged, and the fallacy on which the whole theory rests is instantly apparent.

Yet the explicitness of the language of Ridley, Cranmer, Jewel, the Common Prayer Book, and Dr. Pusey, proves that these ideas are not new, but the doctrines of antiquity, universality, and consent, both in the Romish and English Church. It is truly so, as they were received from the Cerinthian, Gnostic, Donatic, and Ignatian polity, which established the Catholic Church in the second and third centuries; and by the Act of Uniformity, 13 and 14 Charles II., chap. iv., every clergyman must adhere in public worship to the use of the Common Prayer Book, and, moreover, he subscribes to the following articles contained in the 36th canon:—"That he himself will use the form in the said book prescribed in public prayer, and administration of sacraments, and none other." Now this book, in the administration of the sacraments, positively maintains baptismal regeneration. An appeal to the accredited standard of the church—the Prayer Book—is the only safe criterion by which we can with certainty judge of her authorized doctrine. It will not do to depend upon vacillating privy councils, archbishops, bishops, a Pusey, a Phillpots, or a Gorham, when we have to inquire into the religious principles of a community. It is imperative that our judgment should be formed from the formularies adopted and subscribed by the whole body, and established by law, which undoubtedly is baptismal regeneration. This doctrine is taught in the Oxford Tracts, without the slightest reserve, and Dr. Pusey goes so far in the tract on baptism as to say, "Whosoever of us has been baptized was thereby incorporated into Christ." "Our life in Christ begins when we are by baptism made members of Christ and children of God."

They greatly err, who affirm that the baptism of heathen tradition, Judaism, the baptism of John, and the baptism of Christ, make but one baptism. "Judaism," says Dr. Arnold, "within the first century, transfused its spirit into a Christian form, and substituted baptism for circumcision, and thereby, as has happened many times since, perverted Christianity to a fatal extent." (Arnold's Letters.)

The same remark equally applies to Cerinthianism or Gnosticism, when the Jewish baptism came to be confounded with pagan regeneration, and pagan regeneration became associated both with John's and Christ's baptism, as one regenerative principle in man; and the baptism of the pagans, the Jews, John, and Christ, combined into *one* whole, constitute the one Christian baptism, throughout all ages, in the traditional churches throughout the world.

Great contentions have prevailed at different times, both in the Church of Rome and in the Church of England, as to the nature and effect of baptism. "The whole of what they agree in," says Dr. Campbell, "amounts to this,—that in this sacrament, as they call it, something, they know not what, is imprinted, they know not how, on something in the soul of the recipient, they know not where, which can never be detected." (Dr. Halley on the Sacraments.) This is the best foundation they can lay, that their water baptism and Christ's regenerative baptism make but one baptism; although they are distinct in name and character, as we may be assured by the distinction between John's baptism with water and Christ's with the Spirit. Christ's baptism did not accompany John's, to make up one entire baptism: forasmuch as those whom John had baptized had need to be baptized of Christ afterwards. If John's baptism had been one and the same with Christ's, that only had been sufficient; but John's baptizing them with water unto repentance, left them still in need of the sanctifying baptism of the Spirit. As a proof of this we shall here subjoin a few testimonies :—

Augustine said, "It is clear that there was one baptism of John, and another baptism of Christ." (Contra Lit. Petil. 2.)

Pasor, paraphrasing on Heb. vi. 2., on the doctrine of baptism, said, " Here the plural number showeth forth the outward and the inward baptism."

Chrysostom says that " in the apostles' time the baptism of water, and the baptism of the Spirit, were different baptisms, and done at different times." (Magd., 5 Cent., p. 363.)

" The baptism of John gives not spiritual grace, nor remission of sins ; but Christ forgives sins, and gives the Spirit plentifully." (Theophilact. on Matt. iii. 11.)

"John was sent to baptize with water, but the baptism of the Spirit was committed to Christ. John baptized with water inviting to repentance; Christ by his Spirit renews the heart, and sanctifieth by his grace." (Aug. Marlorat on Acts. i. 5.)

Again : " John the Baptist makes Christ the author of spiritual baptism, but himself the minister of outward baptism only." (Aug. Marlorat on Matt. iii. 11.)

Spark, the king's chaplain, in speaking of the pouring forth of the Spirit upon the Apostles, said, " They had before the watery baptism of John, but now the baptism of the Holy Spirit; their tongues were touched with a coal from the heavenly altar. The baptism of John," saith he, " doth not take away sin, but puts them in mind thereof; but Christ's baptism takes away sin ; his Spirit is our Jordan."

Piscator, on Matt. iii., in speaking of 1 Peter iii. 21, saith, " Lest any should think that outward baptism saves us, Peter makes a distinction, and ascribes salvation to inward baptism ; saying, not outward baptism, whereby the filth of the flesh is put off, saves us, but inward baptism—the baptism of the Spirit."

Piscator on Matt. iii. 11, says, " There is a two-fold baptism, the one outward, whereby the body is cleansed; the other inward, whereby men are regenerated and renewed."

" There is a two-fold baptism " (says Trapp, on Matt. iii. 11.), " that is, of water and of the Spirit ; by John's with water, the pollution of the flesh is put away; by Christ's with the Spirit, the answer of a good conscience purged from dead works is known."—(See Thomas Lawson's Works ; A Treatise concerning Baptism, pp. 13-15, A.D. 1703.)

The query now arises: Can the sprinkling of water in the face of little children, or the immersion of adults, be Christian baptism? This was no practice of Christ, neither did he nor his apostles command it. Can a human invention be the proper means of making members of Christ's Church? Can such means ever effect that great change of heart which is necessary to renovate the soul? Can such an empty ceremony ever effect anything of a spiritual nature? Are there not very many of those who have been sprinkled by the priest, and pronounced to be regenerate, and made members of Christ's Church, children of God, and inheritors of the kingdom of heaven, who are never brought to the knowledge of the truth as it is in Jesus, and are scandalous in their lives and conversation—lovers of everything that is evil, and scorners of all good? By their fruits ye shall know them!

Yet the formulary of the Church of England teaches in the baptismal service that, "Forasmuch as all men are conceived and born in sin; and as our Lord and Saviour Jesus Christ said, None can enter into the kingdom of God except he be regenerate and born anew of water and of the Holy Ghost:" —as a natural consequence of this, the Church Catechism teaches "that, in this (water) baptism they are made members of Christ, children of God, and inheritors of the kingdom of heaven ;" "that coming to baptism, they receive remission of sins by spiritual regeneration," as a consequence of being sprinkled with water, as they say that we are not Christians without it;— which is quite inadmissible. Yet they add in the same service, "Seeing now, dearly beloved brethren, that this child is regenerate, and grafted into the body of Christ's Church, we yield thee hearty thanks, most merciful Father, that it hath pleased thee to regenerate this infant with thy Holy Spirit, and to receive him for thine own child by adoption, and to incorporate

F

him into thy holy church, he being dead unto sin, and alive unto righteousness." Wonderful change! can it be realized?* Now let us see what they say to the adult.

In the office of baptism for those of riper years, they say, " Forasmuch as all men are conceived and born in sin, and that which is born of the flesh is flesh, and they that are in the flesh cannot please God, but live in sin, committing many actual transgressions ; and as our Saviour Jesus Christ saith, None can enter into the kingdom of God except he be regenerate and born anew of water and the Holy Ghost :"—of water as the "visible sign of the inward and spiritual grace :" " a death unto sin and a new birth unto righteousness ;" " for being by nature born in sin, and children of wrath, we are hereby made children of grace ;"—"and seeing that these persons are regenerate, and grafted into the body of Christ's Church, let us give thanks to Almighty God for these benefits, that he that believeth and is baptized shall be saved, but he that believeth not shall be damned." (See the Order of Adult Baptism and the Catechism.)

Now it may reasonably be asked, what are the consequences of admitting that the use of water baptism in infancy constitutes Christian baptism, without which none can be saved ? Would it not follow that the salvation of a child may be lost, or even a whole family of children, through the mere neglect or mis-apprehension of their parents, (as in my own case, who am an unbeliever in the effects attributed to it,) without any fault what-ever of the unconscious children ; and that the salvation or damnation would depend on the performance, or omission, of an act over which they had no control, and of which they were not conscious—on what may be termed an accident as regards themselves ?

* The learned Dr. Taylor, in his dissuasive against papacy (p. 117), tells us " that a tradition to baptize infants (in England) relies but upon two witnesses, Origen and Austin : the latter having received it from the former, it relies only on a single individual testimony, which is but a piti-ful argument to prove a tradition apostolical. He is the first that spoke for it, and Tertullian, that was before him, seems to speak against it."

Now let us consult the plain dictates of reason, and consider without prejudice, whether the application of water to an innocent unconscious babe, according to the practice of the Church of Rome, and the Church of England, &c., can cleanse his soul from sin, and make him "a member of Christ, a child of God, and an inheritor of the kingdom of heaven." But here another and previous question arises, and a very important one too: Is there actual sin to be cleansed away with baptismal water? Before he has done or thought evil, is he to be punished everlastingly? The thought is monstrous; and repugnant to all our moral convictions, and to the most adequate ideas which man is able to form of the goodness, mercy, equity, and justice of an Almighty and All-gracious God. The Scriptures declare "that sin is the transgression of the law." And also, "that sin is not imputed where there is no law." That the helpless infant who knew no law, can not actually have committed sin, surely all rational persons must admit. Is he, then, to be condemned eternally for the sins or neglect of his progenitors? Far is this from every Scriptural view of the glorious Divine attributes.

Calvin says expressly, "that infant baptism is not mentioned by any of the evangelists." And in this opinion Luther agrees. And Jeremy Taylor says, "it is against the perpetual analogy of Christ's doctrine to baptize infants." "Christ," he adds, "gave no such command, neither did he nor his apostles baptize any of them." Yet the compilers of the Liturgy of the Church of England, by some unaccountable mistake, declare in the 27th Article, "that baptism of young children is by all means to be retained in the church as the most agreeable with the institution of Christ." Whom are we to believe? Or where are these institutions to be found in Scripture? We know not where! The sprinkling of infants, and the supposed regeneration thereby, derives no authority from the New Testament. This, of itself, is sufficient to prove that whatever else may be said in favour of the practice, it lacks, at all events, a direct Scriptural warrant; it strikes at the root of plain Scripture doctrine, that every man is responsible for his own personal actions. The Prayer Book contains much that is nothing but the dregs of popery, and which was left there by "expediency," for the sake of reconciling the Roman Catholics, at what is called the Reformation.

Having traced the steps of antiquity, and been diligent to search out the origin of sprinkling with water, and of infant baptism, and what we have found relating thereunto, we freely commend the result to our readers for their consideration. We find it recorded, that " the practice of infant baptism was established before the time of Irenæus, A.D. 178, by Elxai, a baptized Jew, who laid great stress upon baptism, to which he attached the forgiveness of sins." (See Schliemann, p. 226, seq.) This idea was faintly maintained, till it was carried up to the days of Fidus, Bishop of Carthage, about A.D. 254, who ordered Cyprian to baptize infants before they were eight days old. When Cyprian, and a council of sixty-six bishops, unanimously agreed that children might be baptized as soon as they were born ; they began exceedingly to magnify water, so that Christ's baptism with the Spirit was nearly lost sight of, they thinking that water baptism saved, regenerated, and took away original sin.

" As water extinguisheth, cleanseth, whiteneth, above other liquors," (saith Algerius,) " so in baptismal water, fleshly lusts are quenched, sin both original and actual washed away, whence innocence begins." Not particular men only, but even general councils, were involved in this erroneous conceit and misapprehension. The Council of Florence taught, " that by water baptism we are spiritually born again, and that it imprints in the soul a character—that is, some spiritual sign indelible, that cannot be blotted out ; and further, that we are thereby made members of Christ, and of the body of the church." (Summa. Concil. et Pontif.)

On what did they ground this doctrine ? Not on any command given by Christ and his apostles, but by an analogical reasoning, and that, too, of the most puerile kind, viz., the traditions of Judaism and Paganism, as interpreted by the philosophy of former ages, which now became mixed up with Christianity ;

and it is sufficient for us to know that from the beginning it was not so.

It has been asserted by some of the advocates of infant baptism, that from the time of Cyprian to A.D. 1158, no society of men ever pretended to say that it was unlawful to baptize infants. This is totally destitute of truth, for if there were none who opposed the baptism of infants, why were there canons made and anathemas affixed to them, against those who denied it? A council of bishops met at Carthage in the year 416, and after much debate adjourned to Mela, in Numidia, and among other decrees, guarded by anathema, was the following:—"It is the pleasure of the bishops present in this holy synod, that whoever denieth that infants are to be baptized, shall be accursed." (Wall's Hist. of Bap., p. 121; Robinson's Hist. of Bap., p. 217.) And the bloody persecutions of the Donatists in Africa for refusing to subscribe to this decree, as well as the murder of 1,200 Christians at Bangor in Wales, A.D. 604, by the influence of Austin the monk, who set the Saxons upon them, for refusing, among other things, to baptize (or give Christendom to) children, are a sufficient refutation of the assertion.

But there was no occasion for this contrivance of men, which, according to history, was got up in the apostasy from the true faith. Yes; it was got up by Elxai, Victor, Fidus, Cyprian, &c. They appear to have been the first who advised the baptism of infants for the purgation of original sin, and the practice became preached up afterwards as necessary.

Dr. Taylor, in his book of prophecy, (page 237,) gives a true and notable account, and "the truth is, that the necessity of pædo-baptism was not fully determined in the church till the canon that was made in the Melevitian council. I grant," says he, "that it was practised in Africa before that time, and they, or some of them, thought well of it; yet none of them did ever pretend it to be necessary,—none to have been a precept of the Gospel. St. Augustine, Bishop of Hippo, was the first that ever preached it to be necessary." Thus far, Taylor. Then remarks D'Anvers, "this Melevitian Council was celebrated by ninety-two bishops; Anselm the pope's legate and Augustine presiding, in the fifth year of Arcadius; and the first of Pope Innocentius, in A.D. 402. The occasion of the council is expressed to be about the difference that happened between Pelagius and Celestius, Augustine, and others, respecting original sin, baptism of children, &c., &c.

Among many other canons in this council we find this—viz., "That it is our will that all that affirm that young children receive everlasting life, albeit they be not, by the sacrament of baptism, renewed; and that will not that young children which are now born shall be baptized, to the taking away of original sin, that they be anathematized." Augustine and his party outvoted the other side, anathematizing them bitterly.

Afterwards, the fifth general council of Carthage, in A.D. 416, decreed to the same purpose in these words :—" We will that whosoever denies that little children by baptism are freed from perdition and eternally saved, that they be accursed."

By this and other innovations in this age, it plainly appears that the spirit of Antichrist which began to work in the days of the apostles, and had increased in the second, third, and fourth centuries, had made great progress in the world, and greatly beclouded and obscured the Christian religion by many inventions and impositions. Here these imperious and imposing Antichrists exhibited their decrees founded on notorious error, by imputing the sin of Adam to all children, so as to affect their eternal salvation, in a style quite contrary to the way of the primitive believers, who had the mind of Christ in what they did.

What an evidence is this, that the doctrine and practice of the Church of Rome and the Church of England is founded on these traditions—the opinions of Elxai, Fidus, Cyprian, the Clementine Constitutions, and the Councils of Carthage and Mela, and not on the Holy Scriptures—" It is our will, we will, and all who oppose our will, let them be accursed." The writer has been " accursed" in the nineteenth century because he could not receive these traditions, which has proved the principal cause of this history being written for the information of others.

Notwithstanding these curses, the Oxford divines, in a convocation held in A.D. 1647, said, "That without the consentaneous judgment and practice of the universal (Romish) church, they should be at a loss, when called upon for proof, in the point of infant baptism."

God's revealed will did not require anything of our first parents beyond what he gave them ability to perform; so it is with us; therefore no infant on earth comes into the world a sinner, or partaking in any degree of the sins of his parents, or under any moral impossibility of conformity to the Divine will so far as it is revealed. No infant is conceived and born a sinner, but is born as free from sin in itself as Adam was created; therefore needs no water baptism to wash away original sin received from its parents. Man is here, on practical principles, to do that which is sealed to him by God's law, by the testimony of Scripture, and by the Holy Spirit, as to what is good and what is evil. If children, as well as adults, would strictly and steadily conform, as they might do, to the Divine will, so far as it is from time to time opened and made known, they would acquire a dominion in the divine life over the evil inclinations in them. For there is no man, we believe, who commits a sin, but feels a rebuke of conscience. Our state in this life is a state of probation—such was the state of our first parents, and such is ours; and being armed with the spirit of Omnipotence, so far as we stand faithful and valiant in the strength afforded us, we are sure of victory. Our strength and help is only in God, but then it is near us, it is in us—a force superior to all opposition—a force that never was, or can be foiled, until we endeavour to be wise above what is written, as was the case with our first parents. When we stand, we know that it is God alone that upholds us; when we fall, we feel that our fall is of ourselves.

Our priestly hierarchy may well confess, which they do, that their faith is founded on the traditions of the ancient fathers! This is the ground on which the Common Prayer Book says, "that man is conceived in sin and born a sinner, and regenerate in (water) baptism." But we obtain a short-sighted view of the question by considering it as referring to the baptismal service only. In looking to the catechism taught before confirmation, we find that every young person previous to undergoing that ordeal, whatever be his state of mind and conduct, even if it be of the most vicious kind, is called upon to affirm, "that in his baptism he was made a member of Christ, a child of God, and an inheritor of the kingdom of heaven." So much for confirmation. They are confirmed as regenerate; and in the partaking of "the eucharist, the faith of this regeneration is said to be sealed to the mind as a passport to heaven." Now it may be asked again, by what authority was this doctrine brought into the church? The old priests were divided in judgment; some thought that the baptism of infants could be proved by Scripture, but Dr. Hammond, Jeremy Taylor, and others, said "that nothing could be more untenable than to rely upon such an argument, but that they must rest it on tradition."

It is the Gospel, and the Gospel alone, that sets forth the true foundation of the Christian religion. But we must give even tradition a fair chance; and when we come to sift tradition, we find that there is not a single word about infant baptism of much importance till the early part of the third century, and then only with regard to Fidus, Cyprian, and the bishops at the Council of Carthage, A.D. 254, who agreed that children *might* be baptized as soon as they were born, and this when 200 years of the Gospel dispensation had passed away, and the "Catholic Church" had embraced a mixture of Judaism and Paganism, and the prelates were regarded as the exclusive organs in the communication of the Holy Ghost in baptism, confirmation, and the eucharist, as we have clearly shown in chapter the first. This is tradition! and the whole system of baptismal regeneration, confirmation, and the eucharist, as given forth in the Common Prayer Book, is subversive of the plan of salvation as laid down in the New Testament. Christ, his Apostles, and the primitive church, taught no such thing; therefore this traditional invention, inconsistent with Divine truth, must be opposed as being traditional and contrary to truth. We can say with

Tertullian, " That is truth that was first ; that was first that was from Christ and his Apostles ;" what the Apostles preached, that they received immediately from Christ, who is the Alpha and Omega. Augustine, Bishop of Hippo, who lived in the early part of the fourth century, said, " That custom is not to be preferred before truth, but *ought* to give place to the truth."

This was expressed by Augustine when a controversy arose among the learned professors of Africa, Greece, and Rome, when the greatest errors and mischiefs were introduced, contested, propagated, and imposed upon the churches, concerning original sin and the manner of its removal. And when the ruling and strongest party—the " Catholic Church"—blindly concluded that little children are guilty of it, so as to affect their safety in eternity, they therefore imagined that something must be done by them to free children from that guilt, and effect regeneration in them, and pitched upon water baptismal regeneration as the means. But the Scripture says, "As in Adam all die, so in Christ shall all be made alive." We are separated from our God, not by the sin of Adam imputed to us, or the neglect of the sacraments of the churches, but by the awful consequence of sin traced as it is to the depravity and corruption of our nature, as the sons of Adam, finding its way into our own souls. Oh ! that we were more alive to this truth ; for mankind generally conduct themselves very differently from what fallen and con- demned sinners ought to do, in dependence on the grace and MERCY of our sovereign Lord God, by applying to the priest to give them a passport to heaven in baptism, the eucharist, and absolution.

What is mercy, my reader ? Mercy is the love that forgives the criminal and bestows the grace. Mercy is the love that obliterates all transgression through the blood of the everlasting covenant. Mercy is the love that delivers us from the bitter pains of eternal death, and bestows upon us great loving-kindness —the precious gift of eternal life through Jesus Christ. Yes ! Jesus Christ came from heaven in his infinite love and mercy, and humbled himself, and became obedient unto death, and bare the burden of all our sins; and by this most important of all facts, God has displayed for our instruction his own immutable holiness and forgiveness, and his boundless love and mercy to a lost and sinful world.   Shall we, then, think lightly of the Gospel of Christ, which is the power of God unto salvation, and cleave to tradition ?   Shall we clip it ?  shall we narrow it by any system of our own ?  shall we circumscribe God's glorious plan of redemption, by setting up tradition and philosophic notions? Oh no !  Let us have the Gospel of Christ in its length, and breadth, and depth, and height, in all its fulness and freeness, without any alloy.   Then we shall see the perfect fitness of the Saviour to the sinner; "As in Adam all die, so in Christ shall all be made alive."   The vail, my readers, is rent for us ; God has consecrated for us a new and living way through the vail, that is, through the crucified flesh of Christ, which was broken for us on the cross.   This is the ground of the Christian's hope, the rock on which his peace is built for ever.

God would not that what he had made should perish.   He willed to perform a greater work than creation.   With compassion and tender mercy he said, Let man be redeemed.   And Christ, the Lord of life, descended from the glory which he had with the Father before the world was, and took on him the nature of helpless man, sin only excepted, that he might redeem sinners, and restore a fallen world to the favour of its God.   So that he that repenteth him of evil, and setteth himself to do good, shall find mercy, and be as though he had not sinned, through the merits of Christ, whom God the Father hath appointed our Redeemer, who is the source and foundation of all good.   He converts the soul from sin unto righteousness, and baptizes us into the way of salvation.   It is he who makes us steadfast to do the thing that is right, and keeps our souls that they be not immersed in vain imaginations.   He has received the Holy Ghost of God the Father, wherewith to baptize us, and to enlighten our souls, whereby his redeemed are purified and rendered holy, and restored to the favour of their God.   He has ransomed and redeemed the souls of men, by enabling them to behold his righteousness, and attain unto righteousness, because he delighteth in mercy.

" This is the condemnation, that light is come into the world," but " men love darkness rather than light, because their deeds are evil." Under this condemnation infants cannot come, until they attain to the condition of moral agents. And let it ever be remembered that this redeeming principle of light they receive from Christ, who is the light and life of the world ; and not from the priest, or their sponsors in baptism.

This doctrine of the possibility of salvation to all men through our Lord Jesus Christ, without the sacraments of the churches, is essential, to be consistent with the attributes of the Deity ; because he cannot be represented to be merciful, or just, or equal in his ways, if this principle is denied. He cannot be represented to be merciful to those to whom he extends no mercy—or just in punishing those who do his will—or equal in dispensing happiness to one who may have been baptized by a priest, and misery to another who has not been so baptized, when both stand in the same relation to God, so far as they themselves are concerned.

If God's love to man is such that he follows him by the light of his own Spirit, and spares him till by disobedience he becomes abandoned to corruption ; what greater evidence can we desire of the universality of his love and mercy; and the long-suffering of his patience ; and to manifest those things which are evil, by violence done to clear convictions? Here death takes place, as in Adam on the day he ate of the forbidden fruit. In this state of death truth is not easily distinguished from error, or good from evil. Therefore evil habits gain strength ; darkness covers the mind ; temptation is yielded to ; and though the Spirit again and again admonishes, and bids beware, the mind, habituated to stifle conviction, too commonly rushes forward, and becomes more and more hardened, and darkened ; until what was at first plainly condemned as evil, by the unflattering witness of God's Holy Spirit, is, at length, maintained to be innocent and sinless—and, sometimes, even necessary to salvation. But "the reproofs of instruction are the way of life" to the soul. They check in secret both before and after temptation is yielded to; warning, beforehand, not to touch or taste; and, afterwards, condemning if we do so—this is the very thing whereby God works in all to will and to do of his own good pleasure; and by which he will, if we cleave to it, and work with it, enable us to work out our own salvation, without any of the traditions of men. Therefore, my readers, despise it not, do no violence to its motions; love it, cherish it, reverence it, hearken to its pleadings, give up, without delay, to its requirings, and obey its teachings. It is God's message of good to the soul; its voice is truly the voice of the living God. Its call is a kind invitation from the throne of grace. Hear it and it will lead thee; obey it and it will save thee from the power of sin and Satan; and baptize thee into newness of life. This baptism was before Fidus, Cyprian, the Council of Carthage, or the Council of Mela. Therefore we cannot but again subscribe to the testimony of Tertullian :—"That is truth that was first; that is first, which was from the beginning; that is from the beginning which was from the apostles."

Now, although it may be admitted that the precepts and example of our Lord have a primary reference to the conduct of individuals, as in the case of the apostles; they can surely be no less binding upon churches and nations, professing allegiance to Christ, the Supreme Ruler, than upon the individuals of whom they are composed. Nor can we be too strongly impressed with the importance of individual, as well as social influence, in the formation of the national mind, with regard to religious principles. If each individual, and each Christian church, wait for others, before they take the course to which his, or the church's convictions lead, it is plain that all religious progress must be stayed. If the principles for which we are pleading be essential parts of pure Christianity, it is for the Christian, even if he stands alone, in simple faith, to act upon them, and set them forth to the world; that the heavenly leaven may be more and more diffused. Let us never forget that the Gospel is not a transitory, but an abiding dispensation; that it is the dispensation under which we now actually live; and that these great principles we are now advocating, are among its most glorious and essential characteristics—spiritual regeneration. To affirm that this is impractical, is to put dishonour upon its Divine Author, and to set at nought his supreme authority. Therefore, it is now, that the Church, and each individual member of it, are bound to prove their allegiance to their Divine Master; and, by their influence, to promote the spreading of his kingdom upon the earth—that kingdom which is righteousness and peace, and joy in the Holy Ghost.

# CHAPTER IV.

SOME Christian communities, and a large number of individuals in others, admit that it may be a mistake to attribute to water baptism any spiritual benefit, or to conclude that this ceremony possesses any vital efficacy in effecting the great work of regeneration. Yet they believe, at the same time, that it is a part of Christian baptism, to be received either in infancy or adult age: and that it was commanded by Christ, (Matt. xxviii. 18,) and practised by the apostles as a gospel ordinance (which cannot be proved by the acts of the apostles), as initiative into his professed church; and "as an outward and visible sign of an inward and spiritual grace," if not conferred, yet signified; as a public token of membership in the church, like circumcision among the Jews; and as a perpetual ordinance to be practised among Christians.

Among this large class of persons, opinions differ very widely, as to the advantages to be derived from the observance: some deny them altogether, and others estimate them more or less highly; but all act on the opinion of the divine authority of the institution; and are therefore careful to retain the sign in some way or other, in order to fulfil the apprehended duty. But, be it remembered, that the types and shadows of the legal dispensation were not abrogated, to be succeeded by other shadows equally outward and figurative with the first. They were not shadows of shadows, but pointed to the living and eternal substance. (See Heb. x.)

There is no warrant in Scripture to lead us to suppose that baptism is the substitute for circumcision as initiative into the

Christian Church. On the contrary, circumcision was administered to every male in virtue of his being already a Jew; while baptism presupposes a belief in Christ as a necessary qualification. Again: the council of the apostles, at Jerusalem, abolished circumcision, without the most remote hint that any other ordinance was substituted in its room.

We can understand the value and necessity of signs in the former dispensation, when they were employed as a distinguishing mark between the Jews and idolatrous Gentiles, to prefigure the spiritual blessings more fully to be enjoyed under the gospel: but when these were come, and realized, through Christ, it appears neither consistent with Scripture, nor with right reason, to suppose that signs of the realities already come, are still to be continued; their reality and end having been already answered: and the danger is very great of mistaking them for the spirituality, and thereby bartering away the crown of Christ, and the cross on which he won it with his own blood, as well as the doctrine of his Divinity.

If our Saviour had ever instituted any sign, or rites, to be perpetually observed in his church, may it not be supposed that particular directions would have been given for the mode of performing them, as in the Law of Moses? Whereas, now, in the absence of such directions, some of those most eminent for piety and learning, after much research, arrive at different and very opposite conclusions, which is a convincing proof that they were never ordained of God.

If, then, a strict compliance with the *falsely supposed* original institution, is by most Christians deemed to be necessary, does not a more serious and enlarged spiritual view of the whole question still demand our attentive consideration? And would it not lead to the conclusion expressed by Christ himself, that "it is the Spirit that quickeneth." Or to the same conclusion conveyed in nearly the same terms by the Apostle Paul, "the Spirit giveth life." The same may apply to the words of our Saviour unto Peter, "If I wash thee not, thou hast no part with me." Augustine, Bishop of Hippo in the fourth century, said

"Christ hath not desisted from baptizing, but even yet practiseth it. Not by the ministry of the body, but by the invisible operations of his power and majesty." Jerome said, "If any man have received only the bodily washing of water, that is outwardly seen by the eye, he hath not put on our Lord Jesus Christ, how then can he be baptized into his body?" Chrysostom said, "the mystery is to be perceived by the inward eye of the soul, that is, spiritually."

Now the inquiry naturally arises, as to what is the benefit of water baptism, confirmation, and the eucharist; since a strong presumptive evidence, or reason, is afforded, for questioning the Divine authority of the rites as practised in Christendom; and for submitting whether there has not been, as we have already shown, some great misapprehension, and erroneous interpretation of the Scriptures, where it was designed that they should be spiritually interpreted, and accepted; and whether the idea of many of the early Christians, as well as of the early Reformers, is not well founded, that this mysterious subject is but ill-understood, and that more light must be sought for upon it; and whether, in fact, the reformation from the darkness, corruption, and superstitions of the Roman Church, which were borrowed from it by our English Episcopal Church, as respects these observances, as well as by other churches,—has attained its intended completeness: we trow not.

Although we can never be living members of Christ's Church, without being baptized by the one Spirit into the one body, and becoming new creatures in Christ Jesus, and being brought to feel that Christ is indeed our light and life, and that the kingdom of God is not in word, but in power, not in meats and drinks, and divers washings, but in righteousness and peace, and joy in the Holy Ghost; yet the religion of Jesus Christ in its full development abrogates all the symbols and rituals of the former dispensation, and destroys the works of the carnal mind, by which, in the time of the apostasy, the priesthood of man was substituted for that of Christ, and outward forms and ceremonies took the place of the unchanging power and holiness of the gospel.

These considerations, deeply momentous as they are to the cause of revealed truth, the writer desires in all tenderness to lay before those who think differently to himself, and to recommend them to their candid and serious thoughtfulness, though they may not accord with their prepossessions and consciousness. Conscientious convictions, my readers, even where the ground *may* be questionable, are entitled to charity and deference from those who may differ in opinion. Therefore, the author hopes he may receive credit, for the expression of the views at which he has arrived after a deep and continuous research into ecclesiastical history for the space of forty years; since the nature of the inquiry demands that the subject should be treated without any reserve, and closely viewed in all its different practical bearings; and we have to do with principles, not men.

With regard to the subject of baptism, the Scripture doctrine requires a true faith in Christ as the Redeemer of men, accompanied with good works, which cannot be by proxy, or in those who are unconscious, as infants; in fact, the concurrence of the sanctified mind is the essential element of all Christian perfection. Believers, who have been converted by the Spirit of God, and who are led to Christ, the Redeemer, who is able and willing to forgive, sanctify, and save them; these are the only scripturally and spiritually baptized ones; it is these who are baptized into Christ, and who put on Christ.

The Lord Jesus Christ gave the command to his apostles to teach baptizingly. At the day of Pentecost, they who gladly received the word were baptized. At Samaria, they who believed were baptized. The eunuch openly avowed his faith, and was baptized; Saul of Tarsus received the Holy Ghost, and was baptized; Cornelius and his friends received the Holy Ghost, and were baptized; the Lord opened Lydia's heart, and she was baptized; the jailor believed with all his heart, and rejoiced in God, and was baptized; Crispus and his house, and many Corinthians, heard, believed, and were baptized. This baptism is connected with the most important doctrines, duties, and principles of the Gospels. The Saviour connects it with a belief in the name of the Father, Son, and Holy Ghost—preaching the Gospel—fulfilling all righteousness—and the promise of salvation. The Apostle Paul connects it with the death, burial, and resurrection of Christ—the believers dying to sin—living unto God—and putting on Christ. He connects it also with one body—one spirit—one hope—one Lord—one faith—one God, and Father of all. Peter connects it with the remission of sins —salvation and a good conscience. This is the Scripture doctrine of baptism. This is practical regenerative baptism; it is the work of God's spirit on the soul of man, bringing him to a spiritual knowledge of the Saviour—redeeming him from all sin. This is not the fruit of traditional baptism, as we have already shown.

Water is but twice alluded to in connection with the sixteen passages of Scripture above advanced. In one instance the question is asked by a heathen convert immediately on his receiving the gospel doctrine contained in Isaiah liii. (which see), "What doth hinder me to be baptized?" In the other instance, Peter who had frequently dissembled for fear of the Jews, asked the question "Can any forbid water that these should not be baptized?" These are very weak foundations to build water baptismal regeneration upon as a gospel ordinance. And the other fourteen passages are diametrically opposed to such an idea. For what has water to do with a belief in the Father, Son, and Holy Ghost—fulfilling of righteousness—the promise of salvation—the death, burial, and resurrection of Christ—of believers dying to sin, and being alive unto God, and putting on Christ—with one body, one spirit, one hope, one Lord, one faith, one God, remission of sins and a good conscience? Nothing! Let us then reject it as unworthy of a thought.

The religious man, however simple, is like a mariner who has a compass on board his vessel, which will always guide him aright, however thick the atmosphere around him, however dark the night. The Christian has a compass within him—a faithful monitor—a clear director—the Spirit of God. If he consult this compass diligently, with a single eye to Christ, he will be sure to form a right decision on every religious question; while the proud philosopher, and the traditional Christian, who know no such teacher, are tossed on the waves of forms, ceremonies, doubt, and confusion. We have many proofs of this in history.

When John the Baptist, the last prophet of the legal dispensation, preached the coming of the kingdom of heaven, and repentance for the remission of sins, he also, according to his special calling, baptized those who came as converts to his doctrine and fellowship according to the Jewish custom. Our blessed Lord, therefore, submitted to this, as he did to all the other ceremonies of the Jewish law, in order to fulfil all the righteousness of that law. John was, however, very careful not to mislead the people by directing their expectations to himself or his baptism; on the contrary, he distinctly pointed their attention to Christ, saying, "Behold the Lamb of God which taketh away the sin of the world." "I indeed have baptized you with water, but he shall baptize you with the Holy Ghost." "He must increase, but I must decrease." These last words foretold a gradual conclusion of the former dispensation, and also a progressive establishment of the new one.

The baptism of John was no new thing, there had been before his appearance divers washings under the law, figuring forth the baptism of Christ, who when he came, would purify the hearts of the disobedient, by the power of his grace. When Christ appeared, there was no longer any need for the typical washings and purifications, for Christ, to whom the symbols pointed, had appeared and taken their place; the symbols had fulfilled their office, and were at an end.

John the Baptist, as the forerunner of Christ, did not belong to the gospel dispensation, but came before to prepare the way of Christ and his baptism; now, as John did not belong to the gospel dispensation, he could not introduce a gospel ordinance. He was but the forerunner of Christ, he came to prepare his way, and then to give place to him and disappear; and Christ, with his spiritual baptism, must increase and swallow up all types and symbols, by giving this spiritual baptism in fulfilment of the gospel promise.

John's baptism was a figure of the baptism of Christ; and seeing that the figure or shadow gives place to the substance projecting it, so the baptism of John ceased in the presence of the baptism of Christ. Therefore, water baptism is not to be continued under the gospel, as forming any part of the new dispensation.

To make water baptism, in any shape, a necessary institution of the Christian religion, which is pure and spiritual, is to derogate from the New Covenant, and to set up the legal rites of a dispensation that has ceased to be, and was only imposed till the time of reformation.

The imposition of the baptism of John could impart nothing heavenly, it only prepared for the heavenly, it could not impart the forgiveness of sins, and the gift of the Holy Spirit; that none but God can do. Christ himself said, that the Spirit could not come down in its fulness, till He had ascended to the Father. Therefore, we perceive that so long as Christ was on earth doing his Father's will there, in the fulfilling of the ceremonial law, there could be no Christian baptism. The true baptism could not be till after the completion of the work of redemption, *i.e.*, the resurrection and glorification of Christ, and the imparting of the Holy Ghost.

In the Holy Scriptures there is the promise of the Old Covenant, and the promise of the New Covenant ; the promise of the Old Covenant was Christ, and the promise of the New is the Spirit. Therefore, well might the Apostle declare, "It is the law of the Spirit of life in Christ Jesus that sets us free from the law of sin and death." And Christ, "that he would send the Comforter to us, even the Spirit of truth, to lead us into all truth."

When Christ's baptism is expressly spoken of, it is generally stated to be with the Holy Ghost, or Spirit ; the phrase "with fire" being occasionally used to show its powerful nature in the destruction of sin, and the contrast to the baptism with water. Thus, John said, " I indeed baptize you with water unto repentance, but He shall baptize you with the Holy Ghost and with fire. He that sent me to baptize with water, the same said unto me, On whom thou shalt see the Spirit descending and remaining on him, the same is he which baptizeth with the Holy Ghost." From this it is quite clear, that the gospel baptism is that of the Holy Ghost, as distinguished from the baptism with water at the hands of the priests.

By this heavenly baptism, that necessary change is accomplished in us "of putting off the old man which is corrupt according to the deceitful lusts; and of being renewed in the spirit of our minds, that we put on the new man, which after God is created in righteousness and true holiness."

It is with doctrinal belief, as it is with moral conduct, that the first step from the strait and narrow way is the most dangerous one. The most vicious conduct has its beginning in what some would term slight deviations from virtue ; and equally true it is, that the most pernicious heresies have originated in what has been called harmless speculations, in philosophy, paganism, and Judaism, when the word "baptism" was borrowed from Judaism, and "regeneration," from philosophic paganism. (See Chaps. 1 & 2.) A doctrine is known by the terms in which it is stated, as "by one Spirit we are all baptized into one body, and all made to drink into one spirit." This doctrine became obscure when it was mixed up with Jewish ceremonies, and heathen traditions ; when the apostolic meaning of the term was changed by the priesthood who had usurped to themselves the character of the priesthood under the Jewish law, and pagan idolatry, when a new term of equivalent meaning to spiritual regeneration was invented ; viz., water baptismal regeneration. It has been uniformly found in all ages of the Church, that when a spiritual doctrine is to be discarded, it is done under a pretence of affixing a new meaning to a term—as water instead of spirit baptism. A man thus disguising his real sentiments may subscribe an orthodox creed, and convey a false impression by tampering with words. If suspicion of his real sentiments is aroused, he attempts to evade conviction by alleging that he differs only in words, although in such a connection words are emphatically things. Those conversant with past and present theological controversies, will not fail to have remarked that the abettors of errors, when subjected to trial, have uniformly endeavoured to shield themselves under the plea that their differences are only verbal, although in the first publication of their opinions, they have insisted upon them as important, if not original views. Thus it was concerning water baptism, confirmation, and the communion in the Church of Rome, &c. Well may we be suspicious, then, when we hear any one characterizing any deviations from the pure gospel doctrine, as too unimportant to disturb the peace of the Church. What is not truth is error, and no error can be inconsiderable, because its tendency must be to unsettle the truth. This has been the case, by introducing water baptism, confirmation, the eucharist, and the catechism, to support them, instead of spiritual baptism, communion, &c.

Many such errors are found in the baptismal service and catechism of the Church of Rome, and the Church of England. It is certain that baptism is not called christening in the New Testament. This is almost universal among Conformists, who much more frequently talk of christening, than of baptizing their children. The natural conclusion is, that they are spiritually regenerated, when they are christened by the parish priest, whose prerogative alone it is to make them members of Christ, children of God, and inheritors of the kingdom of heaven, in their baptism or christening. This opinion is confirmed in the catechism.

This baptism, or christening, is supposed to place the child in a state of complete salvation, to invest it with every Christian grace, so that it becomes as really a Christian in nature, state, and privileges, as was the Apostle Paul himself—regenerated. Indeed, we defy any person to state in terms more plain and significant, the conversion, adoption, and eternal safety, of any true Christian in the world, than is contained in the baptismal service of these churches. Hence, while living in the utter neglect of vital religion, and in direct opposition to the law of God, the bishop confirms them in this faith by the imposition of his hands. Their consciences are, therefore, rendered easy and comfortable, in the midst of their sins. A doctrine more congenial to depraved human nature—more likely to be cordially received, and constantly retained in the unrenewed heart—more adverse to holiness of life—more destructive to the souls of men, or more opposed to the whole scheme of Christianity, could hardly have entered into the minds of mankind.

We will now refer to the unmeaning dialogue entered into between the priest and the sponsors in the baptism of infants· "Then shall the priest say unto the godfathers and godmothers in this wise : This infant must promise by you that are his sureties, until he come of age to take it upon himself, that he will renounce the devil and all his works," &c.

*Minister.*—"Dost thou in the name of this child renounce the devil and all his works," &c.

*Godfather.*—" I renounce them all."

*Minister.*—"Dost thou believe in God the Father Almighty,"&c.

*Godfather.*—" All this I steadfastly believe."

*Minister.*—" Wilt thou be baptized in this faith ?"

*Godfather.*—" That is my desire."

*Minister.*—" Wilt thou obediently keep God's holy will and commandment, and walk in the same all the days of thy life ?"

*Godfather.*—" I will."

The reader will observe here that the infant is presumed really and personally to renounce the devil—to believe the Apostles' Creed—to desire baptism—and to resolve on constant and universal obedience unto God. If this be not an ascertained fact, sponsors are not warranted to say so in its name. But how have they so fully discovered the baby's piety, belief, desires, and resolves? For aught they know it may be a little Quaker or antipædo-Baptist. Therefore, merely to guess, is to venture at a gross misrepresentation ! They are not questioned about the probable future, but the actual present desires and intentions of the unconscious child ; nor are they called upon to state their own personal views and wishes. They are interrogated only as the mouth-piece of the unconscious infant; otherwise the child might as justly be baptized by proxy, as believe by proxy !

A more unmeaning and obscure jargon, on religious subjects, is not to be found in all the compass of ecclesiastical nonsense, of which there is plenty ; and this, too, in the Church of which the mighty, the noble, and those called wise, are enrolled as members, and whose ministers are honoured with distinctions, clad in splendour, and revered as oracles.

It is manifest, that if the sponsors performed all that they undertake, parents are necessarily deprived of their natural oversight and management of the education of their own children, as they are generally refused the sponsorship at the font.* And

---

* The office of Sponsors, though mentioned as early as Tertullian, has no foundation either in example or precept drawn from Scripture, but may have, probably, originated in a custom authorized by Roman law, by which a covenant or contract was witnessed and ratified with great care. The common tradition is, that sponsors were first appointed by Higinus, a Roman bishop, about A. D. 154. The office was in full operation in the fourth and fifth centuries. The names of the sponsors were entered in the baptismal registers, along with that of the baptized person. Certain qualifications were required of those who undertook the duties of sponsors. Thus (1.) the sponsor himself must be a baptized person, in regular communion with the Church. (2.) He must be of adult age, and of a sound mind. (3.) He must know the Creed, the Ten Commandments, the Lord's Prayer, and the leading doctrines of faith and practice, and must duly qualify himself for his duties. (4.) Monks and nuns were, in the early periods of the Church, thought to be peculiarly qualified, by the sanctity of their character, for this office ; but they were excluded from it in the sixth century. (5.) Parents were disqualified for the office of sponsors to their own children in the ninth century; but this order has never been generally enforced. According to the Rubric of the Church of England, " There shall be for every male child to be baptized two god-fathers and one godmother ; and for every female one godfather, and two godmothers." In the Church of Rome, no person is allowed to marry one who has stood to him or her in the relation of sponsor. This prohibition first appears in the code of Justinian, surnamed the Great, and came to be admitted into the canon law about the middle of the sixth century.

it is equally evident, to all considerate persons, that they engage to accomplish what the parson and themselves are, there and then, fully assured cannot be performed by them; and what not one sponsor in a thousand ever attempts to fulfil. Hence they are induced to make vows at the bidding of the Church, with no other intention but of breaking them, in what is called a Christian sacrament.

We are fully convinced that water baptism never was designed to, and never can, convey regeneration, notwithstanding the promises of the sponsors; and has no such promise in Scripture. We confidently conclude that no mortal was ever so regenerated. The expectation thereof is vain, and fallacious. It is one of the great leading errors that first corrupted Christian truth, as we have already shown in the first and second chapters; and, probably will be one of the last to be banished from the Church. It strikes at everything vital in religion—subverts the covenant of promise—makes faith and truth of none effect—and supersedes the genuine work of the Spirit.

Among the Gnostic sects of the early Church there were some, as, for example, the Marcosians, and Valentinians, who rejected water baptism, on the ground that men were saved by faith, and needed no outward ceremonial whatever. The Archontici, also, objected to it, on grounds peculiar to themselves. The Seleucians and Hermians, again, alleged that baptism with water was without validity, not being the baptism instituted by Christ: because John the Baptist compared his own baptism with that of our Lord, saying, " I baptize you with water, but he that cometh after me shall baptize you with the Holy Ghost and with fire." The Manicheans also refused to baptize their disciples, on the principle that baptism with water was of no efficacy to salvation, and ought, therefore, to be rejected. Among the Duchobortsi, the most noted of the Russian sects, baptism and the Lord's supper were both dispensed with, as not consistent, in their view, with the spiritual nature of Christianity. On this ground, Peter Abelard, Peter de Bruis Abbot of Cluny, with Henry, his disciple, in France; Henry and Arnold, of Italy,

Gerard and Dulcimus, of Germany, and their disciples, all taught against infant baptism; for which the first was committed to the flames; the second to imprisonment, where he died; the third was executed; and the others persecuted in various ways.

It is a very noticeable fact, that almost all variations of theological views have, at some time, and in some persons, been regarded as unimportant differences. And, in accordance with this view, it has become a convenient phrase in controversy, that we are not to make a man an offender for a word. Shall the Church be agitated for a shade of opinion between water baptism and non-water baptism? Shall we disturb its harmony in the attempt to make every man pronounce the shibboleth aright? Is no allowance to be made for honest expression of opinion? The popular ear is readily caught by such catch-phrases; and many are intimidated by them from a fearless discharge of their duty. No one covets, we apprehend, the charge of being either a bigot, or a heresy-hunter; and advantage is taken of this to maintain the existing errors, or to introduce into the Church those novelties, or revived errors, which damage the true faith, and awaken controversy, as in the days of the apostles, as well as many times since; if, indeed, there be any bold enough to contend for the truth! What is religious controversy, but the vindication of religious truth, so far as we are permitted to see? But, is not the truth liable to be denied, distorted, corrupted, or frittered away, as in former times? Yes! Has it not ever been, since the second century, entangled with spurious errors—as water-baptismal regeneration—and the renewal of this life in the eucharist, which are productive of false consequences. It was against these things that the early Church contended; and are the friends of the same glorious gospel, at the present day, to stand still, and see its dearest interest jeoparded, without coming forward in its defence? Is there any alternative left them but to enter the lists of controversialists, and endeavour to show truth triumphant? If there are fundamental truths in the gospel, and these truths are assailed by false principles and practices, the truth must be defended: for this we have the highest authority, both of Scripture precept and example. Mention is made of some " whose mouths must be stopped," and " gainsayers put to silence." And we find several of the epistles written with the express design of confuting certain errors of a Judaizing and philosophic character, which had sprung up in the Church, and were making head against the apostles' doctrine. This was the apostles' work. This is our work.

And we have yet to learn that the days in which we live are so highly distinguished above the days of the apostles, as to absolve us from the necessity of controversy. Are errors less rife, over the length and breadth of the world, at this moment, than in the time of the apostles, and our fathers? Is there a more cordial yielding to the pure principles of religion and morality? No! But there is a disposition to relax the vigour of truth, and maintain Jewish and heathen traditions, as was the case in the second and third centuries; and here, if we mistake not, embedded in the flower of charity, lies the baneful canker-worm.

Shortly, or immediately before Christ's ascension, and in the course of his parting conversation with his disciples, he made repeated mention of baptism. Then it was that he gave his apostles their commission to preach the gospel to the Gentiles; " baptizing them in (or into) the name of the Father, and of the Son, and of the Holy Ghost." This was much more likely to be effected by the preaching of the gospel Divinely Commissioned, and under the power of the Holy Ghost, which they had received for the purpose, on the memorable day of Pentecost—than by any washing in water, as this cannot create a true faith in any one, nor preserve us in the life of truth, causing his Spirit of glory and power to rest upon us, and the virtue thereof to spring up day by day. In this point of view, the words doctrine, and baptism, are synonymous—it being, as we have often remarked, the acknowledged principle of the Jews, that when there was a new doctrine, there also, as a matter of course, was a new baptism.

Jesus Christ was accustomed to speak of baptism in a spiritual sense. When he came and spake unto his disciples, about what is generally called the great gospel, or baptismal commission, he said unto them, " All power is given unto me in heaven and in earth. Go ye therefore, and teach all nations, baptizing them in the name of the Father, and of the Son, and of the Holy Ghost: teaching them to observe all things whatsoever I have commanded you: and, lo, I am with you alway, even unto the end of the world." A very proper introduction to command attention, inspire confidence, and show them whence their whole qualification to teach baptizingly was to proceed :—" All power is given unto me in heaven and in earth "—" Go ye therefore," because " I have all power," and can and will qualify you to teach, in my own life and power, so as to baptize the people into the very name, power, virtue, and life of the Father, Son, and Holy Ghost. The commission is not to teach and baptize, as two distinct acts ; but to teach baptizing : and as such a work might seem too great for their faith, he adds, that He, who had " all power," would be with them in the work, and that " to the end of the world."

The apostles, being well confirmed and taught in Christ's school, and furnished with the gift of the Holy Spirit, went out into the world, according to Christ's command, and commended unto others what they had learned of Christ, teaching them to observe all things whatsoever he had commanded them. What they received from Christ, that only they were to teach others. No heathen philosophy, or tradition of men, dropped out of their mouths ; but their living concern was to bring them to learn of Christ, and to witness salvation and eternal life through his baptism.

It is plain, then, that this commission, as it enjoins a peculiar kind of teaching, so it could not be executed but by a super- natural assistance received from God. " Behold," said Christ, "I send the promise of my Father upon you : but tarry ye in the city of Jerusalem, until ye be endued with power from on high." " Ye shall receive power, after that the Holy Ghost is come upon you : and ye shall be witnesses unto me both in Jerusalem and in all Judea, and in Samaria, and to the uttermost parts of the earth." Thus it is evident, that their being living witnesses of Christ, depended upon the power of the Holy Ghost coming upon them ; and that they could never perform his baptism, till they were thereby so endued, as to teach baptizing into the same Spirit into which they themselves were baptized. And in the power thereof, they taught with such baptizing efficacy, that multitudes were pricked in their hearts. The Holy Ghost fell on them that heard the word ; their very enemies were not able to resist the wisdom, and the spirit by which they spake. Thus truly, with great power gave the apostles witness of the resurrection of the Lord Jesus. Thus they preached the gospel unto the people, "with the Holy Ghost sent down from heaven." No wonder, then, that it fell on those of the true faith, who gladly received the gospel in its baptizing power, so that they became baptized into a belief in the Father, Son, and Holy Ghost, having felt the power thereof. In order to understand this doctrine, we must be convinced from the depth of our own experience. To render the knowledge of Scripture truth availing to the progress of the work of religion on the soul, it must be accompanied with a humble subjection of the heart and understanding, to the immediate operation of the Spirit of God. It is the Holy Ghost that makes gospel preachers and baptized hearers. Not by the form, not by any outward element, but by the proclamation of the truth. Under the power of God they baptized the Jews into the name of Jesus—the Gentiles into the name of the Father, and of the Son, and of the Holy Ghost. Well, therefore, might Paul, an undaunted partaker of the great commission, say to the Corinthians, " Christ sent me not to baptize "—with water, "but to preach the gospel ;" and well might he add, " that the preaching of the cross is to them that perish foolishness, but unto us which are saved, it is the power of God." This view of the subject perfectly agrees with " Go ye into all the world, and preach the gospel to every creature ;" " he that believeth, and is baptized, shall be saved."

To say that Christ sent his disciples to baptize with water, is to question the testimony and record of John, who said, "Christ shall baptize with the Holy Spirit." This he did by the power of the apostles' ministry, by bringing those to whom they were sent, to become disciples of Christ, to learn of him, to know his immediate teaching, to take up his yoke, to bear the same, to learn obedience, to come into the self-denying state of discipleship; so the words originally import, say Bullinger, Zwingle, Leigh, Fisher, Trapp, &c. This is what Paul spoke of when he said, "By one Spirit are we all baptized into one body;" so that it was the Spirit that baptized the hearers. Paul, as well as the first disciples, in and through the virtue of him that sent him, opened the eyes of the Gentiles, and turned them from darkness to light, and from the power of Satan unto God; so that these also were witnesses of the spiritual baptism into the name of the Father, and of the Son, and of the Holy Ghost. Zwingle and Piscator, in speaking on the aforesaid Scripture, say expressly that "Christ Jesus did not in these words institute a form of baptism; and that divines had taught falsely, who held it out as a form of (water) baptism."

The word "name" here, is not to be understood literally, but of that Divine power, virtue, and influence, which emphatically denotes and characterizes the Godhead above all other beings and things; which our Lord often expressed by the same words. "I have manifested thy *name* unto the men whom thou gavest me." "I have kept them in thy *name*." And he prayed, "Holy Father, keep through thine own *name* those that thou hast given me." Into the internal virtue of this sacred and all-sufficient name or spirit are all the truly regenerated measurably baptized; "for if any man have not the spirit of Christ he is none of his." The apostles, with many of the primitive brethren, received this baptism into the name, or spirit, of the Godhead to a high degree, without the application of water. On the review of this statement, the unprejudiced inquirer may perhaps agree with us in the statement, that there is no sufficient evidence in the New Testament that water baptism was ordained by Christ;

or that we are required to observe it as a permanent obligation under the Christian dispensation. To continue to observe rites and shadows is at variance with one of the grand features of our common Christianity; they contain no hidden mysterious grace —no regenerating or converting power, whereby the recipients of the ceremony are made partakers of newness of life. In order to substantiate this truth, we have only to recur to the plain Scripture history, and common observation on the subject.

Thus we perceive that the New Testament plainly declares that the subjects of Christ's baptism are the souls, and not the bodies, of men, and that Christ himself is the true baptizer by his Holy Spirit, for by his Spirit are we all baptized into one body. The effect of this baptism "is not the putting away the filth of the flesh, but the answer of a good conscience towards God"—a heart purified by faith—a being baptized into Christ, putting on Christ. It produces a new man, with new desires— new affections—new hopes—new confidence. It is the office of the Spirit of Christ to testify of Christ—to enlighten the understanding—to sanctify the affections—and comfort the heart.

The baptism with the Holy Ghost is the first part of sanctification, which together with justification, is spoken of in the Scriptures under various figures of speech, such as the washing of regeneration—eating Christ's flesh and drinking his blood— being washed from sin in the blood of Christ—sprinkled from an evil conscience—made free by the truth—being born of the Spirit—the robes washed and made white in the blood of the Lamb—the purging out of the old leaven—washed, sanctified, and justified in the name of the Lord Jesus, and by the Spirit of our God—a being "born again." No outward ceremony can effect this great spiritual work, nor *even assist* in producing it, for it is the law of the spirit of life in Christ Jesus alone, that can set us free from the law of sin and death, and create us anew in Jesus Christ our Saviour and Redeemer.

When the multitudes at Jerusalem, Decapolis, and other places, flocked to the banks of Jordan, to be baptized of John, it may be presumed, and it is more than probable, that many of them were sincere in the belief of his doctrine, and were truly brought to repentance towards God. Now of this repentance it may be judged from the analogy of Scripture, that his preaching was the means of their repentance, and the washing in Jordan by which it was accompanied, according to the Jewish practice of receiving proselytes, was nothing more than the appointed Jewish sign. What analogy, then, is there between the preaching of John and Jesus? While Jesus made more disciples than John, though he baptized not with water; yet there can be no doubt that the grace of conversion went forth towards the new believers, under the preaching both of John and of Jesus.

Just similar was the case of the Ethiopian eunuch. The angel of the Lord appeared unto Philip saying, "Arise, and go towards the south unto the way that leadeth down from Jerusalem to Gaza." In his way he met a man of Ethiopia, an eunuch. "Then the Spirit said unto Philip, Go near, and join thyself unto the chariot." And Philip ran to meet him, and heard him read Chapter liii. of Isaiah, which gave a clear description of Christ, and his sufferings. Then Philip said, "Understandest thou what thou readest?" and he said, "How can I, except some man guide me? I pray thee of whom spake the prophet this?" Then Philip took the opportunity to expound to him the gospel from the passages he was then reading; which at once laid open the guilty and miserable condition of mankind in the fall, and their recovery only by the grace of Jesus Christ. He also laid open the nature, end, and effect of Christ's death and resurrection; and the doctrine of justification before God by the knowledge of the same Jesus, and the merits of his blood. The man felt himself guilty and wicked, and the views of the prophecy before us, as laid open by Philip, discovered to him the remedy which it pleased God so powerfully to apply to his heart. Here Philip made no mention of water baptism to the heathen eunuch, and if he had, where would have been the connexion between such instructions on his part and the prophecy referred to? It is by receiving the truth *alone* into our hearts, that we are baptized into Christ. Philip assured him that there was no impediment

to his being really baptized, if he was sincere in the faith of
Christ: yes! this faith is real baptism into Christ. Philip knew
that man is saved by grace through faith in Christ. And that
man is created in Christ Jesus through grace unto good works
by his faith. He knew that so many as were baptized into
Christ, were baptized into his suffering and death, and were
buried with him by baptism into death unto sin, and enabled to
walk in newness of life. Therefore his baptism was a baptism
into the faith concerning the gospel—and a belief in the name
of Jesus Christ as wounded for our transgression, as bruised for
our iniquities, and that with his stripes we are healed; that the
iniquity of us all was laid upon him, that he was cut off for our
transgressions, and that he bore the sins of many, and maketh
intercession for the transgressors. They that gladly received
the word were baptized. But the eunuch, being accustomed to
hear of, and witness, a washing with water of the heathens on
their becoming proselytes to Judaism, proposed to Philip the
propriety of his being so baptized, according to the appointed
sign of Judaism. He openly avowed his faith, and was thus
baptized with water.

The Samaritans, who attended to the preaching of Philip
concerning the kingdom of God, and the name of Jesus, were
baptized both men and women. Thus we perceive that it was a
belief in Philip's doctrine (as it was of the apostle John's at
Jerusalem, Decapolis, and other places, as well as of the Ethiopian
eunuch) concerning the kingdom of God, and the *name* of Jesus
Christ, by which the Samaritans, as well as Cornelius and his
company, received their baptism in his *name*. Simon, the sorcerer,
believed also, and was baptized in the faith of Jesus Christ, and
continued with Philip, wondering, and beholding the miracles and
signs that were done. Now when the apostles which were at
Jerusalem heard that Samaria had received the truth of the
gospel and the name of Jesus as set forth by Philip, in explanation of the 53rd chapter of Isaiah; they sent unto them
Peter and John to confirm them in the faith, who, when they
were come down, prayed for them that they might receive the

H

Holy Ghost, to seal the truth to their hearts, for as yet He was fallen upon none of them, only they were baptized into the belief of the name of Jesus by Philip's preaching the doctrines contained in Isaiah's prophecy of Christ, and him crucified for the sins of the whole world, as in the case of the heathen eunuch. This faith is a real baptism into Christ's name.

The word which began to be preached at Galilee, and was published throughout all Judea *after* the baptism which John preached, proclaimed peace by Jesus Christ as Lord of all; and *how* God anointed Jesus of Nazareth with the Holy Ghost, and with *power*, for God the Father was *with* Him. And to Him gave *all* the prophets and apostles witness, that through His name whosoever believeth in Him shall receive remission of sins. While Peter spake these words, the Holy Ghost fell on all of them which heard them, not because of the word spoken, but because of their belief in Jesus. So they of the circumcision were astonished, because that on the Gentiles—Cornelius and his company—was poured out the gift of the Holy Ghost; for they heard them speak with tongues, and magnify God. Then asked Peter (the Judaizing apostle whom Paul on one occasion withstood to the face), Can any forbid water, that these should not be baptized, who have received the Holy Ghost as well as we of the circumcision? then *he* commanded them (without any precedent or command given to him) to be baptized according to the Jewish custom of baptizing proselytes. (See 10th chapter of the Acts.) Thus it appears that baptism, as commanded by Peter, as well as the Jews, was a proselyting baptism, and as such to be applied only to converts to Christianity from other religions.

"Though many legal types" (says Gell) "continued some considerable time after Christ's death, yet they lost their positive obligatory power, and were used only as *Adiaphora*, things indifferent, in compliance with the inveterate prejudices of new converts, lately brought from Judaism, who could not quickly lay aside the great veneration which they had for the rites of the Mosaic institutions. The same applies equally to the newly-converted Gentiles" from Paganism.

In the case of Saul of Tarsus, and Lydia of Thyatira, whose hearts were already changed by the Holy Ghost, these washings were superfluous, as they did not change the character. " Before *faith* came they were kept under the law (of ceremonies) ; wherefore the (ceremonial) law was to bring them to Christ," as the Scriptures of the New Testament afterwards became to the Gentiles, that they might be justified by faith. For the Jews and the Gentiles became children of God by faith in Jesus Christ, and not by baptismal water. For being baptized by the Holy Spirit into Christ, they put on Christ, and are heirs of God according to the promise. (See Gal. iii.)

Ananias, in his address to Saul of Tarsus, says unto him, " The God of our fathers hath chosen thee, that thoushouldest know his will, and shouldest hear the voice of his mouth. For thou shalt be his witness unto all men of what thou hast seen and heard." Saul was already a believer, therefore baptized into Christ, and already felt the forgiveness of his sins of unbelief; and to complete the work, Ananias exhorted him to arise and " be baptized, and wash away his sins, calling on the name of the Lord." It was by this " calling on the name of the Lord " that his sins were washed away, and his baptism completed. This is the word of faith which Paul preached to the Romans— " The word of faith nigh thee, in thy mouth, and in thy heart." He further adds, in addressing the believers, " That if thou shalt confess with thy mouth the Lord Jesus, and shalt believe in thine heart that God hath raised him from the dead, thou shalt be saved. For with the heart man believeth unto righteousness ; and with the mouth confession is made unto salvation." Here is righteousness, salvation, and true baptism. After that faith in Jesus Christ is come, we are no longer under the law of Jewish ceremonies, much less under the pagan doctrine of baptismal regeneration.

The forgiveness of sins accompanying faith in Jesus Christ is one of the grand principles of the Gospel dispensation. " Be it known unto you therefore, men and brethren," (said the apostle to the believing Gentiles,) " that through this man (Jesus Christ) is preached unto you the forgiveness of sins : and by him all that *believe* are justified from all things, from which they could not be justified by the law of Moses ;"—therefore justified from washing in water. This was exactly the case with the Ethiopian eunuch ; Lydia of Thyatira, and her household ; the jailor and his family at Philippi, with the believing Corinthians, and Ephesians. All these were brought to a knowledge and acceptance of the truth as it is in Jesus, by means of apostolic preaching, and the truth of their doctrine sealed to their hearts by the Holy Ghost, without water baptism. This is the baptism set forth in what is called the great commission to the apostles.

The case of the three thousand converts on the day of Pentecost, and the case of Saul of Tarsus, are undeniable proofs that the true Christian baptism is effected by a living faith, and an immediate act of Divine grace : thus armed, the disciples on the day of Pentecost, as well as Saul of Tarsus, were enabled to go forth under the influence of this faith, and grace, to convert others to the same saving faith which God had wrought in them, which was the baptism of their commission.

In all these cases it surely is very clear, that the grace, virtue, or interior power of regeneration, is not inherent in the ceremony of washing in water. Much less is the inward grace of regeneration contained in this ceremony when applied to unconscious infants. Nevertheless, the Roman Catholic Church, and our English Protestant Episcopal Church, and not a few other Protestants, declare, "*that water* to be the water of regeneration." They even allow of no other regeneration than that which they suppose to be inherent in the water which is sprinkled on the bodies of their children, or in which the adults are immersed. But what is the actual result of such doctrine, which time and experience develop ? A large proportion of these children, and adults too, prove, by their subsequent conduct and character, that they have never been born again of the Spirit. To the inward grace of regeneration they are utter strangers : and while they follow the multitude to do evil, they offer a palpable and unanswerable argument to prove that, whatsoever may be the supposed advantage or authority of the practice, it is destitute of any interior grace.

There are thousands of people scattered up and down this nation, who find in themselves a hunger and thirst for spiritual food. They have been taught, from infancy, that the priests are men of God through whom the blessing must come. They have spent years in running after and listening to these teachers; and, instead of finding their wants supplied, they become more and more sensible of their hunger and thirst. They go hungering and panting to churches, but no nourishment comes home to their spirits; no strength is gathered; no comfort received; no true faith in Jesus confirmed; and they return to their homes in a more miserable condition than before;—I speak from experience—because they feel that they cannot feed upon what they are taught to consider divine food: *i. e.*, water baptismal regeneration, confirmation, the eucharist, and absolution; or, it may be, penances, pilgrimages, indulgences, purgatorial fire, or masses for the dead. Some, thus sensible of the utter unworthiness of this food, turn away to vanity, or drown their spiritual cravings in worldly pursuits or amusements, while others, who have seen the emptiness of these things, settle down into a state of darkness and indifference.

My object, in referring to this class of persons, of which I have been one, is to endeavour to turn them to the truth—the life—the way. To direct them to the fountain, Christ; who said, " I am the way, the truth, and the life "—" I am the bread that cometh down from heaven." This is what the hungry, thirsty, panting soul needs—Christ the life—the Divine principle in his soul. Without the Spirit's baptism none can come to feel the corruptions of his heart cancelled. None escapes the bondage, slavery, darkness, defilements, and reprobate state of his corrupt nature, or feels sin crucified in his mortal body, a being translated into the kingdom of light, nor any cleansing of the soul, no oneness in and with Christ, no putting on Christ. But they who are baptized with the Spirit—they grow in the Spirit—receive a new name, and a new nature—are cleansed from sin—baptized into Christ—having put on Christ—being made one in Christ—and weaned from the traditions of men.

Now the question is, how can this be attained, that the soul may be satisfied? This is the question: and here it is that the sectarian priests cause men to stumble. One cries, "Join our church, be dipped in water, and wash away thy sins." Another says, "Be sprinkled and regenerated, and made a member of Christ, a child of God, and an inheritor of the kingdom of heaven." Another says, "Take a little bread and wine in which both the substance of the bread and wine, and the body and blood of Christ, are also present to refresh the soul." Another says, "Take a little bread and wine as the sign and symbol of the body and blood of Christ, and be baptized in water as a sign of regeneration." Another says, "Be baptized in water, and take a little bread and wine, wherein a certain Divine virtue or efficacy is communicated to the receiver." Another says, "Be baptized, regenerated, confirmed, and take a little bread and wine, of which there is made a conversion of all the substance of the bread into the substance of the body of Christ; and of the substance of the wine into the substance of the blood of Christ, who is present in the eucharist." But miserable comforters are they all!

The true teaching is this: to lead to Christ, who is willing to be their prophet to teach them what is right—willing to be their priest to forgive their transgressions—willing to be their king to rule and reign over them for good. His appearances at first may be small—a little reproof—a little instruction—a little condemnation for wrong doing—a little satisfaction and peace for well doing. But as the little is attended to, more light is received, and as you advance in goodness the path shines more and more unto the perfect day, and joy and gladness will burst forth in your barren spirits, and songs of praise will take the place of mourning, and your path will be more clearly revealed, and you will have no need that any man teach you.

The apostle John said to his brethren, "Ye need not that any man teach you, for the anointing which ye have received of him (Christ) abideth in you, and is truth, and is no lie, and is able to guide into all truth." The whole design of all true preaching is to turn the people to Christ. And when a minister has turned the attention of his hearers to Christ, and established his faith in Him, the work of that minister with that hearer is accomplished. This is a true baptizing ministry.

If our readers desire to know whether we would have all preaching cease, because of the abuses that are in the world, we answer—No! We believe that there are many, who, if they are faithful to the manifestations of truth, will be qualified to preach the gospel with power, in demonstration of the Spirit, the fruit of which would be faith in Christ and salvation from sin to all who would receive it.

These preachers would go forth as the Spirit of God would lead them, as the apostles did, and preach as the Spirit gave them utterance, as did Paul after his conversion. They would be baptized into the spiritual state of the church, as Paul was when he wrote his epistles to the churches, and be qualified to speak to the condition of those before them; to reprove the wicked, encourage the feeble-minded, to comfort the mourner, to strengthen the weak, and give to each his portion in due season. Thus baptizing them in or into the name of the Father, of the Son, and of the Holy Ghost.

How different this kind of ministers from those who know nothing of the gospel except what they get from books, and learn at universities, from philosophic Judaism and Paganism! Again: how different such preaching from these heartless, philosophic, and studied utterances which unanointed priests write on paper: when they have no internal sense of the state of the people, or the power of God! These are they who introduce into their sermons the doctrines of water baptism, confirmation, the eucharist, and absolution; or, it may be, penances, pilgrimages, indulgences, purgatorial fires, and masses for the dead, to make up the void here also.

To be a Christian is to have Christ living in us. The Lord said, by Hosea the prophet, "I will be as the dew unto Israel."—Heavenly dew! But how admirable this gentle dew, when it distils its treasure into Nature's lap! It is neither heard by the quickest ear, nor seen by the sharpest eye: what a striking emblem of that Divine anointing from above which descends on heaven-born souls! The soul that is attentive to the Divine teaching will become more and more sensible of the guiding eye, the leading hand, the directing voice, which says, to those who are wishful not to rest in anything short of it, " the anointing which ye have received of him abideth in you, and ye need not that any man teach you; but as the same anointing teacheth you all things, and is truth and no lie, and even as it hath taught you, ye shall abide in him." By living according to the rule of the Spirit, man becomes the wisest, the best, and the happiest creature he is capable of being.

Several of the Epistles seem to have been written on purpose to dissuade from an attachment to, and retention of, the rituals of the shadowy dispensation which had passed away. Paul, having his knowledge of Christ by immediate revelation, knew that the dispensation of figurative institutions was ended: and that for Christians to receive lifeless signs as gospel ordinances must powerfully divert them from the saving substance: hence he pressingly invites to Christ, and warns against a continuance of ceremonies. His Epistles to the Galatians and Colossians, and a great portion of several others, are full of this purpose. Some troublesome persons had got in among the Galatians, insisting on circumcision and the rituals of the Jewish law, and had so influenced the believers, that this inspired apostle vehemently expostulated with them for being so easily shaken from grace, and turned to elementary observances :—" I marvel that ye are so soon turned from him that called you into the grace of Christ, unto another gospel!" Mark! "which is not another gospel! but there be some that trouble you, and would pervert the gospel of Christ." Indeed, every attempt to establish ceremonial institutions as gospel ordinances, is directly an attempt to pervert the gospel, and frustrate its blessed design. On this ground the apostle pronounces every man, even though it were himself and companions, or an angel from heaven, that should preach any other gospel than that already preached unto them, accursed. The gospel that Paul preached, was Christ within— the word nigh in the heart, and in the mouth; which he expressly calls—" the righteousness which is of faith "—" the word of faith which we preach." A little before he had de- scribed Christ " as the end of the law for righteousness to every one that believeth." Hence it is evident that the word of faith, nigh in the heart and in the mouth, is that which super- sedes and ends the signs and shadows of the ceremonial law to all true believers in Christ.

Paul's commission was to open the eyes of the Gentiles—" to turn them from darkness to light, and from the power of Satan unto God." If any doubt whether this is the same baptizing ministry mentioned in what is called the great commission, let the words of the apostle be duly weighed. He was sent to the Gentiles, as the apostles were sent to the Jews, " that they might receive forgiveness of sins, and an inheritance among them that are sanctified by faith, that is, in Jesus Christ." Hence the Gentiles not only received the forgiveness of sins, but the same inheritance with all the sanctified, and that through the same faith; for thus believing, they were baptized through the powerful ministry of the gospel, which was in the demonstration of the Spirit, into the power and virtue of the same *name*, they were turned unto God. There is not the least doubt but that Paul, in the execution of his mission, as truly baptized into the name of the Father, Son, and Holy Ghost, as ever a disciple of Jesus Christ did under the great commission; yea, did admi- nister the very same baptism therein required. He well knew that this commission contained no precept for water baptism, " as touching the Gentiles which believed;" and says, " we have written and concluded that they observe no such thing." (See Acts xxi.)

Yet, so great was his condescension to the weak state of the people, that he says, " to the weak he became weak—yea, that he was made all things to all men, that he might by all means save some;" and this he says " he did for the gospel's sake."

Yea, further he says, "he caught them with guile."  Hence, on the same principle of condescension, he baptized a few with water because of their attachment to the ceremonial law of Moses; yet, declared that he was not "commanded to do it." And when he saw the abuse made of it, "thanked God that he had baptized no more."

After Paul had discontinued water baptism, he told the Ephesians, "There is one Lord, one faith, one baptism;" and further he tells us what that one baptism really is.  "Know ye not," says he, "that so many of us as have been baptized into Jesus Christ, were baptized into his death?" and adds, "We are buried with him by baptism into death: that like as Christ was raised from the dead by the glory of the Father, even we also should walk in newness of life."  The spiritually baptized ones know that, "as they have been planted into the likeness of his death, they shall be also into the likeness of his resurrection: knowing this, that their old man is crucified with him (as well as baptized into him), that the body (or power) of sin might be destroyed, that henceforth they should not serve sin.  For he that is dead with Christ (or baptized into his death) is free from sin.  For in that Christ died he died unto sin once, but in that he liveth he liveth unto God."  So doth every one who is baptized into the name of the Father, Son, and Holy Ghost.  (See Rom. vi.)

About the twelfth century, one of the Christians (usually called St. Bernard), in speaking of the manifestations of Christ's Spirit to the soul, says, "I was sensible that he was present with me; I remembered it after his visits were over.  You ask me whence I could know that he was present?  I answer, His presence was living and powerful.  It awakened my slumbering soul.  He moved, softened, and wounded my heart, which had been hard, strong, and distempered.  It watered the dry places, it illuminated the dark, it opened those that were shut, inflamed the cold, made the crooked straight, and the rough places plain; so that my soul blessed the Lord, and all that was within me praised his holy name.  I had no evidence of his presence with me by any of the senses, only by the motions of my heart. I understood that he was with me. From the expulson of vice, and the suppression of carnal affections, I perceived the strength of his power. From the discernment and conviction I had of the very intent of my heart, I admired the depth of his wisdom. From some little improvement of my temper and conduct, I can perceive the goodness of his grace. From the renewal of my inward man, I perceived the comeliness of his beauty; and from the joint contemplation of these things I trembled at his majestic greatness. But because of all these, on his departure, I became torpid and cold; I had a signal of his leaving me: my soul must be sad until his return, and my heart be again influenced with his love: and let that be the evidence of his return." This is baptism indeed! Doth the priest's baptism produce such effects? Nay, verily! There is no waking of slumbering souls, no softening and wounding of sinful hearts, no watering of the dry places—inflaming the cold heart—illuminating the dark mind— no suppression of carnal affections—no expulsion of vice—no perception of comeliness and beauty of the way of salvation through a crucified, risen, and glorified Redeemer.

True Protestantism can be nothing less than the renouncing the religion of man's contrivance; and a turning to the religion of God in the soul. Indeed, among all the very pointed and remarkable prophecies concerning Christ and his kingdom, there is not one in all the Old Testament that points him out as the administrator of water baptism, or as establishing a church or kingdom accompanied with any such outward ordinance. The Father, by the prophet Isaiah, speaks of Him as "the Lord's elect, in whom his soul delighteth." Declaring, " I have put my Spirit upon him—given him for a covenant to the people—for a light to the Gentiles—to open the blind eyes—to bring out the prisoners, and them that sit in darkness, out of the prison house. Behold, the former things are come to pass, and new things do I declare: before they spring forth I tell you of them." (See Isa. 42nd chapter.) But not a word among all these new things of water baptism. His work is to bring forth judgment unto truth

—to enlighten the Gentiles—bring out of prison and darkness—
bringing the blind by a way that they know not—a spiritual way
—not the way of signs and shadows and outward ordinances—
these are the old ways. But the new things are—I will lead
them in paths they have not known—a new heart and a new
spirit will I put within them. Such things as these the prophets
foretold, but not once in all their predictions of return, reform,
restoration, and building the waste places, do they mention
Christ baptizing with water, or establishing it in his gospel
church. Nor did Christ when he came, even once that we read
of in the New Testament, call the baptism of water his baptism.
And, moreover, we do not find that Christ ever once called it
by any other name than John's baptism. Is it not wonderful,
that he should constantly call it John's, if it was as truly his own
as John's? Why should he leave his followers, to the world's
end, under the great difficulties and disadvantages of such a total
silence, if he wished them to use it as the baptism of the gospel
dispensation? Was Moses more faithful than Christ? Moses
was very particular in describing the ritual of the law, even to
very minute circumstances; and would Christ ordain a perpetual
institution, and never once call it his own, but always call it
John's? We know that both himself, John, and others, called,
and understood, water baptism to be John's. We also know that
his own was repeatedly placed in direct contra-distinction to it—
and said to be with the Holy Ghost.

When Paul "came to Ephesus and found certain disciples there,
he said unto them, Have ye received the Holy Ghost since ye
believed? and they said unto him, We have not so much as heard
whether there be any Holy Ghost. And he said unto them,
Unto what then were ye baptized?" as much as to say that he
knew no other than that of the Holy Ghost. "They said, Unto
John's baptism. Then said Paul, John verily baptized with
the baptism of repentance, saying unto the people, that they
should believe on him that should come after him, that is, on
Jesus Christ." (See Acts, 19th chapter.) And John, though he
came to fulfil the baptism of the Jewish dispensation, and pre-

pare the way for the Lord, directed the people to a believing
faith in Jesus Christ, and repentance towards God, as the true
Christian baptism into His name. "When they heard this, they
were *baptized* into the *name* of the Lord Jesus. And when Paul
had laid his hands upon them, the Holy Ghost came on them;
and they spake with tongues, and prophesied." What a different
baptism is this to Simon's! not because of baptism in water, but
because of their repentance towards God—faith in Christ—and
the gift of the Holy Ghost. The apostle knew this great truth,
for he tells the Galatians, "that it had pleased God to call *him*
by *His* grace, and to reveal His Son *in* him." This is the gospel
which Paul learned by the revelation of Jesus Christ: "I neither
received it of man, neither was I taught it," says he, "but by
the revelation of Jesus Christ." Hence he could say, " I live,
yet not I, but Christ liveth in me; and the life that I now live
in the flesh, I live by the faith of the Son of God." That is, by
the faith of Christ living in him, he was dead to the ceremonial
law, that he might live unto God. He renounced all ceremonial
religion, and came home to Christ in his own soul. This is true
baptism. (See Gal. i., ii.)

Yet, notwithstanding this great gospel truth, the 20th Article
of the Church of England says, "that the Church hath power to
decree rites and ceremonies"—a point which is strenuously
denied by many dissenters. And although the same article
appears to guard this power claimed by the Church against
abuse, by asserting that "it is not lawful for the Church to
ordain anything that is contrary to God's words written; neither
may it so expound one place of Scripture that it be repugnant
to another;" the caution thus introduced is without avail, since
the Church herself is to be the judge of what is or is not opposed
to the Scriptures of truth. What is this, my readers, but to follow
in the steps of Cerinthus, Carpocrates, Clement, Elxai, Victor,
the Gnostics, and the Jewish and Heathen Philosophers of the
Alexandrian school of the second and third centuries? (See p. 13
to 17.) The great safety of any church is simply to adhere to the
teachings of Christ and his apostles in the Scriptures, and thus
to trench in nothing upon the simplicity of primitive Christianity.

The human mind, once turned to religious ceremonies, and the dogmas of a priestly hierarchy, is hard to be restrained. At all times the mind of man in his degenerate state is, and ever has been, prone to imagery, ceremonies, and idolatry. From this sprang all pagan idolatry, and all advances towards it among the Jews; and its continuation among professing Christians and Mahommedans. The dispensation of signs was ever in condescension to man's weakness, even under the ceremonial law; and although Christ taught his disciples that "the kingdom of God cometh not with observation:" yet, he and his disciples did permit things not properly belonging to the gospel, in condescension to Jewish and heathen prejudices: but which were to decrease and terminate as the light of the gospel day advanced.

As to its permission during the time of John's administration, and the lifetime of Christ upon earth, it might well be practised in the fulfilment of the law, for the Gospel Dispensation had not then fully come in; many things of an outward and typical nature, as well as ancient prophecy, were during that time being fulfilled; and very especially that of the passover, which Christ desired with great desire to eat with his disciples before he suffered. In this the law of ceremonial ordinances ceased for ever.

While certain ceremonies have been instituted in the Christian Church, more especially in the Roman Catholic Church; the question has been again and again proposed, whether the Church is authorized in instituting ceremonies which were not originally enjoined by our Lord and his apostles. One thing is certain, that the conduct of the Jews in this respect, in the days of our Lord, met with his explicit and decided disapproval: thus he plainly declares, "in vain do they worship me, teaching for doctrines the commandment of men." All ceremonies of man's devising, then, are plainly to be condemned. In the History of the ceremonies of the Church of Rome, published by M. Ponce, A.D. 1646, he has traced the rise, growth, and introduction of each rite into the Church, and their gradual abuse as they appeared. Many of them he traces to Judaism, but still more to Heathenism. And this is most fully confirmed in our first chapter.

The epistle to the Galatians indicates a serious defection in their church from the purity and simplicity of evangelical doctrine. Its members consisted of both Jews and Gentile converts, among whom there came several Judaizing teachers, insisting upon the necessity of observing the law of Moses in many of its abolished rites. This explains to a certain extent why the followers of Jesus being Jews, feeling their own uncleanness, and called to a new and devoted service to God, entered upon it by water of separation, called baptism or washing, according to the law of Moses; while the Gentiles introduced the pagan notion of baptismal regeneration, as we have before stated. Such were the circumstances with reference to this matter when Jesus was to depart from this world, and entrust the management of his church to human instrumentality, when the converted Jews carried many of their Jewish habits into their new mission, though they had been warned against the use of them; while at the same time they questioned the apostleship of Paul; who defended his own character, and established his apostleship against those enemies of the gospel; and seriously, but with warm affection, rebuked the Judaizing Galatians, and instructed them clearly in the doctrine of justification and salvation by the righteousness and atonement of Christ. The fruits of this principle, he insists, must be manifest by walking in the Spirit, and glorifying God.

Multitudes have passed through the external ceremony of water baptism, who have lived to attest, by their unhappy conduct and conversation, that they are utter strangers to the purifying influence of the Spirit of Christ. We have instances of this continually before our eyes; such cases prove, demonstrably, that some other baptism than that which consists in an outward washing with water, is necessary to purify the flesh, sanctify the spirit, and save the soul.

We stand on dangerous ground, if we suffer ourselves to be drawn from the blessed Spirit which is given for our profit. Where but within our hearts shall we find the Comforter—the safe guide? Surely the Holy Scriptures direct us to Christ within—the hope of glory. But we are told by many of the

high professors of the Christian name, that all revelation has
ceased; and, that in looking for inward and spiritual grace, and
forsaking the forms and ceremonies usually performed and
practised in the various Christian churches, we subject ourselves
to error. What need have we, then, to dwell where the spirits can
be tried whether they are of God; and where our own spirits can be
kept subordinate to the pure yet steadfast principles of truth!

The apostle Paul earnestly exhorted the Colossians to be
constant in Christ—to beware of philosophy and vain traditions,
and then declared, " Ye are complete in him, in whom also ye
are circumcised with the circumcision made without hands, in
putting off the body of the sins of the flesh by the circumcision
of Christ. And you, being dead in your sins, and the circumcision of your flesh, hath he quickened together with him,
having forgiven you all trespasses." Here the spiritual change
is expressed in a figure derived from the Jewish legal ordinances;
and then the apostle proceeds to explain his own meaning,
establishing a strong analogy between circumcision and baptism
—" buried with him in baptism, wherein also ye are risen with
him, through the faith of the operation of God." Mark!
Through the faith of the operation of God. In all this the
apostle speaks of a spiritual baptism and circumcision, *through
the faith of the operation of God's Spirit*. Not a compound,
including two or three things—the outward visible sign, and the
inward spiritual grace, which the Episcopalians call the one
baptism. But we must remember that human orators, philosophers, and hireling priests, often cloud Divine truth, by
opening doors that lead to darkness, error, and death. Oh, let
us aim at realities! This is a reality—an assertion that has
Divine truth in it!—that the Lord Jesus Christ is the life of the
souls of his people—and that by his living in them, they have a
life which they will feel to be a life in death.

Those who have attained to a full state of manhood in Christ's
kingdom are fed with strong meat—and are taught the deep
mysteries of the kingdom; and are not tossed to and fro, and
carried about with every wind of doctrine (as the priests were in

the time of Henry VIII.; Edward VI.; Mary; Elizabeth; Charles I., and II.; James I. and II., &c.), but speak the truth in love, growing up in Christ in all things, who is the Head—every thought being brought into captivity to the obedience of Christ.

There the adoption of a full state of sonship is attained, and the redemption of man from every evil propensity is effected. So that he becomes *stedfast, immovable*, always abounding in the work of the Lord, knowing that his labour is not in vain in the Lord. Those who perfect holiness in the fear of the Lord, have a degree of divine knowledge more than they can declare, and more certain than the demonstrations of geometry. Our natural light, on the other hand, is like a candle, every wind of doctrine bloweth it out, or maketh the light tremulous. But the light of the Spirit is fixed, and bright, and shines for ever. The treasures of these are in heaven, from whence their light and strength are derived, and their consolations flow; where their hopes are fixed, their affections placed, and their desires tend, expecting there to receive an exceeding recompense of reward—from whence also they look for the Saviour, Jesus Christ, the Lord. Strengthened by such faith as this, and baptized with such a baptism as this, they can adopt the exulting language of Peter:—" Blessed be the God and Father of our Lord Jesus Christ, who according to his abundant mercy hath begotten us again to a lively hope, by the resurrection of Jesus Christ from the dead, to an inheritance incorruptible, and undefiled, that fadeth not away, reserved in heaven for us."

In order to a happy progress in the life of religion, the great thing is to abide in the Divine light, to preserve a clear and distinct sensibility between the flesh and the Spirit. There is no doing this without the steady attention of the mind upon the Divine gift. If the eye go from this, it is blinded by darkness, and the man is led by a counterfeit light. This was evidently the case with the Pharisees, in the time of our Saviour's personal appearance on earth; when they were the most inveterate enemies he had among mankind. What a picture is this of the pharisaical priesthood in all ages since that time! Seeing, then, that frail mortals are liable to such dangerous mistakes, how exceedingly circumspect and watchful ought all to be, in examining into the state of their own hearts, and into the truth of the Gospel, which can be known no otherwise by any, but as the Lord is pleased to be their light and their guide. These are children of God, and co-heirs with Christ, and have their robes washed in the blood of the Lamb, and are made kings and priests unto God—and know this by the testimony of the Holy Spirit in their hearts, whereby they can cry, Abba, Father.

At the time of the transfiguration of Christ while the cloud overshadowed the disciples, Peter proposed to build three tabernacles, one for Moses and his law, one for John and his baptism, and one for Christ and his law written in the heart. They knew not that Moses and John must not be any longer retained; but when the voice of God broke through the cloud, they had their attention called singly to Jesus. And further, that no confirmation should be wanting to seal it for ever, we find that immediately upon their hearing the Divine voice break through the cloud, even " suddenly, when they looked around, they saw no man any more, save Jesus alone with themselves. And there was a voice heard out of the cloud, saying, This is my beloved Son, hear him." A very timely admonition, and sufficient, one might suppose, to prevent all who understand it, from wishing to build three tabernacles, or to retain any of the mere shadows of Moses' law, or John's baptism, since Christ and his law were to be heard in all things.

Seeing, then, that Jesus alone remained to them, and is now our great High Priest that is passed into the heavens, as our baptizer, let us hold fast our profession. " For we have not an High Priest which cannot be touched with the feeling of our infirmities: let us, therefore, come boldly to the throne of grace " (passing by the tabernacle of Moses and Elias, i.e., John) ; "that we may obtain mercy, and find grace to help in every time of need." Christ glorified not himself to be made an High Priest; but God, that said unto him, Thou art my Son. As he says also in another place, Thou art a Priest for ever. Christ, because he continueth ever at his Father's right hand, hath an unchangeable, spiritual priesthood: whereby he is able to save them to the uttermost that come unto God by him, seeing that he ever liveth to baptize them, and make intercession for them. "For such an High Priest became us, who is holy, harmless, undefiled, and separate from sinners, and made higher than the heavens." Now we have an High Priest who is set on the right hand of the throne of the Majesty in the heavens, a minister of the sanctuary, and of the spiritual tabernacle, which God hath pitched and not man. Wherefore it is necessary that this man, Christ, should have somewhat also to offer, namely, spiritual gifts; seeing that there were priests that offered gifts according to the law. But Christ obtained a more excellent ministry—a spiritual one, being the mediator of a better covenant, which was established upon better promises. In finding fault with the old covenant—the ceremonial law—the Lord saith, " Behold, the days come, when I will make a new covenant with the house of Israel and with the house of Judah: not according to the covenant that I made with their fathers, in the day that I took them by the hand to lead them out of the land of Egypt. For this is the covenant that I will make with the house of Israel after those days, saith the Lord : I will put my laws into their minds ; and write them in their hearts; and I will be to them a God, and they shall be to me a people : and they shall not teach every man his neighbour, and every man his brother, saying, Know the Lord ; for they shall all know me, from the least unto the greatest. For I will be merciful to their unrighteousness, and their sins and their iniquities will I remember no more. Now in that he saith, A new covenant, he maketh the first old." (See Heb. viii.) By the eternal priesthood of Christ, the Levitical priesthood of Aaron is abolished, and the temporal covenant with the fathers, by the eternal covenant of the gospel, which is the power of God unto salvation to every one that believeth.

The outward things which had been imparted until the time of reformation, and were exhibited in the transfiguration as not belonging to the gospel, were not absolutely and entirely abrogated till Christ had risen from the dead. It had long, under the law and the prophets, been found extremely difficult to restrain the Jews from the idolatry of the heathens, even though God had so far accommodated himself, and the ceremonial law, to their outward state and dispositions, as to provide them with many signs and ceremonies, and a worldly sanctuary (see Heb. 1), and which the Jewish converts to Christianity were very loath to part with, though enjoined so to do, as the Scriptures abundantly prove. And the Christians of this day are quite as loath to part with them as were the Jews in the apostles' days. And no marvel, as they have been continued from the days of the apostles in what was called the "Catholic Church," in the days of Cyprian and Constantine ; and, shortly after them, it assumed the name of "Roman Catholic Church ;" which name it retains to this day. And our English Episcopal Church borrowed her dogmas from Rome, and is become the fashionable religion of this country ; the prominent reasons for which we have already shown in the first chapter.

Blessed are those who have ears to hear, and hearts to understand the Gospel, and faith to follow the Lamb of God—the Christian's High Priest, wheresoever he leadeth. These shall be established in the truth, and shall never be moved from Christ, who is the way, the truth, and the life : they shall be preserved from touching, tasting, or handling those things that perish with the using without profiting those who use them. Nothing that is extrinsic to the nature of the soul can raise and restore a fallen soul ; nevertheless it must be fashioned anew, and a new meetness for glory formed in the inmost essence of it. Our blessed Lord bare testimony to the necessity of this great change that must pass upon the soul :—"Verily, verily, I say unto thee, except a man be born again, he cannot see the kingdom of God." And did the doctrine of regeneration rest on this text alone, we must allow it sufficiently established ; but this is far from being the case, as it is set forth under a variety of similar expressions, on purpose that we might not be left in uncertainty as to the truth and meaning of it ; as when the true

Christian is said to put on Christ—to have him dwelling in his heart by faith—to be " renewed in the spirit of the mind—and that as many as are led by the Spirit of God, they are the sons of God." In like manner—" the new creature "—"the new man"—"the sanctification of the Spirit"—"to be born of the Spirit" —and "to be alive unto God through Jesus Christ"—do all imply a new life in the soul which it has not in its natural state, as it stands in the fall, and which nothing but the sanctification of the Spirit can give.

What cause shall we assign, then, for that opposition to gospel truth that appears generally among the professors of the Christian name, and for that dislike to those who urge the necessity of regeneration—the spiritual life in the soul ? The true reason is nigh at hand, though others are pretended. Such doctrines are contrary to the maxims and principles that govern the conduct of fallen man, and are contrary to the false interests of flesh and blood, as they declare war against the kingdom of self; and strike at everything that is most near and dear to the corrupt nature of man ; and, therefore, carnal men, of every denomination, think themselves warranted to oppose and discredit such a representation of Christianity as we are endeavouring to establish and uphold. They can be zealous for the opinions of this or that church, and their forms and ceremonies, because they leave them in quiet possession of their ambition, dignity, coveteousness, love of themselves, and love of the world. They can readily take up a profession of faith in a suffering Saviour, nay, bring themselves to trust in an outward covering of his merits and righteousness for salvation through the priests' baptismal regeneration, confirmation, the eucharist, and absolution ; because this costs them nothing ; but to be clothed with humility, to renounce their own wills in total resignation to the will of God, to mortify the fleshly appetites, to be crucified to the world, to strip themselves of all complacency in those endowments which appear great, glorious, and dignified in the eyes of both themselves and others,—in a word to take up their cross and follow Christ in the regeneration, these are hard sayings, they cannot bear them; therefore they set up a baptism of their own, borrowed from Judaism and Heathenism, as we have already shown.

By the Anglo-Catholics of the present day, baptismal regeneration is used to denote justification and sanctification;— a change of state and a change of mind. That the word is employed in this extended sense we learn from the writings of Dr. Pusey, who defines regeneration to be "that act whereby God takes us out of our relation to Adam, and makes us actual members of His Son, and so His sons, being made members of His ever blessed Son," and this through water baptism. The error in teaching this baptismal regeneration originates in confounding ritual with spiritual baptism. The grand distinction between the two was again and again enforced upon the people by John, and Christ himself: "I baptize you with water, but He (Christ) shall baptize you with the Holy Ghost." And Jesus himself spoke to his disciples in similar terms: "John truly baptized with water, but ye shall be baptized with the Holy Ghost." Now let men be never so wise, never so high titled, let their pretensions to learning and dignity be what they will, and their acquaintance with creeds and canons never so extensive, so long as their hearts are unsurrendered to God and the power of Christ's Spirit, they are no better than dry bones, or a tinkling cymbal, as to the divine life; they cannot in such a state receive the things of the Spirit of God, not having the spiritual senses exercised thereto, so these things appear foolishness unto them, and they speak evil of that which they know not. And why? "Because the natural man knoweth not the things of the Spirit of God; for they are foolishness unto him; neither can he know them, because they are spiritually discerned." "But he that is spiritual judgeth all things, comparing spiritual things with spiritual." "That he may know the things that are freely given to him of God." Works done in this grace are acceptable to the Father, in and through his Son.

There is nothing more opposite to the genius of true Christianity than tradition, and bigotry of spirit, which hinder us from seeing the emptiness of all forms and ceremonies, and beholding the beauty of holiness in the character of a sanctified Redeemer, and salvation by and through him : as God does not measure out grace and goodness according to the creeds of certain churches, or to the scanty pattern of the notional, national orthodoxy of man.

Inspiration is the best of God's gifts to men, however the belief of it may be deemed enthusiasm by some, it is the privilege of every true Christian—a power communicated to the soul from God the Father, through Christ the Son; which saving grace is a real participation of the divine nature in which Adam was created. In proportion, then, as he is purified from sin through the Spirit, so far he advances in union and communion with God, and comes into fellowship with the Father and the Son, so that the light of divine truth shines in his heart. For this inspiration the Church of England is taught to pray. But the learned dignitaries thereof, by their false glosses, in the interpretation of the Scriptures, attribute it in all cases to their baptisms, confirmations, and eucharists, and that without these there is no revelation—no regeneration—no communion with God. They, by thus exalting human reason, and tradition, have so explained away the important doctrine of immediate divine revelation, that we no longer wonder that the belief of all internal operations of God in the soul is treated as enthusiasm and fanaticism. But be it remembered, that we are made willing and obedient in the day of God's power, who were unwilling, disobedient, and backsliders, in the days of our weakness. Tradition, forms, and ceremonies, consist well enough with inward impurity, and offer no violence to the corrupt nature, and therefore men are content to be religious at so cheap a rate, and in a manner so congenial to their carnal desires.

Notwithstanding the assertion that our English Church resembles primitive Christianity, and not at all the Church of Rome : the latter appears to be as true as the other is false : as both their liturgies, rites and ceremonies, are a composition of pagan and papal inventions, with some additions of their own ;

and much of primitive Christianity excluded. Therefore as the Church of England does not, in its rites, services, and ceremonies, resemble primitive Christianity, which is a spiritual religion ; it is true that it does closely resemble pagan and popish novelties ; as the proofs make manifest. Fox tells us in his " Acts and Monuments " (vol. 2. p. 1189)—"As for the service in the English tongue, it perchance may seem to you a new service ; and yet indeed it is no other but the old ; the self-same words in English, for nothing is altered, but to speak with knowledge that which was spoken with ignorance." And so saith King Charles II. in his preface to the Common Prayer Book. And Dr. Stillingfleet, in his Irenicum (c. 7, sect. 5, p. 123), speaks to this purpose,—" that the great reason why our first Reformers did so far comply with the Papists, was to gain, and lay a bait for them, which he hoped was never intended to be a hook for the Protestants."

The Church of Rome and the Church of England, in their spiritual aspects as considered in relation to primitive Christianity, are barely to be distinguished ; the one has as effectually eclipsed the glory and beauty of God's salvation as the other. The translator of John Baptist, Van Helmont, says, " Such hath been the subtlety of the serpent, that under the name of Christ, he hath taken up paganish means to build withal, calling them hand-maidens of divinity." This is different from God's command, who said, " Learn not the way of the heathen." Paul of Samosata derived his heresies against the Son of God from Plotinus, and he in the church of Alexandria. Origen also, and after him some of the Pelagians, derived their pestilent errors against the grace of God out of the same school. Arius, a presbyter of the church of Alexandria, imbibed his blasphemies against the divinity of Christ out of the divinity school of Alexandria about A.D. 300. From him sprang the Arians who overran all Christendom.

Some objectors may say "that Dissenters have no cause to separate from the Church of England, for continuing Romish rites and ceremonies which were practised by antiquity before popery came into the world." True, they were many of them practised by the pagans, 700 years before the advent of Christ. This of itself is surely a sufficient reason why Dissenters ought to separate themselves from her communion, for to enforce this heathen standard upon its members, as the professed followers of the Lord Jesus Christ is to dethrone Christ and the spirituality of his kingdom. (See Casaubon's Original Idolatry, translated by Darcy, p. 73, and Moore's Mystery of Iniquity.)

# CHAPTER V.

The question, What is Christian baptism? is not a trivial or unimportant one. Among the latest recorded words of the Saviour before his Ascension, are these, "Go, and teach all nations, baptizing them." It is surely of consequence to those who regard his words as law, to ascertain their meaning. On the day of Pentecost, the multitude, conscience-stricken by sin, are exhorted by Peter, saying, "Repent and be baptized every one of you, in the name of Jesus Christ for the remission of sins." At Damascus, Saul—suddenly arrested in his course of persecution—has a message sent to him on this wise, "Arise and be baptized, and wash away thy sins." It is surely important that all who are in the like condemnation, heirs of the curse, by reason of sin, should ascertain the nature of that baptism which is "for the remission of sins," by which sins are washed away—that baptism by which three thousand souls were added in one day to the Church, by which he who had been "before a blasphemer and persecutor and injurious," was fitted to become an apostle, and to "preach the faith which once he destroyed." On the testimony of one apostle, "as many as have been baptized into Christ, have put on Christ." On the testimony of another, "baptism doth save." It cannot surely be a matter of little moment to those who call themselves Christians, to understand what that baptism is which constitutes the Christian indeed, amid the conflicting opinions that abound in the world. Christ had been wont to speak of spiritual baptism.

Conflicting views on this subject cannot be equally true, or equally harmless. If there be only one view which is Scriptural, no pains should be spared to arrive at an understanding of what it is. To mistake something else for Christian baptism is to pave the way for the most serious evils. Error here might be fatal. For a man to suppose that he has received Christian baptism when he has not, is to view himself as an heir to the kingdom of heaven, when he has neither part nor lot in the matter. If the strong expressions of Scripture are to be received in all their fulness, it is impossible to escape the conclusion that this is one of the most important of all subjects treated of in the New Testament. And its importance is to be estimated only by that of salvation itself. If " baptism doth save," every man who has a soul to be saved ought to be interested in the question, What is baptism? It is spiritual.

And yet, it needs scarcely to be told that the subject is far from being a settled one. Indeed, there are few questions upon which opinion has been more divided, in consequence of starting upon a false principle, in adopting the washings of the Jewish law, or John's Jordan washings, combined with the pagan notion of regeneration; this fact meets us as early as the first and second centuries. And still, though for eighteen centuries the question of baptism has been before the church, disciples have not yet agreed upon its meaning. On one point only in connexion with it, has there been anything like a general agreement. With a very few exceptions, this baptism has been viewed as a command to observe a rite, one feature of which consists in the use of water, in conformity to the practice of the Jews, and the lustrations of the heathens; and another, the idea of regeneration, as borrowed from philosophic Paganism. Beyond these there are a great variety of opinions, mostly rejecting spiritual baptism.

The controversies to which these several opinions have given rise, seem, as at present conducted, to be endless, and we cannot help thinking that before any one of them can be satisfactorily settled, a deeper question must be investigated, and the point which is common to all, and which is generally taken for granted without much proof, must be thoroughly sifted and canvassed. It is assumed by these different parties that baptism is a rite, and hence the question arises, What does it mean? What is its value? How is it to be administered? Who are its subjects? and, Who are to administer it? And if on all these points Scripture is silent, we may cease to wonder at the diversity of opinion which has been elicited by their discussion. We purpose in this inquiry to go a step further back, and to ask—Is Christian baptism a rite? When Christ said, "Go baptize all nations," did he ordain the administration of a rite? What do the words of Christ signify?

The point we purpose to discuss in this section of the work is, not the expediency of water baptism—this we cannot admit. The question we wish to approach is not—Is it a wise institution? but, is it a Christian ordinance? And in discussing this point, and answering this question, we shall go upon the common Protestant canon, of proving Scripture by Scripture, as we have done throughout. We mean not here to entertain the question, Is water baptism a wide-spread fact? Does it exist in many, or in all Christian churches? Had it a being in the sixteenth century? Did it exist in the seventh? Can it be clearly traced to the first? We shall not touch upon these points here, except so far as their solution may be supposed to affect the evidence by which the meaning of the command, "Go baptize all nations," is determined. In any other view we consider these questions irrelevant, till the previous one is answered. Does Christ enjoin it? Has he spoken upon the subject, and to what effect? Do the words baptize all nations, as employed by him, mean baptizing with water? There is not the smallest doubt that the word baptize is used in the New Testament as equivalent to baptizing with water as practised among the Jews, and lustrations among the heathens; but it is equally certain, that this is not its only meaning. We conceive that by examining certain passages in the New Testament in which the word "baptize" is found, and perhaps a few others in which words of similar import occur, we shall have data sufficient to determine its meaning in the passage in question.

We will first examine a few passages in the historical books of the New Testament, in which the subject of baptism is mentioned; relating to the days of John the Baptist. The statements of all the four Evangelists on this subject may be combined and considered together. We will only quote a small portion, as that will be sufficient for our purpose, leaving the reader to satisfy himself, by consulting the entire passages, that no point of importance to our object is omitted or overstrained.

"John did baptize in the wilderness, and preach the baptism of repentance for the remission of sins. And there went out unto him all the land of Judæa, and they of Jerusalem, and were all baptized of him in Jordan, confessing their sins." "And as the people were in expectation, and all men mused in their hearts of John, whether he was the Christ or not; John answered and said unto them all, I indeed baptize you with water; but one mightier than I cometh; he will baptize you with the Holy Ghost, and with fire." "They asked him, and said unto him, Why baptizest thou then, if thou be not that Christ, nor Elias, neither that prophet? John answered them, saying, I baptize with water; but there standeth one among you, whom ye know not; he it is, who coming after me is preferred before me. These things were done in Bethabara, where John at first baptized." John said "This is he of whom I said, After me cometh a man who is preferred before me; for he was before me, and I knew him not; but that he should be made manifest to Israel; and therefore am I come baptizing with water. And John bare record, saying, I saw the Spirit descending from heaven like a dove, and it abode upon him. And I knew him not; but He that sent me to baptize with water, the same said unto me, Upon whom thou shalt see the Spirit descending, and remaining on him, the same is he which baptizeth with the Holy Ghost. And I saw, and bare record that this is the Son of God."

Two kinds of baptism are here distinguished, which may be respectively called water baptism, and the baptism of the Spirit. The meaning of the word baptism as applied above, must be found in something common to the two, but not including the

two to make one baptism, or, to state it in other words, we
are entitled to conclude that the influence of God's Spirit resembles the operation of water in this respect; that it is a
cleansing spirit, in a manner that is common to water as used
under the law. The water in baptism is spoken of not so much
with a view to what it actually accomplishes, but rather with
a view to suggest what the Spirit effects.

The baptism of John was the baptism of repentance for sins.
He said " I baptize you with water unto repentance." So
that the object of *his* baptism was not so much to wash the
body as to point to the cleansing of the soul; deriving its
significance from its reference to the Spiritual baptism of Him
who was to come after him and cleanse the soul, whose forerunner he was. That the idea of cleansing, real or figurative,
enters into the meaning of the word baptize, will further
appear from the consideration that in two of the Evangelists, the
expression " with fire " is added to the Holy Ghost; so as to
bring more prominently to view the cleansing influence of the
Spirit, or the baptism of the Holy Ghost.

Water baptism is connected with the dispensation of the law,
and the name of John, under the law; the baptism of the spirit
with the dispensation of the gospel, and the name of Jesus, under
the gospel. The time for administration of water baptism was
then present; the time for administration of spiritual baptism
was then future: " I baptize with water, He shall baptize with
the Holy Ghost." John was then engaged in his work. Christ
had not yet begun to baptize with the Spirit. For the Spirit
was not yet given in its fulness.

There is a significance in John's baptism, which cannot attach
to the rite in any period after his days. John says that he had
come that the Christ " might be made manifest to Israel." He
was made manifest when on Him alone of all the people baptized
by John, the Holy Ghost descended at his baptism, and He was
pointed out to John so plainly that he could say confidently,
" Behold the Lamb of God which taketh away the sin of the
world." John's words are express, " That he should be made

manifest to Israel, therefore am I come baptizing with water."
At his manifestation, the great end of John's appearance as the
Baptist was accomplished, and whoever shall come baptizing
with water after him, could not ground his exercise of office upon
the same reason— a Divine commission.

We come now to the well-known words, "Go ye, therefore,
because all power is given unto me, and teach all nations, baptizing them into the name of the Father, and of the Son, and
of the Holy Ghost." Water baptism employed under the dispensation of the law, is termed baptism simply, or the baptism
of repentance for the remission of sins ; spiritual baptism is not.
The command is to baptize into the name, power, and life of
the Father, Son, and Holy Ghost.

The narrative of the disciples now tells us of a New Dispensation, called "the kingdom of heaven ;" a dispensation in which
John and Judaism have no place at all.   They tell us further of
a new baptism, associated particularly with the name of Jesus,
the head of this New Dispensation—the ruler of this spiritual
kingdom.   "He shall baptize you with the Holy Ghost and with
fire."   Do not these words import, that spiritual baptism was
the special work of Jesus, and not to be shared in by John or
others, as he declared that "all power was given unto him in
heaven and in earth ?"

In close connection with this is the promise to the disciples,
"Lo, I am with you alway," "ye shall be baptized with the
Holy Ghost—ye shall receive power—and ye shall be witnesses
unto me, both in Jerusalem, and all Judæa, and in Samaria,
and unto the uttermost parts of the earth," "because all power
in heaven and earth is given unto me."   Here we cannot but see
that when disciples are constituted Christ's witnesses, and commanded to baptize into his name, it is after a promise, "The
Holy Ghost shall come upon you."   If we are God's witnesses,
baptizing into his name, we must have God's Spirit, "for the
things of God knoweth no man but the Spirit of God."   If we
are to bear his testimony before men, we must be endued with
power from on high—baptized with the Holy Ghost.

The time to which the command to baptize all nations into the name of the Father, Son, and Holy Ghost refers, is, emphatically, the new era—the Dispensation of the Spirit. All the baptisms previously noticed, were in the era of the law and the prophets, for as we have seen, "the Spirit was not yet given." But intimation had been made that the Gospel Dispensation, the era of the Spirit, was soon to begin. And while the disciples were commanded to preach in all the world the gospel of the kingdom of Christ, they were commanded not to depart from Jerusalem, not to set out on their mission, till they had received the promise of the Father—endued with power from on high. Now here we have the express intimation that the era of shadows would come to a close, and the dispensation of the Spirit would commence, before the command of Jesus was in a single instance complied with, nay, when disciples are expressly enjoined to wait till this period before setting out to preach the gospel and baptize all nations with the Spirit.

If we look at the force of the words "into the name," as used in the Scripture, we shall see that to baptize into the name of any one, is to baptize into the likeness or character of that person. And to apply the passage before us, "to baptize into the name of Father, Son, and Holy Ghost," must be to unite to God, to administer such a baptism as will introduce us into the character of God, and produce a conformity to his righteous law. And this is what the baptism of the Spirit does. They who are the subject of it "put on the new man which is renewed in knowledge, after the image of Him that created him," "to be conformed to the image of God's dear Son," "that therefore they may be like Him."

To baptize with the Spirit, is to do greater works than were done by Jesus himself during his own ministry; to baptize with water is not. Jesus told his disciples that "he that believeth on me, the works that I do, shall he do also; and greater works than these shall he do; because I go to my Father."

Jesus, in his address to the disciples, associates the gift of the Spirit with the fact of his return to the Father, "If I go not away, the Comforter will not come unto you; but if I depart, I will send Him unto you. When the Comforter is come, whom I will send unto you from the Father, even the Spirit of truth, he shall testify of me." This view of the subject does not tend to lower the power and dignity of the person of Jesus. Rightly considered, it tends rather to his honour and exaltation in the conception of his followers. To say that the disciples baptized with the Holy Spirit, into the name of the Godhead through Christ's power in them, is not to take from Him his glory, but to view Him as more glorious than before. It is to say that his work did not terminate with his death; it is to say that having ascended to his Father, his delights were still in the children of men. It is to say, too, that he could work in heaven as well as on the earth, by human instrumentality, as well as in his own person. This is to magnify the grace of God, and to show that from the most unpromising materials, as in Peter and Paul, he can raise up the most powerful instruments for advancing the Gospel, and for the salvation of souls. "Because he lives, they live also;" and his mission is executed by virtue of his promise and his power: "Lo, I am with you alway," "All power is given unto Me." So soon as they forget this, their voice is powerless. While they lean all their faith upon Jesus, their words are with demonstration and power.

We have now reached the point at which John's baptism and the washings of the Jews ceased to be in force. We come now to the period at which Christ's baptism begins to exist. From the day of Pentecost, the prophecy begins to be fulfilled, "He shall baptize with the Holy Ghost." The promise to be verified is, "Ye shall receive the power of the Holy Ghost coming upon you." From this time the disciples were to bring others under the dominion of those influences of which themselves became the subjects, by preaching the Gospel of Christ, who imparts that Spirit which they now receive. In support of this view, it may be remarked that, unless the expression, they "were baptized,"

K

relates to the Spirit's work, there is no account whatever of the fulfilment of the promise.

We will now leave the historical books of the New Testament, and turn our attention to the Epistles. For in these "holy men of God spake as they were moved by the Holy Ghost." They are to be regarded, therefore, as expressing, not the private opinions of Paul, Peter, James, and John, but the mind of the Spirit of God. In the Epistles, the Apostles do not appear swayed by the feelings of the moment, as Peter seemed to be when he dissembled at Antioch, or Paul when he took the vow of the Nazarite, or circumcised Timothy because of the Jews. They are to be viewed, in writing the Epistles, as giving forth doctrines suited to all times, and adapted to all circumstances. If they speak of baptism as a rite, binding on every Christian, we must have been mistaken in the interpretation put upon passages of the Gospels and the Acts. If, on the other hand, their words harmonize with the views previously adduced from the historical books, if they speak of baptism, not as a rite, but as a doctrine, such statements must more than outweigh any inferential reasonings based upon the fact that in a few instances the Apostles themselves practised baptism with water, in condescension to the prejudices of Jewish converts. From the record of their acts, compared with the terms of their commission to "baptize all nations into the name of the Father, Son, and Holy Ghost," we do not gather that baptism with water is a Christian ordinance. When they speak under the influence of the Spirit, which was to lead them into all truth, what is the character of their own testimony? To obtain an answer to this question, let us turn to their writings, and examine those passages in which the subject is mentioned.

"Know ye not," said the Apostle to the Romans, "that so many of us as were baptized *into* Jesus Christ were baptized *into* his death? That like as Christ was raised from the dead by the glory of the Father, even so we also should walk in newness of life." It must be very clear to all unprejudiced minds, that the Apostle speaks here of the spiritual meaning and effect of baptism, regeneration, real conversion, real converts implanted in Christ Jesus—a dying to sin, and living unto righteousness—raised to newness of life—filled with the Spirit—putting off the old man with his deeds—and putting on the new man which after God is created in righteousness and true holiness.

We cannot think so meanly of the wisdom of Jesus, that his parting commission to his disciples can be viewed as enjoining actions which are incompatible in their nature, and incapable of being rightly performed by the same individual. Whatever baptism he enjoined, must be regarded as the proper work of all those who were to preach the Gospel; and least of all can it be viewed as unfitting when dispensed by an Apostle to the Gentiles, who queried, "Is Christ divided? was Paul crucified for you? or were ye baptized into the name of Paul? I thank God that I baptized none of you, but Crispus and Gaius; lest they should say that I baptized in my own name. And I baptized also the household of Stephanas; besides, I know not that I baptized any other. For Christ sent me not to baptize, (with water,) but to preach the gospel: not with the wisdom of words, lest the cross of Christ should be made of none effect."

That water baptism is referred to in this place, and had been administered in some instances by Paul, need not be disputed. But he thanked God that the instances in which he had administered this baptism were not more numerous. This he would not have done had he been speaking of spiritual baptism, for the more he converted, the greater would have been his joy. This conclusion is confirmed by what follows in the same chapter, in which he sets forth the superiority of the Gospel, to what was most valued, either by Jewish doctors or Gentile sages. He adduces two leading errors with regard to Divine revelation, the one prevalent among the Jews, the other among the Gentiles, and says, in opposition to both, "Christ crucified is set forth," and he, Paul, is sent out with a commission to yield to neither the one nor the other. He is neither to baptize with water, nor to use wisdom of words. To do the one would be pleasing to the Jews; to do the other would suit the taste of the Greeks. He is to persist in preaching Christ crucified, unto the Jews a stumbling-block, and to the Greeks foolishness. He is not to become a Jew to the Jew, nor a Greek to the Greek. The Apostle's argument is, that he refrained from baptizing, not because this was a subordinate office to preaching, and that he might leave the lesser, in order more fully to discharge the greater, but because it was a Jewish sign, by the practice of which the cross of Christ might be robbed of its glory. Again, his words intimate that to mix up the Gospel with human philosophy (the effects of which are set forth in our first chapter) was sinful, because it was a departure from the simplicity of Christ, and that to bring into the domain of the Gospel such a sign as water baptism, would be sinful, because this would be to introduce an element not in unison with its spiritual character.

To bring out the Apostle's meaning more clearly, we will set down in parallel columns those parts of the passage which relate severally to the error of the Jews and of the Greeks, placing in the middle the connecting passages which must be read with each column to make the sense complete.

Christ sent me

not to baptize, but to preach the gospel:

(to preach) not with wisdom of words,

lest the cross of Christ should be made of none effect. For the preaching of the cross is to them that perish foolishness; but unto us which are saved it is the power of God. For it is written, I will destroy the wisdom of the wise, and will bring to nothing the understanding of the prudent. Where is the wise? where is the scribe? where is the disputer of this world? hath not God made foolish the wisdom of this world? For after that in the wisdom of God the world by wisdom knew not God, it pleased God by the foolishness of preaching to save them that believe. For

the Jews require a sign,

(and) the Greeks seek after wisdom:

But we preach Christ crucified,

unto the Jews a stumblingblock,

(and) unto the Greeks foolishness;

but unto them which are called,

(both) Jews

(and) Greeks,

Christ

the power of God,

(and) the wisdom of God.

Because

the foolishness of God is wiser than men;

(and) the weakness of God is stronger than men.

For ye see your calling, brethren, how that

not many wise men
after the flesh,

not many mighty, not many noble, are
called : but

God hath chosen the
foolish things of the
world, to confound
the wise ;

(and) God hath
chosen the weak
things of the world
to confound the
things which are
mighty ;

and base things of
the world, and things
which are despised,
hath God chosen, yea,
and the things which
are not, to bring to
nought things that
are : that no flesh
should glory in his
presence.*

It is in the nature of things that the Jews should require
signs, such as they had been accustomed to ; and that the

* Here, be it observed, that the clauses put into the right hand column
make, with the intermediate one (omitting only one or two connecting
words put in brackets), a consistent or harmonious whole, bearing upon
the error of the Greeks, in seeking for worldly wisdom in the Gospel
message. But the clauses thrown into the left-hand column are an exact
counterpart of those in the right-hand ; and ought therefore to form, with
the intermediate ones, likewise, a consistent and harmonious whole, bearing upon the error of the Jews in looking for signs in the Gospel message ;
then the reason why water baptism was not more generally practised by
the apostles, appears to be this, that it partook of the nature of those signs
required by the Jews, but which were not to be granted, because contrary
to the spirit of the Gospel, and by which the cross of Christ might be
robbed of its glory.

Greeks should seek after philosophical wisdom, such as they had received, however contrary to the spirit of the Gospel. Can this be any marvel, when most high professors of the Christian religion in these our days, are found giving forth the statement that "mankind are not formed to live without ceremony and form; and that the inward spiritual grace is very apt to be lost without the external visible signs, and a philosophic mode of preaching." This is not mere theory, it is a fact; but it may be said to those who appeal to philosophy and tradition as their standing-point, that against the truth no rule can make itself valid; no length of time, no authority of persons; there is no pure tradition, or pure philosophy anywhere; elements of falsehood have always mingled with tradition and philosophy (as we have clearly shown in our first and second chapters). And in course of time, falsehood grows strong enough to make head against truth. This has been the case in all ages of the church.

We find that very early in the history of the Christian Church, Jewish rites and heathen philosophy were mixed up with Christian realities. In the fifteenth chapter of the Acts of the Apostles, we read that "certain men which came down from Judæa taught the brethren, and said, Except ye be circumcised after the manner of Moses, ye cannot be saved." And Peter was at one time disposed to compel the Gentiles to live as did the Jews, to judaize, to adopt Jewish rites and practices. Other Jews dissembled with him, and Barnabas was carried away with their dissimulations. The Galatian church, led away by judaizing teachers, was in danger, and Paul sharply reproved them, and speaks of their conduct as a turning again to weak and beggarly elements. The Colossians had well-nigh struck upon the same rock, and Paul writes to them, saying, "Wherefore if ye be dead with Christ from the rudiments of the world, why, as though living in the world, are ye subject to ordinances, after the commandments and doctrines of men?" But in the Epistle to the Hebrews, the distinction between the Law and the Gospel is most strongly insisted on, and the broad announcement is made, that "there is verily a disannulling of the commandment going before, for the weakness and unprofitableness thereof." "He taketh away the first that he may establish the second." Here we find that the Jewish rites were practised when they should have been abstained from, as their end had been served.

The Christian Church is one, animated by one spirit, possessed of one Lord, holding one faith, endowed with one baptism, the creation of one God. The oneness of the baptism is put along with the oneness of the Saviour, of faith, of the godhead. The least that can be inferred is, that there is a spiritual baptism which is common to every member of Christ's Church.

In drawing the subject of baptism to a close, it may be well to sum up, and collect in one view the evidence on the subject, scattered over the preceding pages, which has been adduced from the various passages that have passed in review before us. First, that before the crucifixion, and consequently before giving the commission in Matt. xxviii. 19, a distinction was drawn between the baptism of John and the baptism of Jesus. The first being with water, administered in the lifetime of the Saviour; the second, with the Spirit, to be administered after his death, resurrection, and glorification. Again, that Christian baptism, as enjoined in the commission, was to be administered in the second period, in the *name* or power of the Father, Son, and Holy Ghost: and is really the baptism by Jesus with the Spirit. Again, that such a baptism has been administered by disciples, God being the first cause by the communication of his grace, the Apostles being the conscious agents in preaching the Gospel. Again, that while baptism with water was administered in some cases after Pentecost, there is no reason to believe that this was in compliance with the command of Jesus, but rather in condescension to the prejudices of the Jews and Gentiles. Again, the epistles frequently mention the subject of baptism, but never as a rite, except in one case, and then to condemn it, (see 1 Cor. i. 13-17,) while they often mention it as a doctrine, and affirm of it in this view, that it is one—that it saves—that it implies union to Christ—a putting on of Christ—a burial with Christ—and a resurrection to newness of life—and that its effect is by the Spirit.

Now let me once for all remind the reader that this is not a mere speculative question, in regard to which much may be said on both sides, and either opinion held with equal safety. If the views presented in these pages be the Scriptural ones, then not only is the common practice of sprinkling or dipping erroneous, but it is an error that may be attended with the most serious consequences. " If ye be circumcised," says the Apostle Paul, " Christ shall profit you nothing." And if another rite be put in the place of circumcision, as many high professors say baptism is, we have as little reason to claim a Divine sanction for its administration as we have for circumcision, when it is declared to " profit nothing," but must prove a barrier in the way of true religion. The rite obtains the name of baptism, and this, with most minds, is sufficient to convey the impression, that the characters ascribed to spiritual baptism in Scripture belong to the rite of water baptism. This is the canker-worm that lies at the root of all the mischief. A few men of spiritual discernment may stand forth and say—the burial with Christ—the resurrection with Christ—the union with Christ—these are true, but not of those who only receive the rite, but of those who practise the spirit. But this does not seriously alarm men, their spiritual understanding is darkened, through the traditions of the churches, so that they cannot perceive the truth as it is in Jesus.

But let it once be fairly understood, and become an established fact, that a compliance with the ceremonial rites does not bring men any nearer heaven, and is not required by God ; and then men may be stirred up to ask, What is the bond which unites to the Saviour ? What is true baptism ? Then they may be brought to feel that they have been leaning upon a broken reed, and then flee for refuge to the only rock of safety, the Lord Jesus Christ—the power of his Spirit—the promise of the Father.

If but little has already been done in the way of converting men to the truth, let us never despair of seeing realized the great and glorious things predicted in the Gospel, nor doubt the truth of God's words, nor believe that failure is due to anything but our own indolence and want of faith. If the nations are yet to be baptized with the Spirit, let us not shrink from *our* commission, but seek to discharge it individually, according to the grace given unto us—not in a spirit of self-sufficiency, but with a humble trust in God's promise, " Lo, I am with you alway ; " resting satisfied that if we be with Jesus, greater is he that is on our side than all that can be against us.   " The Spirit and the bride say, Come. And let him that heareth, say, Come. And let him that is athirst, come.   And whosoever will, let him take the water of life freely ;" and say, " Create in me a clean heart, O God, and renew a right spirit within me.   Cast me not away from thy presence ; and take not thy Holy Spirit from me, but uphold me with thy free Spirit.   Then will I teach transgressors thy ways, and sinners shall be converted unto thee."

Such as these are acquainted with the sensible influences of the Spirit of truth, and the absolute need of its influence to the right understanding and saving application of the truth of the Gospel, and take a firm footing upon the only true foundation— Christ Jesus himself.   It is He who changes the whole man, " If any man be in Christ, he is a new creature ; old things are passed away."   They are now ambassadors for Christ and vital Christianity : knowing the fulfilment of those precious words of their Redeemer, when He said, " My Father worketh hitherto, and I work."   The Spirit is one of the blessed gifts of the Redeemer ; it diverts the mind from faith in those vain inventions which the blind zeal and activity of men have mingled with it in all ages, particularly in the Roman, Greek, and other episcopalian churches.

Such as these adhere to the cause of Christ, and the leadings of his Spirit, speak the truth in love, determining to know nothing save Jesus Christ and Him crucified ; seeking nothing, pleading for nothing, save the truth as it is in Him.   They proclaim Him as the Saviour of sinners, the only hope of salvation, the way, the truth, and the life, and that without Him no man can come unto the Father, being in the unity of the Spirit, in the oneness of the faith, baptized with the same baptism, and partaking together, at the same table, of the same bread, ministered to them by their one Lord and sanctifying Redeemer :

therefore, they proclaim his name, vindicate his honour, and testify of that salvation which is through him alone.

Such as these give no countenance to apostolical succession, or the continuance in any form of the sacerdotal office; they maintain, on the contrary, that Christ himself is the ruler in his own church, and that all the Lord's children are members of the church as priests of the living God—all capable of receiving and using the gifts of the Spirit, not admitting for one moment, or on any plea whatever, the worship of any other being but the Eternal Jehovah—Father, Son, and Holy Spirit. They repudiate all the pomps and parade of external rites and ceremonies, and the delusive charms of musical excitement; they light no candles, and burn no incense upon their visible altars, bow down to no graven images, adore no saints, and recognise no object of religious homage in the Virgin Mary. These totally reject the works of supererogation, they perform no pilgrimages to any sacred shrine, they know nothing of the miraculous power of relics, are utter strangers to the imagined flames of purgatory, have no indulgences, no auricular confessions, no sacerdotal absolutions, no masses for the living, no prayers for the dead, and they acknowledge no mediator between God and man but Christ, no justification for sinners but through faith in his blood, no sanctification of the believer but by his Spirit. These are they who are not ashamed to acknowledge a crucified Saviour and risen Lord, as the sole ground of their hope of redemption and everlasting salvation. No! they sink down to the foundation, Christ Jesus, the Rock of Ages.

NOTE.—The Author is free to acknowledge that he has, in this chapter, made many extracts from Robert Macnair's " Christian baptism, Spiritual not Ritual ;" his views being so much in harmony with his own ; and he feels confident that he will not censure him for so doing, knowing that, should his work succeed, it will of necessity create a desire for further acquaintance with his, in which a most critical, learned, and Scriptural, examination of the subject of baptism is contained.

# CHAPTER VI.

In all ages, and among all nations, religious rites have been clothed with a secret grandeur. From the sacredness attached to pagan mysteries, the early "Catholic Church" threw a similar air of hidden grandeur and mystery over certain rites. This remark particularly applies to baptism and the eucharist, to which the word mysteries are especially attached. Isocrates speaks of Demeter, one of the principal divinities of ancient Greece, as having introduced the mysteries, "which," says he, "fill the souls of those who participate in them with the sweetest hopes, both as to this and the future world." Indeed, the ancients generally seem to have entertained the idea that the main secret communicated, was the assurance of a future state of happiness, beyond death and the grave. But from whatever motives the pagan mysteries were received into the paganized "Catholic Church," they, as far as baptism and the eucharist were concerned, led, in process of time, to gross superstition in the "Romish Church," as well as in many others. So far as we can learn from Romish writers, the mysteries at first seem to have been limited to four specific points :—(1) The mode of administering, and the effect produced in baptism. (2) The unction of chrism, or confirmation thereby. (3) The ordination of priests, as organs in the communication of the Holy Ghost. (4) The mode of celebrating the eucharist was more especially a mystery, in consequence of its being an organ through which the communicant received the Holy Ghost, or in other words communion in the sacred mysteries. From this time superstition enveloped and debased the minds of men, and religion was deemed principally to consist in outward acts and ceremonial observances ; spiritual and even miraculous effects were attributed to these, and they were dignified with the title of sacraments.

The Church of Christ, at its first formation, was composed of two distinct classes of converts, those drawn from Judaism, and those drawn from Paganism ; each of them brought into the church many strong prejudices in favour of their own systems. And the profound respect that was paid to the Greek and Roman mysteries and sacrifices, was the cause, no doubt, that induced the priests of the " Catholic Church " to give their religion a mystic air, " in order to put it upon an equal footing in point of dignity with that of the Pagans. Hence originated the doctrine of the real presence in the eucharist ; for it was the opinion of the heathen that the very substance and body of their deities insinuated themselves into the sacrificial victim as it was being offered, and became united to the person who ate of the sacrifice." (See Elsner's Observations, vol. ii., p. 108.) Their notion was, that, thus to participate of, was to assimilate themselves to the gods ; the Greeks and Romans, therefore, had the idea both of a real presence, and of an invisible mystery. Therefore, as pagan Rome borrowed from pagan Greece, so did papal Rome copy from both.

So early as the second century, Irenæus, in his controversial writings, contends that the eucharist should be regarded as a sacrifice ; he takes care, however, to distinguish it from the Jewish sacrifices, alleging it to be of a higher and nobler character than these mere typical ordinances. Clement of Alexandria, Origen, Tertullian, and Cyprian—all of the Alexandrian school —make reference to the eucharist, as the medium through which the priests sustain spiritual life in the church. But it is somewhat strange, that in consulting the writings of the New Testament, and the early apologists of true Christianity, no mention is found of the eucharist or Lord's Supper, by Barnabas, Polycarp, or Clement of Rome ; the earliest apologists for true

Christianity are silent on the subject. But Irenæus contended that the eucharist should be regarded as a "sacrifice." This idea was borrowed from heathenism, and opened a floodgate through which the church was deluged with error.

Cyprian, who was consecrated to the see of Carthage, A.D. 248, was a character extremely energetic in spreading this doctrine, "His works," says Jerome, "shine brighter than the sun." He held by *tradition* the doctrine of the real presence of Christ in the eucharist, which he calls the body and blood of Christ; the grand idea that seems to have prevailed in Cyprian's mind was to bring all sects of religion into harmony, by robbing Christianity of all its high and holy peculiarities, and to amalgamate Christianity and Paganism into one system, called the "Catholic Church." Cyprian of Carthage, and others, adopted this new species of philosophic paganism, and immense harm was done thereby to Christianity. Plain Scripture truth then began to be wrapped up in obscure philosophic language, and unbridled imagination substituted its wildest vagaries for the Sacred Scriptures of truth. The way was thus opened for the rushing in of that flood of erroneous doctrine, which has overwhelmed the Church of Christ, and uprooted the vine of Jehovah's own planting; and many, deceived by the plausibilities of this human system of thought, were, and still are, alienated from the doctrines of the gospel. (See Faiths of the World, Article—Lord's Supper.)

Cyril, Bishop of Jerusalem, A.D. 350, teaches in the clearest manner the real presence of Christ in the eucharist. Of the sacrament, he says: "By it we are made concorporeal and consanguinal with Christ, his body and blood being distributed through our bodies:" and of transubstantiation, he says, "Do not look on the bread and wine as bare and common elements, for they are the body and blood of Christ." (Cat. xxii., n. 1-3.)

Ambrose, Bishop of Milan, A.D. 374, in his book on the Mysteries, held and approved the doctrine of the real presence and transubstantiation. Leo the Great, who filled the see of Rome twenty-one years, from A.D. 440 to 461, taught the real presence of Christ in the sacrament (Ep. xlvi., c. ii., p. 260) ; as well as the sacrifice of the mass. (Ep. cxxv., c. v., p. 337.)

From the sacredness attached to the pagan mysteries, the early-paganised "Catholic Church," with Irenæus, Cyprian, Cyril, Ambrose, Basil, Leo, Chrysostom, Epiphanius, and Constantine at its head, throws an air of hidden mystery over baptism and the eucharist. The origin of these studied mysteries is to be clearly traced to a natural desire on the part of the priesthood to accommodate themselves to the converts from heathenism, who had been accustomed to observe the Eleusinian mysteries, in which the whole of their religion was wrapped, so that it became a paganized Christianity, and has continued so to the present time.

Chrysostom, Bishop of Constantinople, whose writings form a standing bulwark of Catholicity in the latter half of the fourth century, in speaking of the real presence of Christ in the eucharist, says : "He has given us himself to eat, and he puts himself into the state of a victim, being sacrificed for us." (Hom. 1., p. 517, t. 7, ed. Ben.) And again, "He gives you himself to eat—to be revived within you." (Hom. lxxxvii., p. 787.) He also states that, "It is clear that they (the Apostles) did not deliver all things by their epistles, but communicated many things without writing ; and these, too, demand our assent of faith : it is tradition, make no further enquiry." (Hom. iv., in 2 Thess., p. 532.) He teaches the same doctrine in many other places. About the same time, Epiphanius, Archbishop of Salamis, in Cyprus, also wrote his Anchorate, to fix unsettled minds, that they might not be tossed to and fro, and carried about with every wind of doctrine. But how did he do it ? By tradition ! In his work, entitled, "A Box of Antidotes against all Heresies," he says : "Tradition is necessary, all things cannot be learned from the Scriptures. The Apostles left something in writing, others by tradition." By tradition, he justifies the practice of the church. (Hær. lxxvi., c. 7, 8, p. 911, &c.) This peculiar mode of thinking at Constantinople,

Salamis, Rome, and Alexandria, was of great importance in the corruption of Christianity, and the establishment of the Roman Catholic church in Britain, in the sixth and seventh centuries, by Gregory and Austin.

In the second, third, and fourth centuries, notions were prevalent, relating to ritual tradition, which was called the ritual part of Christianity by the Nicene Catholic Church, of which we can discover no trace in the New Testament, if we exclude the Clementines, and the Apostolical Constitution ;* but Cyprian's mind, constructed on the pagan model, and formed to grasp the ideal of government, and highly sensitive to the love of power, found in the Clementines, Constitutions, Recognitions, and the Catholic Church, what at that time was not easily to be met with elsewhere—a sphere of uncontrolled influence, within which a lofty spirit might signalise its energy, putting foremost the priest, and talking more about the rites, as rites ; constantly speaking of baptism and the eucharist as conveying holiness. Or they so held up the rites before the people as led them to pay a superstitious regard to the ceremony, while the moral and spiritual qualities, or state of the heart, were lost sight of.

Chrysostom also, who stands by general consent at the head of the Nicene divines, and who is second to none of them as an

---

* The ancient author of the Synopsis of Holy Scripture, printed among the works of Athanasius, Bishop of Alexandria, about A.D. 360 (tom. ii., p. 154, ed. Paris), in giving some account of the books of the New Testament, says : "The books of the New Testament not universally agreed on are these—the Apostolical Constitutions, and the Clementines, out of which the more genuine and the divinely-inspired portions have been selected, and have been transferred to their proper authors," (See also Epiphanius, Hær. lxx., §§ 10-12 ; xiv., § 5 ; lxxv., § 6 ; lxxx., § 7, and others of the Nicene fathers) ; which show that these grafts from Essene Judaism, the Constitutions and Clementines, were not considered as veritable inspired branches of the Scriptures, although they were regarded to be so by others, and from which the doctrine of the " Nicene or Catholic Church" was received, more especially as they were remodelled between A.D. 211 and 230, and called the " Recognitions of Clement," in which shape they are cited by Origen. (Philocalia, cap. xxiii., p. 81, ed. Spencer, from tom. iii., Comment, in Genes.)

expositor, we bring forward as an authority for the Nicene faith, in his vii. Hom., p. 269 :—where he says, " Although a man should be foul with every vice, the blackest that can be named, yet should he fall into the baptismal pool, he ascends from the Divine water purer than the beams of the moon." This was Chrysostom's view of baptism. Indeed, this is placed beyond doubt by what soon follows :— " They who approach the baptismal font, though fornicators, &c., are not only made clean, but holy also ;" and again, " As a spark thrown into the ocean is instantly extinguished, so is sin, be it what it may, extinguished, when a man is thrown into the laver of regeneration ; he comes forth another man." The highest possible importance was attached to this mere rite, which had been borrowed from the " Pagan Mass," the principal parts of which were the " Asperges," "which was sprinkling with holy water." (See De Laune. p. 115.)

The clergy had a cumbrous machine to work ; and, to keep it in order, they availed themselves of every means which they found would take effect upon it. Hence the mysterious terrors wherewith the eucharistic rite was enveloped. Minds hardened against the genuine motives of the gospel might yet be overawed by the terrors of the eucharistic ceremonials, as set forth by Chrysostom in his Liturgy, (tom. ii., p. 453,) as " the horrific mystery," or " the tremendous sacrifice ;" and (in tom. x., p. 248) as " the cup of blessings." In the same strain speak his illustrious contemporaries of the East and West, Ambrose, Jerome, Augustine, &c., who employed language and conveyed opinions nowhere suggested in the evangelical records,—" That this breaking of bread was a real sacrifice, during the performance of which the angels looked on with amazement as they did when Christ hung on the tree :—that by the words of consecration, what before was bread and wine, had become truly Christ's body, and that the priest to whom such a function is assigned exerts a power to which nothing else either in earth or in heaven can be likened." These are the things we hear of in the Nicene writers, (See Chrysostom's Liturgy,) and which

L

were conveyed to thousands of persons in Judæa, Asia Minor, Egypt,* Africa, and Italy. Indeed, the eucharistic rite may very well be regarded as the hinge of the ecclesiastical economy of the Nicene age.

What faith Gregory and Austin brought into England is plain from this, as well as from Bede's Ecclesiastical History:—"They called the eucharist the true body of Christ, and termed the mass a sacrifice." Rome is to be shunned, therefore, by all Christendom; and for no one thing more than for her sins of the altar. Had these been unopposed in all ages, Christianity would have been extinct in our days, and the world carried back to the worst principles and forms of pagan superstition, for it was out of these, and not from a perverted construction of the phraseology of Scripture, that the eucharistic errors of Rome took their rise, and became grafted upon the civil and ecclesiastical constitutions of Britain.

Inæ, the West Saxon monarch, was the first to impose a sacramental test, A.D. 693. He thus ushered in his law:—

"I, Inæ, by the gift of God, King of the West Saxons, by the advice of Kenred my father, and Hedde my bishop, and with all mine aldermen, and the senior counsellors of my nation, have been consulting the health of our souls, and the stability of our reign, that right law may be settled among our people." He goes on to say:—"If a man be charged with robbing in a very large gang, let him pay his weregild or make his purgation. Half of them that take the oath shall be frequenters of the communion."

This was the first sacramental test in England. It was the test of veracity, and contains principles both of a religious and civil character, and more important than upon the face of the

* "The Egyptians" (saith Theophilus Gale) "so pursued the study of mathematics, that the title of prophet, priest, or wise man, was allowed to none but such as were profoundly instructed therein." While the primitive purity was kept, he that ministered was to do it with the ability which God gave, but this ability being lost in the Nicene Church, schools were erected—heathen learning was entertained, and Rome heathen streamed into Rome Nicene, and nearly swept true Christianity from the earth.

law becomes immediately apparent. In a religious aspect, it was designed by the framers of the law to impress on the mind that there was a more direct and immediate connection between God and the frequenters of the communion, than was secured by any other religious act. Hence the comparative ease with which eucharistic errors were enforced upon the people.

Leaving the West Saxons, and turning our attention to the kingdom of Kent, we find that the 23rd law of Wihtred, A.D. 696, says:—"If any one impeach a servant of God, let his Lord purge him upon his single oath, *if he be a communicant.* If he be not a communicant, let him have another good voucher with him at taking the oath." From this it is evident, that the same principle obtained in Kent as among the West Saxons, in relation to criminal trials. "The communion" imparted higher sanction to the oath.

The laws made by Ecbriht A.D. 740, and Cuthbert A.D. 747, are remarkable, as it was under them that the eucharistic errors received consolidation, influence, and enlargement. At the time when Ecbriht passed the law about to be considered, he most probably thought that he was promoting the interests of the Church. But even pure intentions are not always tests of pure laws. Nay, the very worst laws often proceed from upright motives, as far as the individual making them is concerned ; but which, nevertheless, lay the foundation, if they do not exactly raise the structure, of the edifice. This receives illustration from the fact before us, for we find what Ecbriht began, Cuthbert carried forward, and it remained a despoiling power for 800 years.

In those ages it was common for one kingdom of the Heptarchy to follow the example of another. Among the customs imported into Northumbria, one related to fasts preparative to partaking of the communion ; Ecbriht, therefore, in A.D. 734, said : —

" The custom grew up in the Church of the English, and was holden from the time of Vitalian the Pope, and Theodore, Archbishop of Canterbury, that not only clerks in the monasteries, but also laymen, with their wives and families, went to their confessors, and cleansed themselves with tears and abstinence on twelve days before the nativity of our Lord; that so they might, with the greater purity, partake of the communion of the Lord on his nativity."

The fact here stated is a remarkable evidence of the pains Vitalian and Theodore had taken to indoctrinate the English Church with pagan notions, which they had borrowed from Basil and Cyprian, who lived 350 years before Vitalian and Theodore, and 500 before Cuthbert. Basil maintained auricular confession of sins to a priest, and the validity of absolution conferred, (see Basil in pp. 32 and cp. canon 2, canon 34, &c.,) of which Cyprian said, when addressing himself to sinners, —" Let every one of you make an humble and solemn confession of his sins while his confession can be admitted; while his satisfaction and the pardon given him by the priest are available with God." (Tr. de Laps. n. 14, p. 95.) What an evidence have we here that it is all founded on tradition, and not on Scriptural truth!

Again, one of their laws says :—" It behoved them that would take in hand these holy things, to purify themselves some days before, and to abstain from carnal delights. Being thus prepared they came and stood round the altar." Again : " If they were about any solemn sacrifice to the gods," (mark, *the gods!*) " be the time what it would, it could never be lucky for either not to abstain." (Archæologicæ Atticæ, lib. 2, cap. 4, pp. 57-192, published 1671.) Say which of these authorities—the pagan, Theodore, or Ecbriht the Christian, do you prefer, or are they all alike repulsive ?

Six years afterwards, he promulgated other laws, bearing more expressly upon the eucharist. These last laws are called the " Excerptions of Ecbriht," or "canonical determinations." The important bearing these canons had upon the character and discipline of the church, requires that we should give them special attention. The very preamble is of singular interest; it says :—" priests only are to put in use and read canonical constitutions; for as none but bishops and priests ought to offer the sacrifice, so neither should others put in use those dooms " (laws). Among these are the following in A.D. 740 :—

"That no priest presume to celebrate mass in private houses, nor in any other place than consecrated churches." The previous use of the word "sacrifice" in the preambles, as well as among Jews and heathens, prepared the way for, and seemed to justify, the prohibition. This one word was ominous and fatal. Was it an original idea? Is there anything in Christianity out of which it could arise? There is not so much as the shadow of a word to indicate that it came from Christ or his apostles. The only source from whence it could have been derived was pagan.

The word "Viaticum," appears to have been an improvement upon heathen mythology. Therefore the second canon of Ecbriht demands: — "That all priests with compassion give the Viaticum, and the communion of the body of Christ, to all sick people before the ends of their lives." Third, "that all priests have the eucharist always ready for the sick, lest any die without communion." Fifth, "such seculars as do not communicate on the nativity of our Lord, on Easter, and Pentecost, are not to be esteemed Catholics." Twelfth, "faithful monks especially, ought always to have the eucharist with them."

From these singularly expressive enactments, as well as those we have omitted, it is evident that if Northumbria proudly acknowledged that she had borrowed her religious institutions from Vitalian and Theodore, who had borrowed from Basil and Cyprian, and they from paganism, they must thus have obtained a corrupt religion ; once admit this, and you must go a step further, inducing a preference for human authority ; in fact, you offer a premium to set aside the sole authority of the supreme lawgiver ; and then every particle of true religion will drift off in any direction where sagacity, superstition, or impiety, may for it prepare an under-current.

We now pass into Mercia, one of the most important of the Anglo-Saxon kingdoms. As it joined Northumbria, it was to be expected that, aided by the emissaries of Rome, Mercia would not remain behind any other kingdom in the character of its religious ordinances. In the year 742, Ethelbald, King of

Mercia, held a great council at Cloves-hoo, "and they diligently inquired how matters were ordered in relation to religion, and particularly as to the creed in the infancy of the English Church." The ordinance of Wihtred, King of Kent, was read, "and all that heard it said there never was any such wise decree; and therefore they enacted that it should be firmly kept by all." Ethelbald says he adopted, "those ordinances of the King of Kent for the health of his soul, and the stability of his kingdom, and out of reverence to the venerable Archbishop Cuthbert; and now confirmed by the subscription of his own hand, that the liberty, honour, authority, and security of the church be contradicted by no man." And to add greater solemnity to the whole, he declares, "If an earl, priest, deacon, clerk, or monk, oppose this constitution, let him be deprived of his degree, and separated from the participation of the body and blood of the Lord, and be far from the kingdom of God."

All this, however, was only the beginning. Five years afterwards, Cuthbert hastened to the same place, (Cloves-hoo,) and Ethelbald, King of Mercia is again present " in synod with his princes and dukes." He appears to have been present as approving of the proceedings, for the assembly was purely of an ecclesiastical character. Not one of the thirty laws which were then passed related to secular affairs; not even to the civil rites of priests. These laws will be found at large in Spelman, vol. 1, p. 245, but those only which relate to the eucharist are here inserted. Before, however, these are quoted, it may not be uninteresting to present to our readers the introduction to the whole code. He will perceive by this that no small importance was attached by the bishops assembled to the laws they then adopted. Their own intrinsic merits, and especially the relation in which these laws were intended to place the English church to the Pope of Rome, gave them special interest. It is to be remembered that up to this period the authority of the pope was not completely established in the whole island. This explains the following expressive paragraph in the preamble:—
" When the prelates  .  .  .  .  met at the place of synod,

the writings of Pope Zachary . . . . were in the first place produced, and publicly recited and explained . . . . as he enjoined, in which writings the pontiff admonished in a familiar manner the inhabitants of this Isle of Britain of every rank and degree of quality, and authoritatively charged them, and . . . . . instructed them, and hinted that a sentence of anathema should be certainly published against them that persisted in their pernicious malice and contempt."

These extracts from the introduction will prepare the reader. for a body of laws which paved the way for the most grievous violations of Scriptural truth; and some of which remained in full vigour during the long period of 800 years.

Among the errors now taught and enforced in A.D. 747 were these :—

(1.) "That priests should learn to know how to perform every office belonging to their orders ; to construe and explain in their own tongue, the sacred words which are solemnly pronounced at the celebration of the mass. Let them also take care to learn what these sacraments which are visibly performed in the mass, baptism, and other ecclesiastical offices, do spiritually signify, lest they be found ignorant in those intercessions which they make to God for the atonement of the sins of the people, if they do not know the meaning of their own words."

(2.) " The litanies and rogations shall be kept with great reverence, with fear and trembling, with the sign of Christ's passion, and our eternal redemption, (the cross,) carried before them, together with the relics of saints."

(3.) " The ecclesiastics are admonished to keep themselves always prepared for the holy communion of the body and blood of our Lord ; and rectors shall take diligent care that none of their subjects lead such dissolute and wretched lives, as to be separated from the participation of the eucharist at the altar."

(4.) " Lay boys shall be also admonished often to communicate, lest they grow weak for want of the salutary meat and drink, since our Lord says, ' Except ye eat the flesh of the Son of man, and drink his blood, ye have no life in you.' "

(5.) " The atoning celebration shall be often piously performed by the ministration of great numbers of priests of Christ, for the rest of their souls when they are dead."

If these bishops who were said to be "promoted by God to be masters and teachers of others," were really advanced by heaven to this distinction, how came it to pass that, in commanding others, the priests themselves did not understand the meaning of their own professed Master? When Christ said, "Eat my flesh, and drink my blood," he used these words in a way common among the Jews, and intended not to refer to a ceremony, but to a principle. To eat, as applied to teachers, was then understood to mean to imbibe their doctrine, and related, therefore, to a mental participation of sacred truth, through faith, and not to a corporal partaking of the eucharist. The word is used by the sacred writer as a figurative expression in Revelation x. 9, where its obvious meaning is a deep acquaintance with truth.

The idea of an atoning celebration of the eucharist springs out of a fatally erroneous conception of the Gospel of Christ. His mission was to bring us unto God—as Father, Son, and Holy Spirit, through himself. This was his one grand ulterior purpose; nor can that purpose be realized, except the entire work to be performed present itself to the mind, and sink into the heart; and even then only by its exciting a sympathy in man with the conjoint purpose of Jehovah and Christ, as Father and Son. The Son of God did not so stultify his own work, as to assign to a priest the office of making an atonement by the eucharist.

It was now 186 years since the first eucharistical law was passed by Ina, the West Saxon king. His successors were content to incorporate into their religious and ecclesiastical institutions those several sacramental enactments which had obtained in other kingdoms.

The tenth king from Ina was Alfred the Great, whom we are about to introduce, as enacting a singularly expressive law in relation to the eucharist. He thus ushers it in among other ecclesiastical laws :—

" I, Alfred the King, made a collection of what our predecessors had observed, and which I approved, to be transcribed; and those which I approved not, altered, with the advice of my counsellors, and commanded them to be observed in another manner; for I durst not presume to set down in writing very many of mine own, because I knew not what would please them that are to be after us. What I found in the days of Inæ, my kinsman, or of Offa, King of the Mercians; or of Ethelbert," who was the first of the English nation who received baptism and the dogmas of Rome, "which seemed to me most righteous, I have here collected, and passed over the rest. Then I, Alfred, King of the West Saxons, showed them to my counsellors, and they declared that they approved of them all."

By this singular introduction we obtain a knowledge of the fact that the Saxon monarchs copied from each other's laws. Here are Ethelbert, Inæ, Offa, and Alfred. The connecting link between them all was the ecclesiastical law of each, as received from pagan Greece and Rome. This accounts for the following law made in Northumbria A.D. 950, seventy-three years after that of Alfred. It says:—

" If a priest celebrate mass in an unhallowed house, let him pay twelve ore "—twenty shillings.

This was the first penal law against the priesthood for not performing a religious act. There must have been some special reasons for such a law. They were these: in spite of the interdict of A.D. 740-1, the people continued to celebrate the supper in their own houses. This gave the church an opportunity for complaint, which she instantly accepted, and therefore instantly applied her own remedy.

We now stand upon the threshold of one of the most eventful eras in the English Church. A new class of errors gathered thick round us. The poisonous seeds which Ecbriht and Cuthbert had borrowed from the Nicene Church, and that church from heathen paganism, and had sown more than 200 years before, had grown up, and become matured, so that it is from this seed that the doctrine of transubstantiation was now broached in legal or canonical form; but in such a manner as to cover over the real character of the law itself, and thus reconcile it to the erroneous dogmas of the age.

The first actor in the scene about to be opened before us was Elfric, or Alfric, Archbishop of York, A.D. 957. "He was a very wise man, so that there was no sager man in England" (says Bede, the Anglo-Saxon Chronicler). He is said to have been a prodigy of his age, and was received as an authority by the bishops of both provinces. His canons may, therefore, be said to be national. They appear to have been so designed. These records supply data, which remarkably illustrate the fact that, up to this period, the ecclesiastical path-way of the pope had not been a very easy one. And what did he do? Fall back upon the authority of Scripture, as the only standard of truth? No such thing. He says:—

" There have been four synods in behalf of the true faith in opposition to the heretics. The first was that of Nice, of 318 bishops of all nations. The second was at Constantinople, the third at Ephesus, and the fourth at Chalcedon. All of these were unanimous as to what was decreed at Nice; and they repaired all the breaches that had been made therein. And these four synods are to be regarded as the four books of Christ in his church."

ᵗ With him the eucharist formed the chief burden of his ecclesiastical legislation. Here are some of his laws:—

(1.) " God's house is hallowed to this purpose, that the body of God may be there eaten with faith.

(3.) " The sacrament is Christ's body, that body of which he spoke when he blessed bread and wine for the sacrament one night before his passion, and said of the blessed bread, ' This is my body :' and again of the wine blessed: ' This is my blood, that is shed for many for the remission of sins.'

(4.) " Now know that the Lord, who was able to change the bread into his body before his passion, and the wine into his blood, in a spiritual manner; He himself daily blesseth bread and wine by the hands of his priests into his body and blood.

(5.) " Let the priest always mingle water with the wine. For the wine betokeneth our redemption through Christ's blood; and the water betokeneth the people for whom he suffered.

(8.) " That mass be not celebrated in any house but what is hallowed, except in case of necessity, or if the man be sick."

Such were Elfric's laws. They demand analysis. The first may be said to be an expansion of previously announced notions as to the eucharist being a "sacrifice" in itself, or an "atoning celebration," as Cuthbert had described it. Now, it is "God's body eaten, and eaten in faith." The third utters a positive error, viz., that Christ himself, in speaking certain words, produced a change in the elements of bread and wine. He construes them to mean an act of transformation into his own body. In other words, that the bread and the wine were by Christ's words rendered receptive, and received an element that did not belong to them—Christ's body. This absurdity lies at the foundation of transubstantiation. The fourth is the completed form of the preceding error. Christ "changed the bread into his body, and the wine into his blood ; and that by simply uttering the words, ' This is my body—this is my blood.'" The same words were to be pronounced by the priest, and the same results would follow. Such was the law of Elfric, when he assumed the position of becoming an exponent of the acts of Christ.

The doctrine now urged was the result of previously taught errors. Cuthbert, for instance, had, in the year 747, taught the doctrine, that the mass was a "propitiation—an atonement—for the sins of the living and the dead." It is now "the body of Christ," and it has become that by consecration.

The change thus effected is declared to be so perfect and complete, that, by connection and concomitance, the soul and divinity of Christ co-exist with his flesh and blood under the species of bread and wine; and thus the elements, and every particle thereof, contain Christ whole and entire — divinity, humanity, soul, body, and blood, with all their component parts. According to this doctrine, nothing of the bread and wine remains except the accidents. The whole God and man Christ Jesus is contained in the bread and wine, and in every particle of the bread, and in every drop of the wine. This is an enlargement upon the doctrine of the Nicene Church, as this dogma nowhere occurs in the writings of either the Greek or Latin fathers. The first trace of it is to be found in the eighth century, when the Council of Constantinople, in A.D. 754, having, in opposition to the worship of images, used these words:—— "Our Lord having left no other image of himself but the sacrament, in which the substance of the bread and the wine is the image of his body, we ought not to make any other image of our Lord." The second Council of Nice, in A.D. 787, being resolved to improve upon this doctrine, declared that, "the sacrament after consecration is not the image and antitype of Christ's body and blood, but is, properly, his body and blood." Taking the hint from this last-cited decree, Paschasius Radbert, a Benedictine monk, in the early part of the ninth century, began to advocate the doctrine of a real change in the elements. In A.D. 831, he published a treatise on the subject, which brought into the field of controversy various able writers, who keenly opposed the introduction of this novel doctrine.

"A long period elapsed before the dogma of transubstantiation met with anything approaching to general acceptance. It had been, from the time of Paschasius, the subject of angry contention, and one of its bitterest opponents had been the able scholastic writer, Duns Scotus. For the ninth century, Berengarius and his numerous followers maintained the opinions of Scotus, and opposed those of Paschasius. It was not, indeed, till the fourth Council of Lateran, in A.D. 1215, that transubstantiation was decreed to be a doctrine of the Church, and from that time the name as well as the dogma came to be in current use. The words of the Lateran Decree are as follows :—— 'The body and blood of Christ are contained really in the sacrament of the altar, under the species of bread and wine ; the bread being transubstantiated into the body of Jesus Christ, and the wine into his blood, by the power of God!' This canon, passed in the pontificate of Innocent III., placed transubstantiation among the settled doctrines of the Church of Rome, and accordingly the Council of Trent, in 1551, pronounced an anathema upon all who disbelieved it." (See " Faiths of the World," by the Rev. James Gardner, M.D., A.M., vol. ii., p. 905. Fullarton's Ed.)

Out of this enlarged error sprang all the future notions of transubstantiation; and which, as they unfold themselves in future ages, become a constant source of theological absurdity, and of civil thraldom.

He who was the "Light of the world" had now, for nearly a thousand years, resumed his seat at the right hand of his Father in heaven, when his professed church were congregated together by the peremptory edict of King Ethelred, the last of the Anglo-Saxon monarchs. There sat "Alfeah and Hulfstan, the arch-prelates of Canterbury and York, and a venerable multitude of the great men of England, who conferred together for the recovery of the exercise of the Catholic religion." Their record thus proceeds:—

"These are the ordinances which the English counsellors choose and enact, and strictly charge to be observed, A.D. 1009. And this, in the first place, is the prime decree of the bishops; that we all uniformly maintain one Christianity. And it is our ordinance that right laws be advanced, both in relation to God and the world.

1. "Let every Christian man prepare himself to go to the sacrament thrice a year at least.

2. "He who is in contempt of the right law, either of God or man, let him make satisfaction by mulct or fine."

This enactment is founded upon a principle which in that age was a greatly favoured one. It was "contempt of the right law of God," in which "right law" was included going to the sacrament "thrice a year at least." This neglect was deemed a direct resistance to the law of God, therefore the delinquent must make a money satisfaction. Here the wise counsellors committed an outrage against Christ. He had never said one word which, by any construction, could be made even to imply that the man who did not receive the eucharist thrice a year was to be fined and treated as an evil-doer against civil authority. The singular feature in this enactment is, that while it is copied from Roman law, it is a transcript, not of Roman law, as modified by Christian emperors, but of Roman law as it had existed under pagan emperors.

We will pass over the next fifty years, in which there were no laws of any importance passed concerning the eucharist, and turn our attention to William the Conqueror. "In the fourth year of his reign, by the advice of his barons, he caused the English noblemen, that were men of learning and knowledge in their own law, to be summoned together throughout all the provinces of England, that he might hear their laws, rights, and customs ; which they willingly imparted. Therefore, beginning with the laws of the church, because that by her the king and kingdom stand upon a solid foundation, they declare her laws, liberties, and protection, saying :—Let the protection of God and the holy church be the same with respect to the eucharist as it had been in former years, with this important addition— if any man out of arrogance will not be brought to satisfaction in the bishop's court, let the bishop notify him to the king, and let the king constrain the malefactor to make satisfaction where the forfeiture is due ; that is, first to the bishop, then to himself, so there shall be two swords, and one sword shall help the other." In this last sententious declaration, lies embedded the whole system of religious force which was exercised in the church for 800 years.

Passing over many laws and canons of minor importance in connexion with William Lanfranc, Anselm, and Innocent II., concerning the eucharist, altars, sacrifices, bells, priests, and burials in churchyards, as connected with the eucharist, in A.D. 1070, 1071, 1102, 1108, 1127, and 1138, these laws completing what Elfric commenced in A.D. 957, and the canon of A.D. 1009 had encouraged ; we will now turn our attention to Hubert Walter, whom we find on the episcopal throne, A.D. 1195, in the reign of Richard I., who held ecclesiastical courts in which he ordered the following decrees to be kept :—

" Whereas the salutary Host hath a pre-eminence among the other sacraments of the Church, the devotion of the priest ought to be more particularly employed upon it ; that so it may be consecrated with humility, received with awe, and administered with reverence. And let the minister of the altar be sure that bread and wine, and water be furnished for the 'sacrifice,' and let it not be celebrated without a lettered minister, and let care be taken that the 'Host' be reserved in a clean and decent pyx, and let it be renewed every Lord's-day.

"As often as the communion is to be given to the infirm, let the priest in person carry the Host in a clerical habit, suitable to so great a sacrament, with a light going before him and it.

"We forbid the priest to make a bargain for celebrating mass at a certain price; but that he take that only which is offered at the mass.

"Let the sacrament of the eucharist be consecrated in a silver chalice, where there is sufficient for it."

It is scarcely possible to estimate the baneful effect which thus giving a pre-eminence to the eucharist, and a lettered priest, has had upon the minds of men in all ages. It may be said to be the cardinal error of Christendom; for it cuts up every principle of piety. Unhappily the error still prevails among Protestants, who never suspect from whence they borrowed the idea—"pagan Greece and Rome." To sit down or kneel at the communion-table is regarded by too many as the crowning point of a religious profession. And the priests love to have it so; for if this crowning point is destroyed, the whole fabric falls.

We must pass over the canons of the Council of Westminster, of Edmund of Abingdon, also of Otho and Othobon, a period of about 60 years, which period is employed almost exclusively about vestments, washings of priests' fingers, communicants being drunk, penances, letting the altar and the eucharist to farm, and selling the eucharist at a certain price, which caused Othobon to say,—"It is a great indignity to spiritual things to traffic for them with money."

We have now to introduce Friar John Peckham, who tells us that "the chief pontiff had enjoined him, with the lively oracles of his own voice, to obviate certain abuses:" from him, therefore, we may reasonably expect some rare things upon the eucharist. He says, A.D. 1279:—

"We charge that, for the future, the sacrament of the eucharist be kept in a tabernacle to be made in every church, with a decent enclo-

sure, according to the greatness of the cure [*i.e.* charge]. . . . .
And we charge that the venerable sacrament be renewed every Lord's-
day, and that the priests who are negligent in keeping the eucharist
be punished according to the rule of the Lateran Council of A.D. 1216
(c. 20). We decree also that this sacrament be carried with due
reverence to the sick, the priest having on his surplice and stole, with
a light in a lanthorn before him, and a bell to excite the people to
reverence, who are to be discreetly informed by the priest that they
prostrate themselves, or at least make humble adoration, wherever the
King of glory is carried under the cover of bread. And let archdeacons
be very solicitous on this point, that they may obtain remission of
their sins; and let them with the vigour of discipline chastise those
whom they find negligent in this respect."

Three years more, and Friar John re-appears, to declare
that, "the Most High had created a medicine for the body of
men in the seven sacraments of the church. Here, then,"
he adds, "we begin our correction of abuses, and especially in
the sacrament of the Lord's body, which is a sacrament, and the
sacrifice of a sacrament, sanctifying those who eat it; and a
sacrifice, which by its oblation is profitable for all in whose
behalf it is made, as well the living as the dead." The whole of
the eucharistic mystery is conveyed and comprehended in the
various words which bespeak the latent mischief. At first it was
a designation, "the venerable solemnity," then "the sacrifice,"
then "the viaticum," then "the mystery," after that "the
atoning celebration," then "the propitiation for the souls of the
dead," after that "the sacrament," "the sacrament of the
eucharist," "the sacrifice of a sacrament;" until we arrive, at
last, at the whole, true, and living Christ, under the species of
bread and wine. So rapidly did not pagans advance in religious
absurdity.

Yet we must not stop here; we must proceed to the commencement of the fourteenth century, which was not less
superstitious upon this matter than any preceding period. At a
council held at Oxford, A.D. 1322, Archbishop Reynolds, after
repeating a portion of Friar John Peckham's law, commands

that "rectors and priests be diligent in what concerns the honour of the altar, especially when the holy body is reserved, and mass is celebrated, out of regard to the presence of our Saviour and of the whole court of heaven, which is undoubtedly present at the sacrament of the altar, while it is consecrating, and after it is consecrated; and let the words of the canon be fully and exactly pronounced, and with the greatest devotion of mind, with especial regard to those words which concern the holy sacrament of the eucharist."

Such was the learned nonsense of the expositors of canonical folly. These may be said to form some of the most remarkable of the laws of the Church of Rome. They demand, therefore, special attention. Had the credit of the Christian religion depended upon these men and their laws, the whole system of Christianity would have exploded. But no! there were "a few names who had not defiled their garments." And although on the side of the ecclesiastical rulers there was the power of the spoiler, there were still left in the kingdom of Christ, as there ever had been, many bold and heaven-born renovators. By Friar John Peckham they had been denounced as "innovators, tramplers upon apostolical sanctions, exhalations from the infernal pit;" and by Winchelsey, Archbishop of Canterbury, as "perverse men." But their rage proved harmless against the Nonconformists. Instead of crushing them, they appear to have gathered strength; for in A.D. 1363—that is, 82 years after this violent tirade against them—they were, by the Constitutions of Archbishop Thorsby, to be excommunicated "who adhered to the heretics, to the subversion of the faith, and in contempt of the church and its sacraments." They were despised; contemptuous expressions were used against them, and every parish church was made to ring with their names publicly announced in a sentence of excommunication; and while it was being read, the bells tolled, and as the priest drew near to the end of the sentence, he seized the lighted candle at the altar, and said, "Just as this candle is deprived of its present light, so let them be deprived of their souls in hell;" and all the people were

M

commanded to say, "So be it, be it so." Nor was this all. Civil punishment followed. They were imprisoned, excluded from every civil privilege, and lost all legal status.

Fifteen years after this, another denunciation was fulminated against them. A new canon was passed A.D. 1378, which said—" Whosoever does not receive the sacrament of the eucharist at Easter, let him be forbidden entrance into the church while he lives, and be deprived of Christian burial when dead." Was this law a dead letter? No; it was a living power. There we have pagan Greece, pagan Rome, and papal Rome, all standing side by side to crush the religion of Jesus.

But did not the inhabitants of the isle of Britain, more than six hundred years ago, most solemnly swear that they would obey the pontiff? Thus the Anglo-Saxons brought their necks under the papal yoke. That oath they not only renewed, but enlarged, when, within a little more than three hundred years, they said, "There shall be two swords, and one shall help the other." "Now, O king!" said the priests, "you know that these engagements were sincerely made, and ought to be faithfully performed. Canon law cannot put down the rapidly rising opposition to the pontiff. Come at once and help us with your sword, as we have helped you with our own." The king heard, and obeyed the mandate, A.D. 1383. The 5th Richard II., cap. 5, therefore says :—

" Forasmuch as it is openly known that there be divers evil persons within this realm, . . . . who, by their subtle and ingenious words, do maintain the people in their errors : it is ordained in this present Parliament, that the king's commission be directed to the sheriffs, . . . . to arrest all such persons, preachers, their fauters, maintainers, and abettors, and to hold them in arrest and strong prisons till they shall justify themselves according to the law of Holy Church."

There we perceive that the last Anglo-Saxon king signalized his reign and his character, by becoming a party to the law which threatened the mass of the people who neglected to appear thrice in the year at the eucharist, with the loss of honour, estate, and the infliction of public indignation ; and the last of the restored Saxon monarchs distinguished himself by approving a statute which placed liberty of speech and the right of conscience at the mercy of the prelates, who now crowd round the throne of a Plantagenet sovereign, when priestcraft, kingcraft, and persecution, are about to develop themselves in an augmented and more revolting form, and to take a more deadly and wider range of operations.

To Henry IV. is attached the distinction of being the first English sovereign who burnt heretics. Of these he found hosts. They were designated Lollards ; respecting whom the king sent a message to the convocation, saying that he was determined to extirpate all heresy. " Crush them," exclaimed the monarch ; " they are rebels against my throne." "Crush them," responded the Church ; " they are enemies of the Pope." It was now resolved to extinguish them altogether and for ever.

This is the law, 2nd Henry IV., c. 15, A. D. 1400 :—

(1.) " Whereas, it is shown to our sovereign lord the king, on behalf of the prelates and clergy of this realm, that, although the catholic faith, built upon Christ and his apostles, and the Holy Church, hath been among all the realms of the world most devoutly observed, and the Church of England by its noble progenitors and ancestors, laudably endowed ; yet, nevertheless, divers false and perverse people of a certain new sect of the said faith,—of the sacraments of the Church, and authority of the same, damnably thinking (1) Against the law of God and the Church usurping the office of preaching . . . do preach and teach new doctrines, contrary to the same faith and blessed determination of Holy Church, &c., &c., &c.

(3.) " Upon which novelties above referred to, (as well as some omitted,) the prelates and clergy have sought that this wicked sect, preaching doctrines and opinions (contrary to those of the Church) should henceforth cease and be utterly destroyed.

(5.) " And if any persons be before the diocesan convicted according to the canonical decrees, the sheriff of the county, mayor of a city, or town, or borough, after such sentence promulged, shall them receive, and them before the people, in high place, put to be burnt, that such punishment may strike fear to the minds of others."

The Church authorities having obtained this aid from the State, could more safely than ever fall back upon their own power. They again issued canon law. The Constitutions of Thomas Arundel, Archbishop of Canterbury, legate of the Roman See, are replete with indignation against the Lollards. He begins thus:—

" To all . . . our fellow bishops . . . and laics whatsoever: . . . He does an injury to the most reverend synod who examines its determinations: . . . as the authority of civil law (*i. e.* the Roman law, which Austin had induced Ethelbert to adopt) teaches us that much more grievously are they to be punished, and cut off as putrid members from the church militant, who, leaning to their own wisdom, violate, oppose, and despise, by various doctrines, words, and deeds, the laws and canons made by the key-keeper of eternal life and death."

He then proceeds to denounce the new sect of preachers, and says :—

" Because that part which does not agree with its whole is rotten : We decree and ordain that no preacher of the word of God, or other person, do teach, preach, or observe anything in relation to the sacrament of the altar, anything but what hath been determined by Holy Mother Church ; nor call in question anything that hath been decided by her ; nor let him knowingly speak scandalously, either publicly or in private, concerning these things ; nor let him preach up, teach, or observe any sect, or sort of heresy, contrary to the sound doctrine of the Church."

Heretics and relapsed converts are to suffer the loss of "goods," which shall be deemed "confiscated and seized by those to whom they shall belong." He then denounces the works of John Wickliffe, whose books were not to be " read or taught in any school, hall, inn, or other places in the University of Oxford or Cambridge," nor any " translation of any text of Scripture into the English tongue, or any other by way of book or treatise."

He then goes on :—" Let no one presume to dispute of things determined on by the Church; especially concerning the adoration of the glorious cross, the veneration of images of saints, or pilgrimages to their places and relics ; but let all henceforth preach up the veneration of the cross, and of the image of the crucifix, with processions, genuflexions, bowings, incensings, oblations, pilgrimages, illuminations, and all other modes and forms whatsoever used in the times of us and our predecessors." Here, latent fears called up vindictive rage ; for, says the Archbishop, " new and unusual emergencies require new and mature applications, and the greater the danger, the more caution and opposition is necessary."

Now we may inquire, " Whence this great danger ? " It sprang from the men whom the common people, by way of derision, called Lollards, but whom Arundel more expressly honoured, by saying, " they were stirred up by the old sophist, to erect for himself a church of malignants," they having dared "to dispute the determinations of Holy Church," and to declare that the " lying miracles attributed to the sacramental bread lead almost all men to idolatry." This was the front of their offence. And who that is acquainted with ecclesiastical history, has not read the intensity, extent, and duration of their sufferings, and those of the main body whom they had led on to the never-fading glory, of having sought to emancipate the Church of Christ from the revolting contaminations of the Church of Rome ? They had to struggle often and severely, and they succeeded to some extent as often as they struggled. But Rome could and did easily trample down every sacred and indefeasible immunity while monarchs were serfs ; legislators transmuted into instruments of cruelty ; law prostrated at the shrine of ecclesiastics ; and religion itself scattered to the four winds of heaven.

Ecclesiastics, however, had not completed their work. On they went. And in the second year of the reign of Henry V., they prevailed upon him to exact from all his officers, from the Lord Chancellor down to the lowest officers of the state, having governance of the people, at the time of their appointment, an oath that they would assist "the ordinaries in extirpating heresies," who were to suffer, not only the loss of "goods and lands, but life also."

Surely this was enough ! No ! This apparatus proved incomplete. Again the Church applied itself to supply the deficiency.

This was under the auspices of Archbishop Crichley, A.D. 1416, who, in his Constitutions, says :—

" Whereas, the taking of heretics . . . ought to be our principal care . . . we ordain that every one of our suffragans, and the archdeacons, do by themselves or commissioners, diligently make inquiry, twice at least in every year, for persons suspected of heresy, and cause three or four men of good report in every deanery or parish in which heretics are said to dwell, to swear on God's Holy Gospel, that if they know of any heretics who keep private conventicles, or differ in their life and manners from the faithful, or who maintain heresies, or who have suspected books . . . or entertain persons suspected of heresies, or that favour such . . . who resort to such places ; they will inform against . . . those persons to our suffragans, archdeacons, or commissioners. And if any person be committed before them, whom they do not deliver to the secular court (to be burnt), let them in good earnest commit them to perpetual or temporary imprisonment, at least till the next convocation."

And this for neglecting to partake of the eucharist at least once in the year! So much for ecclesiastical and statute law.

The Real Presence was the watchword of these crusaders against the Lollards. The Lollards denied that a piece of bread contained " the real living and true Christ." This was a sufficient offence, the punishment for which was the consuming their bodies in the fire. Thus were executed two laws at the same time, the law of burning for heresy, and the law of non-burial for the neglect of going to confession and the mass.

We will now turn our attention to the house of the Tudors, where we find the victims to papal cruelty innumerable. The offences with which they were charged became at length so varied and so complex, that it was almost impossible to specify the distinct crime for which they suffered burning. To put an end to this difficulty, it was proposed to consolidate the penal laws upon religion ; but as this might occupy more time than was desirable, to allow men to become emboldened in their opposition to Rome, Henry VIII. exclaimed, "Leave that to me ;" and he and his spiritual lords selected six cardinal points, respecting each of which an appropriate penalty was to be attached. These six points were, therefore, to be embodied in a statute, designated the "Six Article Act." The eucharist, of course, formed an important point. Here is the law, 31 Henry VIII., cap. 14, sec. 8 & 9 :—

"If any person do teach, preach, dispute, or hold opinion, that in the blessed sacrament of the altar, in the form of bread and wine, after the consecration thereof, there is not present really the natural body and blood of our Saviour Jesus Christ, conceived of the Virgin Mary ; or that after the consecration there remaineth any substance of bread and wine ; or, any but the substance of Christ, God and man, or that in the flesh under the form of bread is not the very body of Christ, or that with the blood under the form of wine is not the very flesh of Christ, as well apart as though they were both together ; or affirm the said sacrament to be any other substance than is aforesaid ; or depraveth the said blessed sacrament ; he shall be judged an heretic, and suffer death by burning, and shall forfeit to the king all his lands, tenements, goods, and chattels, as in high treason."

The enormity of this climax of wickedness was equalled only by the dexterity of the theological skill displayed in framing the enactment. For the law, as passed by the Senate, was the law supplied by the Convocation. The preamble of this Act, entitled, "An Act for Abolishing Diversity of Opinion," states, that—

"Forasmuch as in the Synod and Convocation there were certain articles set forth, which the king, of his most excellent goodness, commanded should be deliberately and advisedly, by his said archbishops, bishops, and other learned men of the clergy, debated, whereupon, after great and long, deliberate, and advised disputation and consultation had, concerning the said articles, as well by the consent of the lords spiritual and other learned men in their convocation, it is with the consent of the Commons assembled," &c., &c.

One important principle is illustrated by this offensive law. It is this. The principle of a Christian theocracy received, in this Act, a full and complete form of manifestation. The "high treason" for which heretics were burnt, because they denied the real presence, was "treason" against the Church, rather than the Crown ; the mode of putting the law in execution proves this. To behead the traitor was the secular form of maintaining the majesty of secular law.; to burn the traitor was the mode of vindicating the supremacy of the Church. The treason is against us, said the ecclesiastics ; for wherever the priest goes with the eucharist, he carries along with him "the King of glory, under the cover of bread." (See canon of A.D. 1279.) To deny this, is direct rebellion against Him whose throne we are appointed to guard, and whose sceptre we are delegated to sway. So we see that, under our Christian theocracy, to deny the real presence of Christ in the eucharist is an overt act of rebellion against "the laws of the vicegerent of God." (See canon A.D. 1408.)

Henry, and his convocation of priests, believed all this. They had before expressly said by law (25 Henry VIII., cap. 21, sect. 19), "that they did not intend to decline in anything concerning the articles of the Catholic faith of Christendom."

We will now turn our attention to Edward VI., whom some authors extol to the skies. He occupied himself with the eucharistic question immediately upon coming to the throne, and complained that the said sacrament had been of late marvellously abused by the Lollards, who had condemned it in their hearts, and depraved and despised the most holy and blessed sacrament. There cannot be a greater proof than this, that he and his convocation of bishops had faith in the great and high mysteries thereof. Yes! He, as a deed of piety, gave the cup to the laity, from whom it had been withheld for centuries. This is the only act of importance in his reign.

And the matured superstition of his sister Mary induced her to watch, with an increasing interest, the trembling grasp with which her brother held his sceptre ; and she had become more and more intent upon undoing all that he had undertaken, the moment his throne should become vacant. The first record of her government, A.D. 1553, says :—

"Whereas much false and erroneous doctrine hath been taught, by reason whereof the spiritualty and temporalty have swerved from obedience to the See Apostolic, and declined from the unity of the Church, and so have continued until such time as your majesty was raised up by God; and then by his divine and gracious providence, . . . . . we, as repentant children, are received into the bosom and unity of the Church; and thus this noble realm is delivered from excommunication and all other censures ecclesiastical, which have hung over our heads for our defaults since the time of the schism—(the twentieth year of Henry VIII.,) and which was upon condition to repeal and abrogate such acts as had been made against the supremacy of the See Apostolic." (See 1 and 2 Mary, cap. 8.)

If Rome felt proud of her "repentant children," England had reason to feel ashamed of her sovereign. She signalized the commencement of her reign by the second Act which she passed, A.D. 1553, and which enacted that "all such divine service and administration of sacraments as were most commonly used in England in the last year of Henry VIII., shall be used throughout the realm, after the 20th of December 1553, and no other kind of service or administration of sacraments." (1 Mary, cap. 2.) By this one law, Mary secured her great object, which was the restoration of the mass and transubstantiation; and by virtue of this law, and the old laws of Henry VIII., and his predecessor Henry IV., the fires of persecution were again lighted up, and hosts of victims were dragged to the stake. Yet this is called Christianity! Unworthy name! Placed by the side of heathen persecution, for this is no better, pagan idolatry stands out as a benignant religion. But Mary's reign is not for long; Elizabeth is on the throne.

Steps were now taken respecting the rites and ceremonies of the Church. The Puritans sought, by petition and remonstrance, to get the popish customs removed. A paper was laid before the Convocation, signed by thirty-three of the most eminent men among them, desiring a reformation in the Church, specifying many customs which they wished to be laid aside. This petition being rejected, another somewhat modified in its demands was presented, which also was unsuccessful. Elizabeth was certainly a Protestant in a certain sense, inasmuch as she resolutely opposed the authority of the Pope in the ecclesiastical affairs of her kingdom, and instituted those changes which made it at once a separate communion from that of Rome, but retaining all its antichristian dogmas; and an ecclesiastical establishment, quite as powerful, important, intolerant, and antichristian in deeds, was during this reign set up. The sovereign, Elizabeth, was legally qualified to correct all abuses of doctrine, and to remove all manner of errors, heresies, &c.; to oppress the consciences of the people, and to grind them into whatever form of worship, and administration of sacraments, caprice or bigotry might establish; and to force subjects to the observance of any rites, ceremonies, and absurdities which superstition or tyranny might suggest; and to punish all opposition to the same, by the infliction of any penalties or tortures which cruelty or arbitrary will might design. From this time, the ecclesiastical system of this country—with the Sovereign at its head, and its more than half-popish constitution—is uniformly called the Church of England. Church-of-Englandism, like Popery, from which it had its origin, is an ecclesiastical manufactory, which professes to supply all the machinery necessary for religious worship, and all the means of man's salvation, and to frame all the articles of religious belief which the human mind need adopt. Antichristian and intolerant in its character, Church-of-Englandism admits of no liberty of conscience, of no religious teaching, and of no religious obligations to God, beyond the limits of its own establishment.

But notwithstanding the power and authority with which the Church of England was invested, and which it exercised, and the severe threats which were held out against all those who should presume to differ from her communion, the Puritans still continued to protest against her popish ceremonies, and her antichristian requirements; and thus began those struggles, persecutions, and miseries, which so early demonstrated the character and evil tendency of Church-of-Englandism, which continued in their vigour for two hundred years, while the long train of events which followed proves the strength of the principles which animated the upholders and defenders of religious liberty.

The principal parts of the distinct ecclesiastical government established in the reign of Elizabeth, are found in 1 Eliz., cap. 1, sect. 36. This clause defined the standard by which heresy was then determined, and a strange medley it is. All the old decisions of the constitutions, canon, and statute law are recognized, as well as the canonical Scriptures. Heresy was to be "only such as heretofore had been determined to be heresy by the authority of canonical Scripture, or by the four first general councils, or any of them; or by any other general council wherein the same was declared heresy by the express and plain words of the said canonical Scriptures; or such as shall hereafter be ordered or determined to be heresy by the high court of Parliament, with the consent of the clergy in convocation."

Not a word is here uttered which can convey the remotest idea that she wished to repeal the Constitutions of Arundel, or Henry's law of the Six Articles. More than this; one rule of construction in the law courts will here apply—which is, that when one law quotes the words of a preceding law, it affirms only so much of that law as is quoted; and all the words that are not quoted it sets aside. And still more; when any renunciatory words are dropped, the thing which is not renounced is held *pro tanto* to be revived. Hence the opinions of Elfric, Ethelred, Alfeah, Hulfstan, Hubert Walter, Lanfranc, Anselm, Innocent III., Friar John Peckham, Archbishop Reynolds, Bishop Thorsby, Arundel Archbishop of Canterbury, and King Henry VIII., their laws and constitutions, are all in full force.

Take, then, the Elizabethan articles of faith. They expressed the opinions of her own times. They did more. They linked in not only with the past, but also with the future. The theory, "that the body of Christ is received in the supper," was a very ancient dogma at the time she announced it. Neither had it become so worn out by age as to sink into decrepitude and dotage. Though venerable in years, it was vigorous in power: so much so that it allowed itself to re-appear, bedecked with a new sanction and a new power. Nor must we stop here ; for Elizabeth not only went back to an Anglo-Saxon bishop for her model of theology, but to an Anglo-Saxon principle of legislation also, for her method of enforcing it. Her statute law about the "communion" is this :—

"If any person shall refuse to receive the holy communion, as it is now received in the Church of England, or hold any errors, in matters of religion or doctrines, not received and allowed in the said Church of England, he shall be liable to be cited into any consistory court, the bishop of which may feel it a point of conscience to cite him."

Such are the provisions of the unrepealed statute (5 Eliz., cap. 23, sect. 13), as it applies to the Episcopalians of the present day.

The throne is again unoccupied, and we will now examine the eucharistic laws passed by the Stuart dynasty. A new code of canon law was ratified by James I. He says, in confirmation of them, that they were adopted in convocation "for the good and quiet of the Church, and the better government thereof." Hence the addition of canonical denunciations against "impugners of the public worship," "impugners of the articles," "impugners of the rites and ceremonies," "impugners of the government," "impugners of the consecration of archbishops and bishops of the Church of England" (see canons 4, 5, 6, 7, and 8). And hence, too, the excommunications denounced against "authors of schisms," "maintainers of schismatics," "maintainers of conventicles," "and maintainers of constitutions made in conventicles" (see canons 9, 10, 11, and 12). Nine distinct classes of offenders appear from these canons to have been particularised as objects of censure—an evident proof that there was a very strong opposition to the dogmas of the Church, especially the fatal error that "the body and blood of Christ are verily and indeed taken in the Lord's Supper" (see Catechism).

We now pass over the Commonwealth, and turn our attention to the ecclesiastical laws passed during the reign of Charles II. ; as though no interruption in the royal succession had occurred. The preservation of the public peace, both in

Church and State, became the rallying point of the friends of the Restoration; not as a matter of choice, but from necessity, as the enlightened policy of Cromwell's reign had shown to the kingdom the necessity of a reformation both in Church and State. Therefore, as a matter of State policy, "those persons who were well affected to his Majesty and the State Church," were to be kept in all the municipal corporations of the kingdom; and all others who were either suspected, or whose religious habits might induce a suspicion against them, were to be kept out; especially those who had been supporters of the Commonwealth, and of the doctrine of transubstantiation in the reign of Mary. It was therefore enacted (13 Charles II., statute 2, chapter 1, A.D. 1661), as a matter of policy, that—

"No person or persons shall ever hereafter be placed, elected, or chosen in or to any office of mayor, alderman, recorder, bailiff, town-clerk, common council-man, or any other place of magistracy or trust, or employment relating to the government of cities, corporations, boroughs, cinque ports, or other port towns, that shall not, within one year next, before such election or choice, have taken the sacrament of the Lord's Supper, according to the rites of the Church of England."

All this spoliation of freedom was followed by other acts of excision, for the purpose of "quieting the minds of his Majesty's good subjects," when Charles II. (A.D. 1673) declared that—

"As well peers as commoners, that bear office, civil or military, shall receive the sacrament of the Lord's Supper, according to the usages of the Church of England, in some parish church, immediately after divine service and sermon.

"And shall likewise make and subscribe this declaration:—'I do declare, that I do believe (the new doctrine) that there is not any transubstantiation in the sacrament of the Lord's Supper, or in the elements of the bread and wine, at or after the consecration thereof by any person whatever.'" (25 Charles II., cap. 2.)

Failure attended this effort, as there was great opposition, and the law did not extend itself at full length. An addition was made to it (30 Charles II., cap. 1, stat. 2), which declared that—

" No person that now is, or hereafter shall be, a peer or member of the House of Commons, shall vote or sit, till he shall audibly repeat the declaration—' I do solemnly and sincerely, in the presence of God, declare that I do believe that in the sacrament of the Lord's Supper there is not any transubstantiation of the elements of bread and wine into the body and blood of Christ, at or after the consecration thereof, by any person whatsoever.' "

Each of the three last sacramental tests was based upon the plan of policy and protection, rather than of religious conviction. The policy of the king, and the design of his government, were to meet the reforming spirit of the age, and yet teach a doctrine which pressed hard upon the real presence or transubstantiation —under the appellation of the body and blood of Christ; not accidentally, but intentionally. The nation was, or thought it was, in danger from the religious opinions of certain men in high stations in the kingdom, who believed in transubstantiation, as well as some others who had been supporters of the Commonwealth, and who erred, on the other hand, in denying the bodily presence. These men were by law, in order to weaken their influence, excluded from civil rights and honours. The design of the king and his government was to place those persons who were well affected to both him and his government, and his newly-formed church, and its dogmas, by way of retaliation, in all municipal corporations of the kingdom. This was quite in accordance with the Theodosian, Valentinian, and Justinian codes.

And all others who were either suspected of error, or of a belief in transubstantiation, or the real presence in the eucharist, as maintained by Arundel, Henry, and Mary, &c., were to be kept out as enemies to the government, and despoilers of the newly-formed church. This policy was in accordance with the spirit of the times—retaliation. In imposing these tests, the Legislators laid hold of the highest point of their religious creed; and, brandishing their views of the eucharist in derisive condemnation over the heads of objectors, declared that such religionists should not be men of the State. This was to act on a grand scheme of retaliation. The Roman and English churches had burnt the men who believed not in transubstantiation, or the real presence. The English Parliament now declared, in violation of the 31 Henry VIII., cap. 14, sect. 8 and 9, and 1 Mary, cap. 2, that those who believed that doctrine should be punished, not, indeed, with being hurried to the stake, as in former times; but by being driven off from municipal associations, from the army and navy, from Parliament, and the councils of the Sovereign.

Notwithstanding these prohibitory laws, which were enacted as a matter of State policy, not from choice, but necessity, to meet the reforming spirit of the age, the Common Prayer-Book compiled in this reign sets forth the bodily presence of Christ in the eucharist. The words of consecration are :—

"Most merciful Father, we beseech thee ! and with thy Holy Spirit and word, vouchsafe to bless and sanctify these thy creatures of bread and wine, that they may be unto us the body and blood of thy most dearly beloved Son, Christ Jesus."

Immediately after the prayer of consecration, follows the prayer of oblation, in which is contained these words :—

"We humbly beseech thee, that whosoever shall partake of this holy communion may receive the most precious body and blood of thy Son, Jesus Christ, and be made one body with him, that he may dwell in them, and they in him."

In the office for the administration of the Lord's Supper, the priest says, "I purpose to administer the most comfortable sacrament of the body and blood of Christ, in remembrance of his most meritorious cross and passion; whereby alone we receive remission of sins, and are made partakers of the kingdom of heaven." If further proof is wanted to establish the fact,—in the Church Catechism, taught to all the members of the Church, and contained in the Common Prayer-Book, is also this question and answer :—"What is the inward part, or thing signified, in the Lord's Supper?" "The body and blood of Christ, which are verily and indeed taken by the faithful in the Lord's Supper." This was the creed of the Church A.D. 1604; and 1662, when the

Act of Uniformity was passed by Charles II. and his Parliament, to enforce uniformity therein; and is the creed also of A.D. 1863.

Is it not so? Look at this history. Does it not prove that from A.D. 597, the time when Austin and the forty monks landed in England, to A.D. 1678, the space of 1081 years, the Church has been almost exclusively occupied in contriving and enforcing its sacraments upon all Christians who have stood without its pale; and all that, while not only accumulating errors, alike false in theory and fatal in practice, and by such errors actually setting aside the law of Heaven; but also enforcing upon men the belief that these seven sacraments were either essential to, or necessary appendages to, the salvation of souls? And after having spent all this time in doing homage to its seven sacraments, it was compelled to reduce them to two; and has it not again principally occupied itself nearly two centuries in enforcing these two by proscriptions, denunciations, sinful divisions, and still more sinful hostilities?

Has Christianity, then, been aided by sacramental efficacy? Has it not rather suffered a thousand-fold more by the sacraments being retained, than it would have suffered had they been surrendered? The entire body of sacramentarians, be they who they may, or where they may, are challenged to prove wherein Christianity, taken as a whole, has had the gain. Make them seven sacraments, or reduce them to two; declare these two necessary to salvation; clothe them with all the sacredness invention can suggest; arm them with authority as positive institutions; and what then? Why, as positive institutions, they must have had specific purposes, and could establish the fact of their utility, only as those specific purposes have been answered. Will any sacramentarian dare to affirm that the Lord's Supper has answered the specific purpose which it is declared to do by many; rather, will not the fact previously adduced demonstrate that the specific purpose has been contravened, frustrated, and set at nought; nay, more, so perverted as to bring about the very thing it was said to destroy? The great and eternal principle in the moral government of God—that where any positive institution in his Church causes other results to accrue to himself or to it than he designed, he steps in and places that institution in abeyance. What shall we say, then, of the two sacraments retained in the Church of England, as they strike at the root of everything that is vital in religion, and lead men to trust in a shadow?

Obedience to the authority of Christ is the only security for the preservation of the Christian Church. The obedience must be entire. The law of love to God and man, in its entire manifestation, must be the standard. There must not be any denunciations of "impugners of rites and ceremonies," or of those who do not "partake of the sacraments." Has this been the standard of the Church of Rome, with its seven sacraments? Has it been the standard of the Church of England, with its two? No. Is it not time, then, that we had this heaven-born law of Christ commended to men in the manner it deserves, instead of baptism and the eucharist?

View this law of Christ in connection with the remembrance of his death, and to what does it amount? To this: that the Christian religion is a religion of facts, not of traditional ceremonies; but facts supported by evidence; evidence that so expands the mind as to repel every attempt to cripple its powers, which does not tolerate any such attempt, simply because, if they are once crippled in religion, they become crippled in everything else, and lead back to tradition. Therefore it is that Christ's law of love is as readily understood by a child as it is admired by a philosopher; so understood by the one as to draw out his mental capabilities, and thus qualify him for all the duties of after-life; and so admired by the other as to enkindle, and yet exceed, his researches, clear his perception, direct his decisions, and appropriate his very being to the honour of God and the happiness of mankind.

Faithful men in Jesus, say—Is not the sole authority of Christ of infinitely higher magnitude than the decrees of erring councils or statute laws, whether they be Grecian, Roman, or Anglican

—the opinions of doting fathers—the dogmas of priests, be they sinister or sincere—the selfishness of partisans whose livings are at stake—or the repulsiveness of cold formalists? They will all of them blame any and every effort to bring either them or others to the simplicity that is in Christ Jesus. We have had an undeniable proof of this for 1800 years. What an evidence that they are not in the true church. But by as much as they resist, by so much must we adhere to, the authority of Christ, and reject their dogmas.

# CHAPTER VII.

## THE TRUE LORD'S SUPPER.

As the baptism of Christ is purely spiritual, so is the communion which is truly the Lord's Supper. For, saith the Apostle Paul, "By one Spirit are we all baptized into one body, whether we be Jew or Gentile, whether we be bond or free ; and have been all made to drink into one Spirit." This indicates that the communion of the real Christian, whereby he partakes of Divine strength and consolation, is in the one Spirit with which he is baptized.

The commencement of the new life in the soul is when the Holy Spirit breathes, and the sinful heart is subdued beneath its influence—when the soul has been wounded, and is healed—when the broken heart has been bound up. Reader, cast not aside these momentous truths as unworthy thy attention—cast them not away, for they bring before thee the most momentous question,—Art thou born again of God's Spirit?—a question which in the present day is most needful to ask, because so many guides are leading astray, and denying the baptism and communion of the Holy Ghost, declaring that all Divine Revelation has ceased, except what is virtually conveyed through the dipping in, or sprinkling with, consecrated water,* and through the partaking of consecrated bread and wine.

---

* Water used in the ceremony of baptism, and the bread and wine used in the eucharist in the Church of England as well as the Church of Rome, are previously consecrated by the priests, and this is deemed indispensable. It is then deemed to be endowed with the virtue of the Holy Ghost, and the cleansing virtue of the blood of the Saviour : herein they adopt the opinions of Jerome, Nazianzen, and other fathers, as they are called, who maintained that the recipients of baptism were " washed in the laver of

This doctrine is as absurd as it is untrue, and has been amply refuted in the preceding chapters, where it is shown to be at direct issue with the doctrine of Christ and his apostles. Regeneration by the Holy Ghost is the great work of religion ; yes ! religion itself; there is no religion without it. True Christian religion is regeneration, and regeneration is the expeperimental, operative, revelation · of the Spirit of God in man. And this revelation is a fruit of his Omnipresence. What ! Divine revelation, and the baptism and communion of the Holy Ghost ceased ? Nay, verily ! " God, who at sundry times, and in divers manners, spake in times past unto the fathers by the prophets, hath in these last days spoken unto us by his Son." God, who, in all his former communications, treated man in a way suited to his complex nature, consisting of soul and body, has in his last gospel communication treated him in like manner, addressing spiritual truth to the conceptions and feelings of the soul, and exhibiting that truth in the elements of the visible creation, to the senses of the body. We have seen the application of this as regards baptism ; and we are now to consider it in regard to what is called the Lord's Supper, or Communion, in which we shall find a very close analogy.

During the personal ministry of Jesus on the earth, he expressed many of the sublime truths of his spiritual religion in figurative language. All Scripture, indeed, abounds with figures of speech ; and for the right understanding of Scripture, it is

regeneration," and "dipped in the blood of Christ." (See Bingham's Antiq., 16., 10-4.) Thus we see the origin and ground of the system of consecration, and its alleged effect—regeneration.

That which is called " the consecration of the elements," in the eucharist, is a somewhat similar rite to that of baptism, but applied to bread and wine apparently with greater professed effects in creating the " real body and blood of Christ." (See Wilberforce on the Eucharist, p. 78.) All such consecrations, or creations, suppose a power in the priest to give holiness and moral virtue to physical inanimate objects, even to the creation of Christ himself. Two results of these practices especially contribute to uphold them ; the one that they obtain from the ignorant, credulous multitude a superstitious regard and veneration for the performers ; and the other, the means of filling their pockets with cash.

absolutely indispensable that careful attention be paid to the nature of such language, and the source from whence it is derived. The nature of it is simply this: the expression of an inward and invisible truth by an outward and visible object; the force of which expression is derived from the harmony which, as a matter of fact, is found to exist between outward objects and inward truths, and the consequent suitability of the one to represent the other. For example, we wish to express this precious truth, that the invisible God is aware of our necessities and infirmities, and in his kind, tender care, and watchful love, is constantly supplying all our wants. To say this briefly, comprehensively, and expressly, we say, "God is my shepherd." Here is an outward and visible object, made use of to express our meaning. This is a figure. The office of a shepherd towards his sheep, his knowledge of their habits, and his watchful care over them, going out and coming in, supplying them with pasture convenient for them,—these constitute the suitability which renders the figure expressive. In the letter it is a falsehood; as a figure, it is a life-giving truth.

The sources from whence such figures are derived are various. The most fertile are the natural creation, and the instituted types of the Jewish ceremonial law. When John says, "God is light," he takes a figure from the natural creation. When Paul calls "Christ our passover," he takes a figure from the law of Moses. Concerning the ceremonial law of the Jews, we read that it was arranged for the express purpose of setting forth figuratively the everlasting truth of the gospel, for "See," said God, "that thou make all things after the pattern showed thee in the mount." The great original of that pattern was the everlasting gospel which Jehovah purposed in Jesus to his own glory.

The suitableness, therefore, of the figures derived from the Mosaic types, as baptisms and the passover, to express the spiritual things of Christ, is not accidental, but designed of God. The same is true concerning the objects of external nature. Creation, as well as Judaism, was designed to prefigure and bear witness to the truth which God purposed in his dear Son to his own glory. Hence everything is what it is. Hence the analogy between external nature and revealed religion, which Bishop Butler and others have pointed out with so much sagacity and power, to prove that the author of nature is also the author of Scripture and of all true religion. Hence, also, the interpretation of Scripture, to express the truth of God as it is in Jesus Christ, and in the church of Jesus Christ. The figurative language so used is popular and plain, not scientific ; and therefore the properties of matter and things referred to, are such as are generally and practically known. The new creation of the church of God out of the darkness of sin, the ceremonies of the figurative dispensation, and the Mosaic law, are expressed in language derived from the creation of order, light, and beauty. " For God, who commanded the light to shine out of darkness, hath shined in our hearts, to give the light of the knowledge of the glory of God in the face of Jesus Christ," " who is the way, the truth, and the life."

Words are useful, or not useful. This is a truism. But let us consider *how* words are useful or not useful. They are not useful in themselves as mere words. Words are useful, then, not merely as sounds, but as conveyors of meanings. We have a thought in our minds, or a knowledge in our hearts, which we wish to convey to other minds, so that it may be perceived by the mind and understood by the heart. How shall we do it? We are acquainted with certain sounds which will express our meaning, and we know the fact that others are acquainted with the same sounds ; we speak them, and in an instant we convey into their minds the thought that was in our own. If, however, we use these words, or any of them, in a figurative sense, or in a different sense from that in which the auditors understand them, instead of conveying the thoughts of our minds and their true import into theirs, we convey some other thoughts which might be of a totally different character ; and this has been the case in nearly all the corruptions of doctrine that have crept into the churches in all ages—understanding the Scripture figurative language literally. Thus, in order to be useful and properly understood, words must not only be in the same language which the auditors of them understand, but they must be used in the same sense which these auditors habitually ascribe to them. If the language be known, but the sense in which the speaker uses it be not known, words are deceitful and mischievous, as the whole of ecclesiastical history abundantly proves, and we have abundantly shown in the corruptions of the church ; so that, finally, it is only when the language, and the sense in which the speaker uses it, are known, that words are really useful.

We shall now apply these remarks to one of the most striking and instructive dissertations recorded in the New Testament. Jesus said to his disciples and a surrounding multitude of Jews, "As the living Father hath sent me, and I live by the Father, so he that eateth me shall live by me." Here our attention is turned to the nature of true religion, as enjoyed by living members of Christ's true church. The expression "eating" is the peculiar one in the passage. It was introduced into the conversation by the Jews in their cavils against Jesus. They had followed him because of the miracle of the loaves. Here they insinuated, that as he had grounded his claims to be received as the Messiah upon miracles, they ought to be of a more extensive kind. His having fed about five thousand men with a few loaves, was nothing when compared with what Moses did, who, they said, fed the whole congregation of Israel without any loaves, with manna brought down from heaven. Jesus, as his manner was, availed himself of the incident before him to proclaim essential eternal truth. He takes, as it were, his text from their allusion to the manna in the wilderness, and preaches the gospel in language borrowed from the wants and supplies of the body. Then said Jesus unto them, " Verily, verily, I say unto you, Moses gave you not that true bread from heaven, but my Father giveth you the true bread from heaven. For the bread of God is he which cometh down from heaven, and giveth life unto the world." Not perceiving the spiritual turn he was giving the subject, nor understanding its spirituality, they asked him for a continual supply. "Then said they unto him, Lord, evermore give us this bread." He answered them more plainly, "I am the bread of life, he that cometh to me shall never hunger, and he that believeth on me shall never thirst." Here we learn to identify three modes of expression—eating him, coming to him, and believing on him. That which naturally puts an end to hunger is eating; but Jesus says, "He that cometh to me shall never hunger;" therefore, coming and eating mean the same thing. That which naturally puts an end to thirst is drinking; but Jesus says, "He that believeth on me shall never thirst." Therefore, believing and drinking mean the same thing. Whichever of these expressions is afterwards used throughout the discourse, still one and the same thing is intended—inward, living, spiritual, satisfying, strengthening, communion with him. See what light this throws upon the whole train of what follows,— Ye have seen me and believe not—ye do not come unto me— ye do not eat me. All that the Father giveth me come unto me; shall believe in me; shall eat me. And he that cometh, believeth, eateth, I will in no wise cast out.

This explains the remarkable parallel in the words already quoted :—"As the living Father hath sent me, and I live by the Father," in a spiritual, satisfying, strengthening communion, finding it my meat and my drink to do the will of my Father, so he that eateth me as the bread, cometh to me as the way, believeth on me as the truth, even he shall live by me. What, then, is the eating of Christ, and living by Christ, which is the privilege of every believer? We answer by asking another question. What was the living by the Father which was the happy privilege of Jesus? Was it the actual literal eating of his flesh by the mouth of the body? The supposition is absurd : the Father never took flesh, and the Son could not live upon the Father literally. It is false, therefore, to suppose that the Christian so lives upon the Son, though the Roman Catholic Church, and the Episcopal English Church, as well as some others, declare it to be so.

"It is the Spirit that quickeneth." "If any man have not the Spirit of Christ, he is none of his." "But he that is joined to the Lord," by hunger, by thirst, or by faith, "is one spirit with him." This is the bread which cometh down from heaven—the way opened into heaven—the faith revealed from heaven—he that eateth of this bread—he that cometh this way—he that believeth this truth,—shall live for ever. Many of Christ's disciples, as well as many in all ages since, understand Christ's words literally and carnally, fixing their attention upon the word "eating," and blind to its identity with coming and believing, say, "This is a hard saying, who can hear it?"

Now, suppose the meaning to be what some of the disciples thought it to be, and many in all ages think it was, it would have been a hard saying—a contradictory saying; for he called himself both flesh and bread: "Whosoever eateth my flesh." "He that eateth this bread." Now, flesh is not bread, and bread is not flesh; so that, taking his words in the letter, his sayings were contradictory. Their murmurs led to an explanation. When Jesus knew that his disciples murmured, he said unto them, "Doth this offend you?" Now, while I am with you, it is within the bounds of physical possibility that you should eat my flesh and drink my blood; yet such an interpretation offends you, and very justly. When I ascend up where I was before, and take my flesh with me, there will be an absolute impossibility that you should eat my flesh in the way you mean. O yes! says the Church of Rome; O yes! says the Church of England; O yes! say Archdeacon Wilberforce and the Puseyites, we can, by our consecrations, transubstantiate a little bread and wine into the real flesh and blood of Christ as it appeared on earth; and in the participation thereof the communicant partakes of the real body and blood of Christ. No! said Christ, "It is the Spirit that quickeneth; the flesh profiteth nothing: the words that I speak unto you, they are spirit, and they are life." Mark also the corroborating connection in the two following verses: "But there are some of you who believe not. For Jesus knew from the beginning who they were who believed not. And he said, Therefore said I unto you, that no man can come unto me except it were given him of my Father." The secret mysteries of a divine life,—a new nature, eating Christ, Christ formed in our hearts by faith,—cannot be written or spoken, language cannot reach them, neither can they be understood, except the soul itself be awakened into the life of them, except it be given them of God, and they have chosen Christ.

What is called the holy sacrament of bread and wine, is a commemorative ceremony belonging to the Jewish dispensation, which Christ fulfilled and ended when he partook of the passover supper with his disciples, the night before he offered up his body on the cross, a propitiatory sacrifice for the sins of the whole world.

Now, Christ was made under the law, and must fulfil it and all its symbols and ceremonies, in order to deliver men from its obligations, and blot out the handwriting of ordinances that was against us under the law.

When the proper time was come for him to fulfil and end the feast of the passover, as it had been observed by the Jews as typical of the shedding of his blood, he sent his disciples to prepare a room for that purpose. In that room he partook, with his disciples, of this feast, blessing the cup and the bread as typical of the sacrifice of his body and blood, as it had been commemorative of the sacrificial lamb in Egypt. Not to perpetuate that ceremony, or to establish another in its stead as a gospel ordinance, but to fulfil it as a ceremony of the Jewish law, and put it aside as useless after " he, our passover, was sacrificed for us." So that it has nothing to do with the gospel dispensation.

For God declared (Exod. xii. 25-27), " It shall come to pass, when ye be come to the land which the Lord will give you, according as he hath promised, that ye shall keep this service. And it shall come to pass, when your children shall say unto you, What mean ye by this service? that ye shall say, It is the sacrifice of the Lord's passover, who passed over the houses of the children of Israel, when he smote the Egyptians, and delivered our houses." Again (Exod. xiii. 14-16), "And it shall be, when thy son asketh thee in time to come, saying, What is this? that thou shalt say unto him, By strength of hand the Lord brought us out from Egypt, from the house of bondage: and it came to pass, when Pharaoh would hardly let us go, that the Lord slew all the first-born in the land of Egypt, both the first-born of man, and the first-born of beast; but all the first-born of the children of Israel I redeem." Now, this passover supper was kept, we observe, in commemoration of this great deliverance in the land which the Lord gave the Israelites according as he had promised, that they should keep this service there, to be kept for their generations. Then came the day when the passover must be killed, and Jesus sent Peter and John to prepare this passover that they might eat it. And when the hour was come, he sat down with his disciples, and said, "I have desired to eat this passover with you before I suffer." Here is no command for a new institution, only a commemoration of past mercies.

The redemption of Israel from the idolatry and oppression of Pharaoh king of Egypt, by virtue of the blood of the paschal lamb, was the type of our redemption from sin by the precious blood of Christ, as were all the other ceremonies of the legal dispensation. Hence the apostle says, "Christ, our passover, was sacrificed for us." So that it clearly appears that the rites of the Levitical law of ceremonies were types of Jesus Christ, and fulfilled in him.

At the paschal supper of which Christ partook with his disciples, in order to inculcate the great truths of redemption, and the benefit to be received from the shedding of his blood, then soon to take place, he associated that sacrifice of himself on the cross with the idea of the nourishment of their bodies. "Take, eat, this is my" sacrificial "body," figuratively. "This is my blood of the new testament, which is shed for many for the remission of sins," figuratively. And the calls for food being of a nature so often to occur, and so absolute in their demands, were calculated to fix deeply in their minds the necessity of that spiritual

bread which they were to receive through him, who was about to
shed his precious blood for the sins of the whole world.

"Almost all things were by the law purged with blood, and
without shedding of blood there was no remission." "Wherefore Jesus, that he might sanctify the people with his own blood,
suffered without the gates of Jerusalem." For as the life of the
flesh is in the blood, and God gave it to the Israelites upon the
altar to make an atonement for their souls, for it was the blood
that made the atonement for the soul under the law, so " God
set forth," or fore-ordained, " his Son to be a propitiation through
faith in his blood." Therefore, according to the legal construction of the words, Christ might truly say, This is figurative of
" my blood of the new testament, which is shed for many for
the remission of sins;"—and the apostle Paul, " In whom we
have redemption through his blood, even the forgiveness of sins,
according to the riches of his grace."

Christ taught his disciples that the true gospel communion
was spiritual—that if they opened their hearts to him, he would
come in and sup with them, and they with him. He was to
become their guest, taking up his abode in their hearts. " I in
you and you in me," said he to his disciples. There is a sweet
union between Jesus who shed his blood for us and the truly
justified ones. He creates his own image in them, and they see
the source of their redemption in him as the sacrifice for their
sins; and they embrace one another, he with the arms of mercy,
and they with a filial love. And as they have peace with God
therein, so they have a peace whereof God is the immediate
author and cause. This is union and communion, indeed; Christ
dwells in their hearts by faith and love through grace, and they
are thereby " members of his body, of his flesh, and of his bones."
His divine virtue crucifies their old sinful nature in conformity
to his crucifixion; and when, in consequence of this, the divine
and quickening Spirit becomes master in them, bearing sway in
their souls, it raises them up into a new life. Thus, by dying
unto sin, they are made conformable unto the death of Christ;
and by walking in newness of life, they represent his resurrection

from the dead; by the sacrifice of the old man, the new man is gained, and by dying unto sin they are made alive unto righteousness.

The reader will notice here that this is not a matter of human opinion, liable to error, and open to correction; but a plain matter of Scriptural fact. And if it be a primary duty, as without doubt it is, to give diligent heed to the truth, as revealed in the Holy Scriptures, there is no reasonable ground to suppose that the Lord's Supper (so called) was ever instituted as a gospel ordinance, either by Christ or his apostles. And it is clear that the passover supper of which Christ partook was the fulfilment, and end for ever, of the Jewish passover, as he came "to fulfil the law." And if it was intended to be repeated at all in remembrance of Christ (which is very questionable), that could only be till he came again in spirit, which we read he did on the day of Pentecost. This was the commencement of the new dispensation, when all shadows were to give place to the spiritual substance, and the ceremonial law to end. "I will pray the Father," said Christ the Son, "and he shall give you another Comforter, that he may abide with you for ever." "Behold," said Christ, to the angel of the Church of Laodicea, "I stand at the door and knock: if any man hear my voice, and open the door, I will come in to him and will sup with him, and he with me." This is the true supper of the Lord.

It was the character of the ceremonial law that it stood only in sacrifices, meats, and drinks, and divers washings, and carnal ordinances imposed until the time of reformation, or until Christ came to establish his spiritual kingdom. Now let us consider what is implied in the term "carnal ordinances." Doth it not mean an ordinance relating chiefly to the flesh, in contradistinction to an ordinance relating to the spirit, or of a spiritual and edifying character? Some of the carnal ordinances are enumerated by the apostle, "as meats, and drinks, and divers washings." What, then, are the two sacraments now in use among Christians, but observances precisely of this description,—the one a meat and drink, the other a washing, according to the practice of the Jews under the law, and the lustrations of the pagans at the same period of time?

Is it alleged by any that these carnal ordinances are of a sacramental character? Yes, it is so. And it may well be lamented that an idea, apparently so full of pagan and popish superstition, should obtain credit in any Protestant church; but so it is. No such wonderful effects appear to have been attributed by the Jews to any of their baptisms or feasts, as the Christians attribute to theirs. No; the idea is of heathen origin, as we have shown in the first chapter of this work. The fact, if it really did exist, would be a standing miracle—a contravention of the laws of nature and of God.

When our Lord first spoke to his disciples of their eating his flesh and drinking his blood, he was heard with astonishment, and they exclaimed, "How can this man give us his flesh to eat? This is a hard saying; who can hear it?" This shows that they construed his words literally, when his meaning was altogether spiritual. But be it remembered that the great effusion of the gospel light had not then commenced, as the law was then unfulfilled. Therefore, it was a natural consequence that they should understand his words literally. This has been the case, with relation to the flesh and blood of Christ, from that day to the present hour; notwithstanding that the light of the gospel has shone in the hearts of millions, who have seen that it is a spiritual eating and drinking, that can nourish the soul, and enable man to hold communion with his God.

Some, taking the words of our Lord in the most literal signification, "This is my body," and "This is my blood of the new testament," and "This do in remembrance of me," have supposed that they are authorized to repeat this paschal supper under the gospel; and that the consecrated bread and wine become the very body and blood of Christ. Others, revolting from these gross conceptions, have variously modified their opinions, until they have brought it down to an outward and visible sign of an inward and spiritual grace; and even thus modified into "a sign of spiritual grace," it is contended for as an ordinance in the

Christian church, without which salvation cannot be obtained. But be it ever remembered, that the man who is destitute of a lively faith and redeeming grace, though he receive the consecrated bread and wine, is in no wise a partaker of Christ ; and the man who possesses a lively faith through grace, though he does not receive the consecrated elements, doth spiritually eat and drink the body and blood of Christ in a scriptural sense, to the salvation of his soul.

Among the various errors which have darkened the light of truth, transubstantiation—a prominent doctrine of the Church of Rome, and may we not say, also, of the Church of England? (see chapter vi.)—stands as an instructive yet melancholy example of the deep delusion into which the human mind may fall, when the Scriptures of truth cease to be the only standard of faith, and human reason and tradition are set up in place thereof. The deviation is, indeed, so egregious, that were it not a matter of historic fact, as well as of every-day experience, we might doubt whether it were possible for any calling themselves reasonable beings, to propound and defend so untenable a proposition.

These preposterous notions have no other origin than the direful pagan superstition of Greece and Rome at the advent of Christ ; and which, not very long after the time of the Apostles, began to brood like a cloud in Clementinism, Cyprianism, Ammonianism, Arianism, and Pelagianism ; and which involved the Church of Christ, by degrees, in gross and perilous darkness. Now, there is a clear and definite reason why Christ cannot be understood as declaring that the bread which he had broken was actually his body—namely, that his body was not yet broken—not yet offered up as a sacrifice, but a veritable body, which his disciples saw, handled, and heard, and which was occupying a portion of space distinct from that which the bread occupied, while the very words, " This is my body," were flowing from his lips. The corporal eating of Christ must therefore be regarded as fictitious, and contrary to Scripture doctrine. It is irrelevant, therefore, to argue whether such an eating conveys grace to the soul. That which has no existence can have no effect. But in the notion that the body of Christ is eaten at the passover supper, or in the sacrament of the churches, and that this carnal eating is necessary to salvation, there is surely much that degrades the cause of truth—much that directs the minds of those who are honestly seeking for their salvation, into wrong channels—much that is calculated to divert from a simple reliance on the crucified, risen, glorified, and reigning Saviour, and to substitute for him an idol of man's own imagining. In so corrupt a superstition—so gross a perversion of the great realities of the gospel—there cannot be any inherent virtue, no saving grace. Yet how many poor, bewildered sinners have been taught on their death-beds, both in the Church of Rome and the Church of England, to regard the eucharist, with its supposed hidden mysteries, as their passport to heaven.

But Bishop Burnet says it is not so. In his second letter to William Law, he says,—"Even they (the sacraments) are not strictly means of grace, nor does our salvation absolutely depend on them." Speaking of the eucharist, he says,—"The effect of the prayer (meaning what is called the prayer of consecration) is not converting the bread and wine into the means of grace by a human benediction. Converting is a term," he says, "I can never hear without fearing that, by degrees, the old doctrine of transubstantiation is to be stolen in upon us again. There is no such conversion wrought by the prayer of consecration, nor are there any means of grace there, but the disposition of the heart." So says the author, and so say millions of pious souls.

We believe that the receiving and retaining the eucharist, has a general tendency to settle the minds of the professors of the Christian name in unnecessary forms, and to prevent their aspiring after the practice of real, vital Christianity. The importance attached by the churches to the eucharist, we conceive, justifies our apprehensions; and the abuses which frequently attend the administration, must, we think, greatly exceed its use.

The Ascodrutes, a Gnostic sect in the second century, are mentioned by Bingham as a body "who did not use the sacraments" (Bing. Christ. Antiq., xv. 2–9); and, under pretence of adhering to spiritual worship alone, would admit of no external or corporeal symbols whatever. " They asserted," as Theodoret describes them, " that divine mysteries being the images of invisible things, are not to be set forth by visible things ; nor incorporeal things represented by sensible and corporeal things. Therefore they never baptized any that were of their sect, nor celebrated the mystery of the eucharist among them." (See Faiths of the World, vol. i., p. 202.)

Irenæus, also, who lived in the second century, mentions Christians called Valentinians, who disused the ceremony of baptism and the supper, saying " that the mystery of the unspeakable, invisible power ought not to be performed by visible and corruptible elements, nor that of incomprehensible and corporeal things ; but that the true knowledge of the unspeakable majesty is itself perfect redemption or baptism." If of baptism, so also of communion. (Tertullian on Baptism, Lib. i., cap. 10.)

Ignatius, who lived in the second century after the apostles, appears to be of the same faith. He says,—" Ye, therefore, with meekness of spirit, possess yourselves in faith, which is the flesh of the Lord, and in love, which is the blood of Jesus Christ." And Augustine, bishop of Hippo, in the fourth century, was of the same mind. He says,—" Believe and thou hast eaten. To believe in him is to eat the living bread."

There was, in the fourth century, a spiritually-minded sect named Massalians, in the East, sometimes called Bogomiles, who subsisted through several hundred years, and became a powerful body in the twelfth century. " They rejected baptism with water, holding that the only Christian baptism was a baptism of the Spirit, to be imparted simply by calling upon the Holy Ghost ; and as they refused to admit an outward celebration of baptism, so they were equally opposed to the outward celebration of the Lord's Supper." (See Faiths, vol. i., p. 367.)

Basil said,—" There is an intellectual mouth of the inward man, at which he is fed who partakes of the word of life, which is the bread which came down from heaven." (See Basil on 33rd Psalm.) Augustine says,—" Dost thou prepare thy teeth and thy stomach ? Believe, and thou hast eaten. He eats who believes on him." (See Tracts 25 and 26, on John, 6th chapter.) "The bread of the heart is that whereon we feed, who eat inwardly, not outwardly—with the heart, not with the teeth." (See on Psalm 48.) "The Donatists, in the fourth and fifth centuries, denied the validity of the eucharist." (See Bing. Antiq., xv. 2–9.)

Fauchelin in Flanders, and Peter de Brues, with Henry, his disciple, in France, and the Bogomiles in the Grecian empire, and their followers, held that the sacraments were no longer to be administered or admitted. Many united with them in Flanders, France, and Italy; among whom was John Scotus Erigena, Beringarius, and Arnold of Brescia. (See Dupin.)

William of Newbury mentions thirty religious persons who came into England from Germany, in A.D. 1170, "who denied the eucharist." The Waldenses became generally known about the same time; they also held "that baptism with water, and the other sacraments of the Church of Rome, profit nothing to salvation."

During the fifteenth century there were a great number of persons in England, as well as on the Continent, "who denied the necessity of the eucharist; and held that Christian people were sufficiently baptized into the blood of Christ, to enable them to hold communion with him, without the eucharistic bread and wine."

Dr. Redman, an early English protestant, being asked, in the time of his illness, whether he thought the body of Christ was received with the mouth in the eucharist or not, paused awhile, and then replied, "I will not say so; it is a hard question; but surely we receive Christ in our soul by faith. When you speak of it otherwise, it soundeth grossly. I fear lest that sacrament hath robbed Christ of a great part of his honour." (Fox's Acts and Mon., vol 2.)

Robert Smith, of Windsor, who proved by death the sincerity of his faith, said, "I do not esteem the sacrament in any point, because it hath neither God's ordinance, either in name or other usage, but rather is erected to mock God." (Fox's Acts and Mon., vol 3.)

That there were not a few spiritually minded and faithful ones in the darkest ages of popery, is very clear; and Walter Brute, of Hereford, who lived about A.D. 1405, was not one of the least of them; he had very clear and spiritual views on many points of Christian faith and practice. On the communion of the body and blood of Christ he expresses himself as follows :—

"I believe and know that Christ is the true bread of God, which descended from heaven and giveth life to the world. Of which bread whosoever eateth shall live for ever, as is declared in the Sixth Chapter of John. By the faith which we have in Christ as the true Son of God, who came down from heaven to redeem us, we are justified from sin, and so live by him; which is the true bread and meat of the soul. And the bread which Christ gave is his flesh, given for the life of the world. As we believe that he is the true God, so must we believe that he is a true man, and then do we eat the bread of heaven, and the flesh of Christ. If we believe that he did voluntarily shed his blood for our redemption, then we do drink his blood. Except we thus eat the flesh of the Son of Man, and drink his blood, we have not eternal life in us: because the flesh of Christ, verily, is meat, and his blood is drink indeed; and whosoever eateth his flesh and drinketh his blood abideth in Christ, and Christ in him. But the priests," says he, "be greatly deceived, and also greatly deceive others. For the people believe that they see the body of Christ, nay, rather Christ himself, between the hands of the priests, for so is the common oath they swear, ' by him whom I saw this day between the priest's hands.' And they believe that they eat not the body of Christ but at Easter, or when they be upon their death beds, and receive with their bodily mouths the sacrament of his body. But since the body of Christ is the soul's food, and not the food of the body, whosoever believeth doth eat spiritually and really, at any time when he so believeth; and it is manifest that they do greatly err which believe that they eat not the body of Christ but when they eat with their teeth the sacrament of his body. The priests, therefore, are in great peril, most dangerously seducing themselves and the people." (Fox's Acts and Mon., vol 1, p. 564.)

William Thorp, of Shrewsbury, being examined before Archbishop Arundel, about the same time, as to his faith, declared, " I said to the people, the virtue of the most holy sacrament of the altar stands much more in the belief that you ought to have it in your souls than in the outward rite thereof. And, therefore, we are better to stand still quietly to hear God's word, because by hearing thereof men come to true belief." He requested the people that they would abstain from the sacraments of the corrupt Romish priests, saying, "No need to be afraid to die without taking any sacrament of those enemies of Christ, since Christ himself will not fail to minister all sacraments lawful, healthful, and necessary, at all times, especially at the end, to all them that are in the true faith, and steadfast hope, and perfect charity." The archbishop and the bishops were very bitter against him, and he is supposed to have died in prison. (See Fox's Acts and Mon., vol 1, p. 564.)

When a man hath through faith, and the powerful prevalence of the Divine principle, obtained a victory over evil, his soul abounds with evidence and tokens of his happy attainments through the Lord Jesus Christ; then he apprehends the *all* of God and the nothingness of himself, as well as the nothingness of the priests and their traditions. He has got a truth, whose benefit no words can express. When our religion is founded on this it has the firmness of a rock, and its height reaches unto heaven.

But fallen, degenerate men have in all ages since the advent of Christ endeavoured to destroy this rock, and those who build on it. When we look closely into the truths advanced in our history, we cannot but be convinced that the dogmas of the "Catholic Church" were borrowed from Judaism and Philosophic Paganism, being chiefly drawn from the idealistic system of the Grecian Plato and the mystic theosophy of the Oriental philosophers, rather than from the doctrine of the Gospel, and they have maintained the same character to the present day.

During the dark ages, as they are called, when irreligion and superstition reigned in all their power, and when the Scriptures were withheld from the laity, this church inflicted every act of cruelty which the art of man could devise, to crush and destroy the followers of Christ and his gospel, for he has ever had his 7,000 faithful ones who have not bowed the knee to Baal.

# CHAPTER VIII.

God created man in his own image, to enjoy communion with him; but in his fall he lost the image and life of God in his soul; he died on the very day of his transgression to the image in which he was created; he became a fallen earthly creature, and subject to the temptations of Satan; but the goodness and mercy of God did not leave him long in this condition—redemption from it was granted; and the bruiser of the serpent's head was promised, who was to restore the Divine life once more into human nature. All men, therefore, in consequence of the redemption that cometh by Christ, have in them the seed of the Divine life, as a treasure hid in the centre of their souls, to bring forth by degrees, as it is watered and cultivated, a new birth of that life which was lost in Paradise. No son of Adam can be lost, except by turning away from, and rejecting, the Spirit of God within him. The only religion that can save us must be that which can create a new life in the soul. As nothing can enter into the vegetable kingdom till it have vegetable life in it, or be a member of the animal kingdom till it have the animal life, so all nature joins with the gospel in affirming that no man can enter into the kingdom of God till the heavenly life is born in him. Nothing can be our righteousness or recovery but the Divine nature of Jesus Christ restored to our souls, which may, in a figurative sense, be said to be " eating his flesh and drinking his blood."

As a consequence of the transgression of our first parents, all the posterity of Adam are involved in a proneness to sin. And in order to counteract this proneness to sin " the seed of the woman " was promised, " who should bruise the head of the

serpent." This promise was reserved unto Abraham. "In thy
seed shall all the nations of the earth be blessed." This seed of
the woman—this seed of Abraham, is our Lord Jesus Christ, who
was "wounded for our transgressions—bruised for our iniquities—the chastisement of our peace was upon Him, and with his
stripes we are healed." He gave Himself for us, an offering and
a sacrifice to God ; therefore we have redemption through his
blood, even the forgiveness of sins. He is the "Lord our
righteousness." We have also, through the same compassionate
God and Saviour, granted unto us the gift of the Holy Spirit, to
guide us into all truth. To be guided by the Spirit of truth is
the practical application of the Christian religion—to eat Christ's
flesh, and drink his blood, and to be baptized into Him. This
is the appointed means of restoring us out of the fall, and bringing us into a state of holiness, without which none can see the
Lord. This is not a doctrine of traditional mysticism, but of
practical piety.

They who truly fear God have a secret guidance of a far
higher wisdom than what is barely human—the Spirit of truth,
which does really, though secretly, prevent, and direct them. Any
man that sincerely and truly fears Almighty God, and calls and
relies on him for direction, has it as really as a son hath the counsel
and direction of his father ; and though the voice be not audible,
yet it is actually as real as if a man heard a voice saying, "This
is the way, walk in it." I believe there is no Christian man who
contemplates the perpetration of a crime but feels a compunction
of mind that bids beware, and after its perpetration, condemns
for the act. A strict observance of the secret admonition of the
Spirit of God in the heart is an effectual means to sanctify and
cleanse us.

Pythagoras calls this Divine principle, "the great light and
salt of ages." Anaxagoras call it "the Divine mind." Socrates
calls it, "a good Spirit." Timæus styles it, "an unbegotten
principle and author of all light." Hieron, Pythagoras, Epictetus, and Seneca say, "it is God in man, or God within."
Plato calls it, "the eternal, ineffable, and perfect principle of

truth, the light and spirit of God." Plotinus calls it, "the root of the soul, the Divine principle in man." Philo, "the Divine power—the ineffable immortal law in the mind of man." And Plutarch denominates it, "the law and living rule of the mind, the interior guide of the soul, and the everlasting foundation of virtue." The writings of Thomas à Kempis abound with senti-ments of this kind. "He is that Divine principle that speaks in our hearts; and without which there cannot be just appre-hensions nor rectitude of judgment."

It is impossible for us to enjoy the light and influence of this Spirit until we are deeply sensible of our own sinfulness, nothingness, and emptiness, and our minds are broken down with sorrow, and laid in the dust, under a sense of our condition as we stand in the fall. The Spirit of Christ is indeed a humbling spirit; the more we have of it the more shall we be humbled; and it is a sign that either we have it not, or that it is yet over-powered by our corruptions, if our hearts be still haughty, and we glory in our own strength in anything we do.

Practical Christianity, then, is the actual operation of Christian principle. It is a standing on the watch-tower for occasions to exemplify them. It is exercising ourselves unto godliness. A real Christian will try to keep his heart open, his mind prepared, and his affections alive to do whatever may occur in the way of duty, which comes within the sphere of his calling, for the exaltation of truth and the destruction of error. It is only by the influence of Divine illumination that poor fallen man is capacitated to apprehend the things of God. Therefore it is as man's power of mind becomes illuminated by Divine princi-ples, that the mists and fogs of tradition and prejudice are dispelled, and reason restored to its proper use, and furnished with a clear sense of duty, and ability to perform it, in pulling down the strongholds of error in the Christian Church.

In our inquiry into the decisions of Christianity upon the question of State Churches and their dogmas, we have to refer to the general tendency of Divine Revelation, to the individual declarations of Jesus Christ; to his practice; to the sentiments

and practices of his commissioned followers, to the opinions respecting its lawfulness which were held by their immediate converts, and to some other kinds of Christian evidence.

It is, perhaps, the capital error of those who have attempted
to instruct others in the duties of religion, that they have not
been willing to enforce the rules of the Christian Scriptures in
their full extent, because it crossed their natural inclinations.
Therefore, as a substitute for this, they have set up baptisms,
confirmations, the eucharist, absolutions, masses, purgatory, and
indulgences for sin. Almost every denomination of Christians
stops somewhere short of the point which the Scriptures prescribe;
and this stop is made at a greater or less distance from the
Christian standard, in proportion to the admission, in a greater
or less degree, of principles and practices which have been
superadded to the principles of the gospel. The Church of
Rome, therefore, bears the palm. They who reject truth are
not likely to escape error. Having mingled with Christianity
principles and practices which it never taught, they are not
likely to be consistent with truth or with themselves; and,
accordingly, he who seeks for directions from these professed
teachers of religion, finds his mind bewildered in conflicting
theories, and his judgment embarrassed by contradictory instructions. All who have proposed any other standard of religion
than that laid down in the Holy Scriptures, or who have mixed
any foreign principles with the truth there laid down and taught,
have hitherto proved that they have been sporting themselves
with their own deceivings.

Our great misfortune, in the examination of the duties and
principles of Christianity, is, that we do not contemplate them
with sufficient simplicity. We do not estimate them without
some additions or abatement of our own. There is almost always
some intervening medium. A sort of half-transparent glass is
hung before each individual, which possesses endless shades of
colour and degrees of opacity, and which presents objects with
endless varieties of distortion, and in nothing more so than on
the subject of the eucharist. This glass is coloured by our

education, the influence of priestcraft, and our passions for forms and ceremonies, and things that glitter. Our business is to endeavour to render these things clear and transparent. We know that we have been referred to the determinations of councils, constitutions, and canon and statute laws. But we believe that, when Christianity advances in her purity and her power in the same degree, she will sweep these things from the earth with the besom of destruction.

To attempt to pursue the consequences of State churches, through all their ramifications of evil, in all ages, would be endless and vain. They are a moral gangrene, which diffuses its humours throughout the whole religious, political, and social system. To expose its mischiefs would be endless, for there is no evil which it does not occasion to a greater or less degree ; and it has much that is peculiar to itself, in upholding false principles founded only on traditions, and enforcing conformity to them. To what a situation is a rational and responsible being reduced, who commits actions, good or bad, at the bidding of the Church. We can conceive of no greater degradation. Christianity, as set forth in the Sacred Scriptures, has never stated any case in which personal responsibility ceases. If she admits such a case, she has not told us so ; but she has told us repeatedly and explicitly that she does require individual obedience, and imposes individual responsibility ; she has made no exception to the imperativeness of her obligations.

Are we, then, regulated by the injunctions of God, or are we not ? This is the question ! If there be any lesson of importance for mankind to learn, it is the necessity of simply performing the duties of Christianity, without reference to the creed of any church, or to consequences. The world has had many such examples of fidelity and confidence in those who have been the Christian martyrs of all ages.

Hierarchism, or the religion of the priest ; rationalism, or the religion of man ; Christianity, or the religion of God ; are the three systems which, in our days, as well as the three first centuries, share Christendom among them. But there is no safety either for man or society in hierarchism or rationalism, but only in Christianity, that recognizes Christ alone as its Head, who gives spiritual life to the world; but, unhappily, of the three dominant systems, it is not the true Church that counts the greatest number of followers; followers, however, it has, who are doing its work of leading to Christ as the Redeemer of man.

Whenever religious truth is in question, three objects engage the attention—the priest, man, and God. This was the case in paganism at the Advent of Christ! The ministers of paganism were in a manner the gods whom the pagans worshipped. They thought that salvation was of the priests. The religions of the earth form an earthly religion. The religion of the heathen Greeks and Romans told men that heaven would be given them, and the Holy Ghost communicated to them, by the intervention of the priest; and they, being led away by the charms which pagan Greece and Rome had for ages exercised over the nations, took pleasure in paying to the bishop the honour which belonged to God only. This assumed power grew like an avalanche, and Rome smiled when she saw the nations throwing themselves into her arms, when the priests were likened to the Jewish and heathen priests; and those who separated from them—the true Christians—were put in the same class with Korah, Dathan, and Abiram.

From an individual priesthood, such as the Gospel enjoins, to a sovereign · priesthood, such as Rome and Greece enjoin, the step was easy. The patriarchal institution, as well as the Greek and Roman pagan institutions, contributed to the rise of the priesthood of the "Catholic Church." But, be it ever remembered, that custom without truth, in any church, is the antiquity of error. But the bishops of Asia, Greece, and Rome, to truth joined pagan custom. From that time the evil ceased not to grow, and the hierarchical power to rise higher and higher; thus the whole Christian economy of grace became disturbed, the source of spiritual life from Jesus alone sealed up, and Christianity overturned to its basis. That which lowered grace elevated the priest. Salvation taken out of the hands of God fell into the hands of priests who put themselves in the Lord's place. (See p. 10, 11.)

When the equality of souls before God is lost, and Christendom at the bidding of a priest is divided into two unequal camps—in the one we find a caste of priests who dare to usurp the name of a "Catholic Church," and pretend to be invested in the eyes of the Lord with higher privileges ; in the other, servile herds, called the laity, reduced to blind and passive submission—a people gagged and muzzled. Every tribe, language, and nation of Christendom fell under the dominion of these spiritual kings. Thus everything in the Church of Christ is changed for the traditions of men. Thus papacy and episcopacy became an immense wall between men and their God. The papacy interposes the priest between God and men ; Christianity makes them meet face to face.

One of the principal errors on which the whole system of Romanism and Episcopalianism is built, is the doctrine of Apostolical Succession, as maintained by Dr. Hook ; he says :—" Our ordination descends in an unbroken line from Peter and Paul. The great apostles successively ordained Linus, Cletus, and Clement bishops of Rome ; and the apostolic succession was regularly continued from them to Celestine, Gregory, and Vitalianus, who ordained Patrick, bishop of the Irish, and Austin and Theodore for the English. And from these times," he adds, " an uninterrupted series of valid ordinations has carried down the apostolical succession in our churches to the present day. There is not a bishop, priest, or deacon amongst us, who may not, if he please, trace his spiritual descent from Peter and Paul." These are bold assertions, but unfortunately for Dr. Hook, they proceed upon an assumption which no Roman or Anglo-Catholic can possibly prove to be well founded—that the apostolic office admits of succession. The office of the apostles was peculiar, extraordinary, and miraculous, and, therefore, necessarily temporary. They were inspired men, and this quality being strictly supernatural, it was impossible that they could communicate it to others. And as to the succession of which Dr. Hook speaks, it is a fiction, not a reality. Peter, Linus, Cletus, Clement: such is the order of the first bishops of Rome, as given in the quotations we have just made, and if he had gone one step further, he would, in all probability, have added Anacletus. Is the testimony of the early church unanimous on this point? Far from it. Tertullian, Rufinus, and several others, place Clement next to Peter; Irenæus and Eusebius set Anacletus before Clement; Epiphanus and Optatus place both Anacletus and Cletus before him; while Augustine and Demasus make Anacletus, Cletus, and Linus all to precede him. Well may Stillingfleet say, in noticing the diversity of opinion in reference to the very first links of this chain of succession, "How shall we extricate ourselves from this labyrinth?"

But even were the chain unbroken in point of persons, how shall we secure it being unbroken in point of virtue? If all that is required in the church to make ordination valid, in the case of every individual link in the chain, were not complied with; nay, if in one single case there was a failure, the boasted succession becomes an utter nullity. Well may Chillingworth remark, "That of ten thousand requisites, whereof any one may fail, not one should be wanted, this, to me, is extremely improbable and impossible." And yet on this doubtful foundation the Anglo-Catholics, in common with the most bigoted Romanists, build an arrogant and presumptuous claim.

At first the priests pretended that their object was to defend spiritual order. But when they had begun to handle such weapons as apostolical succession, the church's spirituality was at an end. Her arm could not become temporal without rendering her heart temporal also. It was with a view to strengthen this idea that the succession, and the sacraments of baptism, confirmation, the eucharist, and absolution, &c., were instituted. These, in the priests' hands, became the means of promoting their worldly interest, even to the sale of indulgences for sin. But take away the salvation that God gives, and place it upon men, and you take away purity of heart and life. This has been proved by the events of all ages. Salvation considered as coming from man and his traditions, is the creating principle of all error and abuse.

Sacramental efficacy, or the power of the sacraments in themselves, is a grand principle of the Romish and the English churches. This doctrine, indeed, is intimately connected with those already noticed. God's grace and our salvation depend, according to this theory, on the virtue of the sacraments, and that virtue itself depends upon the apostolical succession of those who administer these sacraments. On these points conjointly viewed, the whole system of Catholicism is founded. The efficacy of the sacraments, *ex opere operato*, has ever been a favourite doctrine of the Romish and English churches, tending, as it does, to exalt the clergy in the estimation of the people, by holding them forth as possessed of a mysterious power of communicating effectually the only means of salvation. Thus they come to be regarded with the deepest reverence, and the sacraments are converted into a species of magical charm, which works in some mysterious way altogether independent of the concurrence of the person to whom they are administered. Such tenets meet not with the slightest countenance from the Sacred Scriptures. On the contrary, the whole efficacy of man's regeneration depends on Christ, and the working of his Spirit ; for an apostle expressly declares, " So then neither is he that planteth anything, neither he that watereth, but God that giveth the increase." Christ comforteth his disciples with the hope of heaven, professing himself " the way, the truth, and the life," and "one with the Father," assuring their prayers in his name to be effectual, promising the Holy Ghost, the Comforter, even the Spirit of truth, that He should abide with them for ever.

All false religions are inherent in the constitution of fallen, unredeemed man. But, from these, true Christians stand separate and apart. Revelation and communion, then, are necessary to man, and not unworthy of God ; accordingly, it has been bestowed. The revelation thus imparted is the Spirit of God the Father, through Christ the Son, and is found, in its holy and purifying influence on the minds of those, whether individuals or communities, who sincerely embrace it. It enlarges the mind in the reception of religious truth ; it refines the taste for the reception of truth and the rejection of error; and purifies the heart ; a purer, loftier, and more powerful principle of holy living animates the whole man than has hitherto been created in his bosom. Impelled by this holy, this ennobling principle, his mind is elevated to the contemplation of objects the purest and most sublime, with his whole soul devoted, not to the eucharist as a sacrifice for sin, but to the service and glory of his redeeming God.

The love and Spirit of Jesus is of singular force and efficacy ; and when it has got an entrance into the heart, and is faithfully entertained there, it is as the sap in the vine, it ceases not its Divine operations till it has consumed man's corruptions, and rid him of whatever is opposed to its generous motions and tendencies. Then it prevails within him, displays its agreeable heat, satisfying the soul, and carrying it, and all its faculties and powers along with it, whithersoever it pleaseth. This is communion, indeed.

This doctrine of grace (says the High Church) annuls the sacraments and contradicts baptismal regeneration ; this is an evidence that they take salvation out of the hands of Christ, and place it in the hands of the priests through the sacraments, and not in grace through Christ our Redeemer. What an evidence is this, that the Church has lost the life that was peculiar to it in its first promulgation by Christ and his apostles. It must put itself again in communication with its native principle—that is, the grace of God through Jesus Christ. The light, the warmth, and the power, came from heaven on the day of Pentecost, as well as on the conversion of Paul ; and the new creation was completed, so it must ever be. He who has no faith to be saved of Christ alone is not of Christ's Church. He frustrates the grace of God, the death of Christ, and the merits of his passion.

It is by knowing our own nothingness, and the nothingness of the traditional religion of men, and that we have no capacity for good but what we receive from God the Father through Christ by the Holy Spirit, that self and tradition become wholly denied, their kingdom destroyed, and we are saved from a traditional holiness and faith in a eucharistic communion, and a multitude of errors the most dangerous to our souls; but when we once apprehend the all-sufficiency of God's power, and the nothing-ness of ourselves and of a humanly-devised religion, we have got a truth whose benefit no words can express. When our religion is founded on this it has the firmness of a rock. Consonant with this is that similitude of the apostle Paul when he describes Christ as the head: "From whom the whole body fitly joined to-gether, and compacted by that which every joint supplieth, according to the effectual working in the measure of every part, maketh increase of the body unto the edifying of itself in love." Blessed union—the life which prevails in the Head, Christ, and all the members being the same, though different in degree, as the measure compared with the fulness.

"There is one body and one spirit, even as ye are called in one hope of your calling; one Lord, one faith, one baptism, one God and Father of all, who is above all, and through all, and in you all. Unto every one of us is given grace according to the measure of the gift of Christ. * * * Till we all come in the unity of the faith, and of the knowledge of the Son of God unto a perfect man, unto the measure of the stature of the fulness of Christ: that we henceforth be no more children, tossed to and fro, and carried about with every wind of doctrine, by the sleight of men, and cunning craftiness, whereby they lie in wait to deceive; but speaking the truth in love, may grow up into him in all things, which is the Head." (Ephesians iv.)

We never think of Christ and his apostles, and the day of Pentecost, but with wonder and admiration, especially when we consider their character and prejudices until that day, and con-trast it with what it was after that memorable event. They were holy men after their conversion, not before, though they had conformed, in the strictest manner, to the ceremonies of the Jewish law. This grand event was surprising, glorious, and honourable to the Christian religion, and the Divine mission of its triumphant author.   For no sooner had the apostles received the precious gift, this celestial guide, than their ignorance was turned into knowledge, their darkness into light, their doubts into certainties, their fears into a firm and invincible fortitude, and their former backwardness into an ardent and inextinguishable zeal, which led them to take their sacred offices with the utmost intrepidity and alacrity of mind.   They were filled with a persuasion founded on Christ's express promise, that the Divine Spirit would perpetually accompany them, and show itself by miraculous interpositions, as often as the success of their ministry should render it necessary.

The conversion and apostleship of Paul alone, duly considered, was and is a demonstration sufficient to prove Christianity to be an immediate Divine revelation.   But many, yea most, who profess Christianity, are fallen into such gross carnality, that to speak to them of a spiritual appearance, and the work of God in the soul, seems so strange, so new, so incredible, that they can in nowise pay any regard to it, but rather deride it, as if they had never read the Holy Scriptures, whose testimony thereunto, from the beginning to the end, is as clear to the spiritually minded man as the noon-day sun.

This is an evident sign that the eyes of the unbelievers are closed to the truth—their hearts and ears are gross and dull of hearing, and their understandings dark, and their minds so carnal that they are dead—dead to God—dead to Christ—dead to the gospel of Christ.   And no marvel, the apostles of Jesus Christ were so before the day of Pentecost, and the apostle Paul before his conversion ; although the former had heard Christ's words and seen his miracles ; and the latter had been exceedingly zealous for the ceremonies of the law, who, after his conversion, declared that "the natural man knoweth not the things of the Spirit of God, neither can he know them, because they are spiritually discerned."

"Every good gift and every perfect gift is from above, and cometh down from the Father of lights, with whom is no variableness, neither shadow of turning.   By his own will begat he us," says the apostle, "with the word of truth, that we should be a kind of first-fruits of his creatures." Yes! God sent his only begotten Son into the world that we might live by him, who is equal in power with the Father,—" In him was life, and the life was the light of men." It was under the influence of this life and light that Christ sent Paul "to open the eyes of the Gentiles, and to turn them from darkness to light, and from the power of Satan unto God, that they might receive forgiveness of sins, and inheritance among them that are sanctified by faith, which is in Jesus Christ."

The apostle Paul's conversion (of whom it does not appear that he had any personal knowledge of Christ during his public ministry, or much intercourse with the twelve apostles) was the work of revelation; and his acquaintance with the doctrines of the gospel was equal, if not superior, to theirs. He declares,— " I neither received it of man, neither was I taught it, but by the revelation of Jesus Christ." By this revelation he testified, "that Christ was once offered to bear the sins of many," and that he is made of God unto us wisdom and righteousness, sanctification and redemption. "And unto them that look for him shall he appear the second time without sin unto salvation." John, also, who spake by Divine revelation, declared,—" We know that the Son of God is come, and hath given us an understanding, that we may know him that is true, and we are in him that is true, even in Jesus Christ." This knowledge of the great gospel mystery, it seems, the priestly hierarchies of nearly all denominations cannot receive or understand; they have been hid, to a large degree, through unbelief, from ages and generations, and forms and shadows put in their place; but, according to the apostle's doctrine, "are made manifest to the saints by the appearing of our Saviour Jesus Christ, who hath abolished death, and brought life and immortality to light through the gospel, to whom (the saints) God would make known what is the riches of the glory of this mystery among the Gentiles, which is Christ, in them the hope of glory." These are they who are come to God, the judge of all—and to Jesus, the mediator of the New

P

Testament—these are they who sit in heavenly places in Christ
Jesus.    No! saith the priesthood; these are they who are
doomed to eternal perdition ; for no man can come unto God, or
be a Christian, a saint, but through the medium we have set up in
our church—baptism—confirmation—the eucharist—absolution
—penance—pilgrimages—purgatory—masses—and indulgences
for sin, and that only through the medium of apostolical succession, and a right ordination.

Where do they glean this information ?  From pagan tradition, eighteen hundred years ago ; for this doctrine is
not so much as alluded to in Paul's epistles to the Romans,
the Galatians, the Ephesians, the Philippians, the Colossians,
and the Thessalonians.   In his epistles to Timothy and Titus,
where some instruction on the subject, if they had been
gospel ordinances, might have been expected, there is no allusion to them.   The same is true of his epistle to Philemon.   In
the epistle general of James there is no allusion to them.   In the
three epistles of John there is no allusion to them.   And, above
all, in the two epistles of Peter, on whom they profess to build
their church, there is no allusion to them.   This, surely, of itself,
is enough to convince any unprejudiced inquirer that there are
no such institutions under the gospel dispensation.

There is a very close analogy between the above doctrine
of what are  now called Christian churches, and that which
heathens have generally formed of idols—namely, that after they
are consecrated, the gods come down and take up their abode in
them, so that the images are honoured as the mansions of the
gods—the uniting of invisible spirits with images forming them
into one body.  Augustine, in giving an account of the Egyptian
Hermas Trismegistus, says—" He maintained images to be, as
it were, the bodies of the gods, certain spirits having their residence in them.   This uniting of invisible spirits with images,
forming them into one body, he termed the making of gods,
and held that there were people who were masters of the great
and wonderful art."   This was the common opinion among the
heathens.   Dr. Pocock asserts, "That the adoration which the
ancient Arabs paid to their idol gods was founded on this in-

dwelling principle." (See Faiths, vol. ii. p. 107.) The same idea was received into the "Catholic Church" in the second and third centuries of the Christian era, by Irenæus, Tertullian, Cæcilian Natalis, and Cyprian. Hence arose the doctrines of baptismal regeneration, transubstantiation, and the bodily presence of Christ in the eucharist, after the consecration of the elements by the priests, when they were supposed to become Christ himself, and the bread and wine to become wholly deified. One of the most peculiar characteristic doctrines of the Church of Rome is that of transubstantiation. This, indeed, is the great central peculiarity of the whole Roman system. It is thus described by the council of Trent :—" Whosoever shall deny that, in the most Holy Sacrament of the eucharist, there are, truly, really, and substantially, contained, the body and blood of our Lord Jesus Christ, together with his soul and divinity, and, consequently, Christ entire ; but shall affirm that he is present therein only in a sign and figure, or by his power—let them be accursed." Again, " Whosoever shall affirm that, in the most Holy Sacrament of the eucharist there remains the substance of bread and wine, together with the body and blood of our Lord Jesus Christ, and shall deny that wonderful and peculiar conversion of the whole substance of the bread into his body, and of the whole substance of the wine into his blood, the species only of bread and wine remaining, which conversion the Catholic Church most fitly terms 'transubstantiation;'—let him be accursed." Again, in the Romish Catechism we are expressly told—" In the eucharist, that which before consecration was bread and wine, becomes, after consecration, really and substantially the body and blood of our Lord." And again,—" The pastor will also inform the faithful that Christ, whole and entire, is contained, not only under either species, but also in each particle of each species." From such statements it is plain that, in the view of Romanists, after the words of consecration have been uttered by the priests, there is, in place of the substance of the bread and wine, the substance of the body of Christ truly, really, and substantially, together with his soul and divinity ; and hence the consecrated host becomes an object of adoration." (Faiths, vol. ii. pp. 767, 768.) And, as the Church of Rome and the Anglo-Catholics say, corporeally present—analogous to his divine nature. Such an image as the pagans made of their gods, do the Christians adore in the *Host* which they call a god.

We will now advance a few arguments to prove that when Jesus said to his disciples—"Except ye eat the flesh of the Son of man, and drink his blood, ye have no life in you," they are not meant of sacramental eating and drinking, in order to show that Christian churches have failed in their claim to truth on this point.

If this be meant of sacramental eating and drinking, it will follow that no man can be saved without it. For Christ said, "Except ye eat the flesh of the Son of man, and drink his blood, ye have no life in you." But a man may be saved without sacramental eating and drinking, for John the Baptist testified, "that he that believeth on the Son hath everlasting life." And Christ himself said, "He that heareth my words, and believeth on Him that sent me, hath everlasting life, and shall not come into condemnation, but is passed from death unto life." So that life and salvation are not tied to, or consequent on, the sacrament, but on true faith in Christ, and obedience to him, which is involved in all true faith.

Christ, in speaking of eating and drinking which is accompanied with salvation, says, "Whosoever eateth my flesh and drinketh my blood hath eternal life." But, surely, none will be bold enough to say, that every one that eateth and drinketh sacramentally hath eternal life ; for then all who partake, though fornicators, adulterers, &c., &c., are saved ; whereas, the apostle declares the contrary ; he says, "Know ye not, that the unrighteous shall not inherit the kingdom of God ? Be not deceived ; neither fornicators, nor idolaters, nor adulterers, nor thieves, nor covetous, nor drunkards, nor revilers, nor extortioners, shall inherit the kingdom of God." Will any one be bold enough to say, that none of these have ever partaken of the sacrament of bread and wine ? Nay ! Verily !

Again, the eating and drinking of Christ is a mutual inhabitation; the communicant dwells in Christ, and Christ in him. "He that eateth my flesh, and drinketh my blood, dwelleth in me, and I in him." But this cannot be said of every one who eateth of the outward bread and drinketh of the outward wine. Judas ate and drank thereof, and he betrayed his Master. Nay, Christ said, "He hath a devil." Did he, then, dwell in Christ, and Christ in him? No! And yet this will follow, if Christ's words are to be understood literally.

Again, Christ saith, "As the living Father hath sent me, and I live by the Father, so he that eateth me shall live by me." "This is the bread which came down from heaven, he that eateth of this bread shall live for ever." But sacramental bread doth not come down from heaven, but from the earth; neither hath it power to give eternal life to its eater, and therefore is not the bread here spoken of, for this bread is heavenly, and giveth eternal life to the receiver.

Again, the eating of the flesh of Christ, and the drinking of the blood of Christ, cannot be understood of sacramental eating and drinking, because they here speak of present eating and drinking in the fulfilment of the Jewish Passover-supper, and the ending of the law of ceremonies, for "he came to fulfil the law and the prophets." To eat Christ, to drink Christ, to feed on Christ, to dwell in Christ, are uttered in a figurative sense in many parts of the New Testament, and thereby give us to understand, that Christ is our spiritual meat and spiritual drink.

Again, when Christ's hearers murmured at his sayings, as hard and not to be heard, Christ corrected their fleshly imaginations, and informed them that by these similitudes of outward and carnal eating and drinking, he understood and intended that which was inward and spiritual; and that it was the import of his whole discourse on the subject that "It is the Spirit that quickeneth; the flesh profiteth nothing: the words that I speak unto you, they are spirit and they are life."

Again, to put it out of all doubt, that his kingdom was to be understood of inward and spiritual communion, and not of sacramental eating, he adds, "But there are some of you that believe not." "Verily, verily, I say unto you, he that believeth on me hath everlasting life. I am the bread of life." It was the unbeliever that could not receive these sayings, and it is the unbeliever now that mistakes them, and either with the papists asserts a corporeal or real presence—an eating and drinking of the real flesh and blood of Christ as manifested on the earth; or, with Calvin and Wycliffe, reject the doctrine of transubstantiation, yet admit a real spiritual presence of Christ in the bread and wine; or, with Zuingle, look upon the bread and wine as the signs and symbols of Christ's absent body. These conflicting opinions have been a bone of contention ever since the second and third centuries. when the "Catholic Church" amalgamated Christianity, Judaism, and Heathenism into one heterogeneous mass, and called it the "Catholic Church."          ·

How opposed this doctrine of the different churches is to the code of doctrines laid down in the New Testament, wherein God provides for us a way of escape from sin, in his own free pardoning grace, through the sacrifice of his Son, Jesus Christ, our Lord —it has been our sole aim to set forth in this history; as God hath appointed this sacrifice, in its nature propitiatory, as the means of atonement and reconciliation, and hath therein at once displayed his mercy to sinners, and his judgment upon sin. This pardoning of sinners for Christ's sake is our justification.

It has been a humiliating task to expose these popish mummeries! But respect for our holy religion has induced the desire that these drivelling inanities were banished from the world, and God and man raised to their true dignity; and that man would cast from him those swaddling bands of superstition with which he has been bound. This is our high calling—this is our heavenly mission.

In those sublime and instructive conversations which our Saviour had with his disciples a short time previous to his sufferings, he has shown that the great purpose of his mission was to reveal the way of truth, and to establish a spiritual communion and communication with himself and the Father through the Holy Spirit, for our help and direction in the way of righteousness :—

"I will pray the Father," said Christ, "and he shall give you another Comforter, that he may abide with you for ever ; even the Spirit of truth ; whom the world cannot receive, because it seeth him not, neither knoweth him : but ye know him ; because he dwelleth in you, and shall be in you. I will not leave you comfortless : I will come to you. Because I live, ye shall live also. At that day ye shall know that I am in my Father, and ye in me, and I in you. These things I have spoken unto you, being yet present with you. But the Comforter, which is the Holy Ghost, whom the Father will send in my name, he shall teach you all things, and bring all things to your remembrance, whatsoever I have said unto you." (See John xiv. 16-26.) "I am the true vine, and my Father is the husbandman. Every branch in me that beareth not fruit is taken away : and every branch that beareth fruit, he purgeth it, that it may bring forth more fruit. Abide in me, and I in you. As the branch cannot bear fruit of itself, except it abide in the vine ; no more can ye, except ye abide in me. I am the vine, ye are the branches : He that abideth in me, and I in him, the same bringeth forth much fruit : for without me ye can do nothing. But when the Comforter is come, whom I will send unto you from the Father, even the Spirit of truth, which proceedeth from the Father, he shall testify of me : and ye also shall bear witness, because ye have been with me from the beginning." (See John xv.)

The necessity of keeping up this communion, in order to the production of truth, is beautifully set forth in the parable of the vine and the branches ; comprehending everything that can relate to salvation or the knowledge of God. The declarations are decisive, and as they are elucidated by the apostles, become further confirmed. The manner in which the apostles have reasoned on the operations of the Spirit, and declare its effects, clearly shows that to it they attributed their conversion and progress in the Christian life.

The Apostle Paul declared that, "a manifestation of the Spirit is given to every man to profit withal." This shows its general intention with respect to mankind at large. And the many extraordinary gifts he enumerates had the same tendency, by an unusual display of Divine power, to strike conviction to the minds of the most unenlightened, as well as to remove the opposition and prejudices of the Jews and Pagans, who had become so much attached to the ritual law, and philosophical paganism drawn from the idealistic systems of Greece and Rome, and the mystic theosophy of Oriental philosophers, that it was with difficulty they could admit the evidences of a religion so pure and spiritual as Christianity.

Our own experience teaches us how slowly we admit an outward fact, when the mind is foreclosed against it. But the true Christian feels the Spirit of truth reproving him for his evil thoughts and deeds; and constrains him to aspire after greater purity of life; and humbles him under a sense of his weakness and imperfections; and having this feeling, he knoweth that it exists, and that he receives it not of man, neither by man, but by the revelation of Jesus Christ; even though it may be difficult or impossible for him to define the exact way of its operations to those who are indisposed to acknowledge the same influence or the same religious truth. And why? "Because the natural man"—the unregenerate man – the unsanctified man— "knoweth not the things of God, neither can he know them, because they are spiritually discerned." Nevertheless, good thoughts are often suggested, and heavenly affections enkindled and inflamed in the hearts of the faithful ones—these are often prompted to holy actions — drawn to duty — persuaded — quickened in such a manner, that he would be unjust to the Spirit of God, who would question its agency. Hast thou never felt Him, my reader, like another soul in thy soul, actuating thy faculties, exciting thy graces, purifying thy passions, exalting thy views of a redemption in Christ, and begetting in thee an abhorrence of sin and a love of God and holiness? Is not this feeling an argument of God's presence as truly as if thou saw him ? This is to eat Christ's flesh and drink his blood—to dwell in Christ—to live by the Father, the Son, and the Spirit—and to partake of the sap of the vine of Jehovah's own planting, and to experience the new birth of the Spirit, and in the new birth a new life ; and in the new life a new sense purifying their souls in obeying the truth through the Spirit. This is not a doctrine of mysticism—but practical piety. Oh, may all embrace it !

# APPENDICES.

## APPENDIX A.
### (p. 12.)

As regards the fall, Pelagius held truly, that the disobedience of Adam and Eve had changed their position from blessedness and purity to sorrow, and a degree of estrangement from God; and that the subtle temptation of Satan had led them, and continued to lead their descendants, into sin; and that the example they had set to their children made sin against God familiar to them, and this from generation to generation. But Pelagius differed widely from Augustine and the Catholic Church in regard to the posterity of Adam having Adam's sin unconditionally imputed to them. He believed it utterly contrary to the teaching of Christ and his apostles, who addressed every man as accountable for his own sins, and not as being doomed to unconditional punishment for the sins of others. Pelagius also differed widely from Augustine and the Catholic Church, by not imputing either a sanctifying or spiritual life to the rite of water baptism, as maintained by Augustine and his church. Yet that Pelagius did not believe in the communication of a Divine life through Christ, is a thought not to be entertained for a moment.

While the recognition of a divine life, according to Augustine's view, and redemption from inherited sin in the predestined, is effaced through the rite of water baptism, Pelagius, on the contrary, not only ignored the doctrine of inherent sin from Adam, but also redemption from it through the baptismal rite, as dishonouring to God; and maintained that it was only they who, knowing God's will, obeyed it, who could be saved, as God's elect. This we believe to be the great characteristic difference between the Pelagian and Augustinian or Catholic doctrines; and this arose out of the two great roots, "unconditional predestination, and the damnation of the unbaptized in the Catholic Church."

We apprehend that Theophilus Gale has fallen into the same error as many of the fathers of the "Catholic Church," respecting the opinions of Pelagius, and his being overwhelmed in so many monstrous errors, as these errors are much more applicable to Augustine than to Pelagius, as may be proved from many authors of Ecclesiastical history: namely, Cyril of Jerusalem, Basil, Gregory of Nazianzen, Ambrose of Milan, and Chrysostom of Constantinople, &c., &c., &c. While thus writing, I am not unmindful of the admonition, " Busy not thyself in searching into other men's lives ; the errors of thy own are more than thou canst answer for ; it more commends thee to mend one fault in thyself, than to find out a thousand in others." But, at the same time, I feel it incumbent upon me to declare, that the whole of the Christian religion lies in this : " Faith in Jesus Christ is the means of salvation, the Gospel the source of light, the Spirit of God our guide, the love of God our law, heaven our home, eternal life our end." Therefore I am bold to write in the defence of truth.

---

## APPENDIX B.
### (p. 17.)

Foremost among the Pagan clergy was placed, under the name of Sovereign Pontiff (See Alexander ab Alexandro, Genial, book ii., Titus Livius, and Plutarch), the visible head of the religion. This Sovereign Pontiff received even the name of the Deity, as Virgil informs us. (Virgil, Eclogue 1.) We are willing, however, to suppose that he did not pretend to be God himself, but merely the earthly representative of the God of Heaven, who was known among the Romans by the name of Jupiter, and among the Scythians by that of Pope (See Herodotus, book iv., 59), an appellation which, though thus primarily peculiar to the deity, was wholly transferred to the person on earth, invested, in the minds of the heathen, with the chief religious authority, who was hence commonly known among the Romans by the name of Papa or Pope. (See " Pagan Rome," pp. 7 and 8, by Thomas Pyne, A.M.)

In order to give a fuller idea of these pagan Roman pontiffs, we cannot do better than cite, verbatim, an author of the age to which we refer. " They possess," he observes, (that is, the sovereign pontiffs possess,) " an absolute authority even over matters of the greatest moment ; for they are judges in all causes relating to sacred things, as well between private individuals as between the magistrates and the ministers of the gods. They establish new laws by their sole authority, on points in which none have been prescribed. They have the right of inspection over all the priests, and generally over all those who hold the higher offices in the sacrifices and ceremonials attached to their gods, and if they see any disobedient to their commands, they punish them at their discretion." (See Dionysius Halicarnassus, "Roman Antiquities," book ii., and "Pagan Rome," pp. 9 and 10.)

## APPENDIX C.
### (p. 25.)

About A.D. 84 Paganism reigned almost alone in the metropolis of the Roman nation. Scarcely were any true Christians found amidst its immense population. A demoralization the most frightful and universal accompanied the idolatry at this time; and what will appear strange, the more immoral were the people, the more they were attached to their pagan religious rights. (See "Pagan Rome," p. 5.)

Between the rites and ceremonies of heathen worship and the popish church there is a close resemblance. The paganism of ancient Rome, in the second and third centuries, exerted its influence in their introduction into the Catholic Church at Rome and Carthage; and the paganism of modern times looks upon them with something of friendly recognition, both in the Church of Rome and the Church of England, &c., &c. But these things find no authority in Scripture.

## APPENDIX D.
### (p. 30.)

The Council of Trent has given the following definition of a sacrament :—" A sacrament is a thing subject to the senses, and possesses the power of signifying sanctity and justice, and of imparting both to the receiver." (See "Catechism of Coun. Trent," cap i., q. 8.) The application of the word "sacrament" to baptism and the eucharist is not sanctioned by remote antiquity, for the expression "sacramentum" was first employed by the Latin fathers as synonymous with mystery. But by the Tridentine definition of a sacrament, as by the whole polity of the Church of Rome, the distinction between justification and sanctification is completely obliterated. Justification is the act of God, the acquittal of our judge, the pronouncing of pardon. Sanctification is the process carried on in the heart of the discharged criminal, by which he is purified and perfected. The one removes the curse of transgression, the other removes its consequences. This the priests and the sacraments cannot do, it is God's work alone.

## APPENDIX E.
### (p. 31.)

Among the early superstitions which crept into the "Catholic Church," the use of "holy water" has been assigned to the year 120. But it is hard to conjecture for what purpose it could have been used at first, even in paganism. But it is well known that at a later period the followers of Christ and his Apostles had such an invincible horror of the superstition, which they linked with the heathen incense, and, as a consequence thereof, their bitter enemy, Julian, (see Gibbon,) caused holy water to be sprinkled over the meat and other food in the market, that they might be compelled to take it against their conscience, or starve. True it is, that in the course of time, it became a custom to bless the water used for baptism in the "Catholic Church," who had received the dogma from paganism, by mixing it with oil and chrism. This "blessed water" is also used on various other occasions. (See Elliott, "Delineation," p. 124.)

## APPENDIX F.
### (p. 36.)

In the second century, Justin Martyr, in his Apology addressed to the Emperor Antoninus Pius, and in the third century, Cyprian, treated of baptismal regeneration in such a way, that if it did not indicate confusion of mind in those who wrote, it was at least very likely to mislead those who read their writings ; and, indeed, these facts have often been appealed to by other authors, in proof of their having held the doctrine of baptismal regeneration. And about the middle of the third century, the North African churches generally received the notion that baptism was unconditionally necessary to salvation, from whence it spread into Greece, Egypt, and Italy, and more especially to Rome, Antioch, Alexandria, and Carthage.

---

## APPENDIX G.
### (p. 72.)

This entirely accords with Tertullian's Work ("Of the Military Crown, p. 337) in the third century, where he, in speaking on baptism, indicates that a spirit of self-righteousness and superstition had overwhelmed some, if not all the churches of Africa, and adds, " If thou requirest a law in the Scriptures for it, thou shalt find none. Tradition must be pleaded as originating it, custom as confirming it, and faith as observing it."

The doctrine of sacramental efficacy is as old as the second century, and, as it gained strength, gradually brought dimness and darkness upon the gracious and saving truths of the gospel in after times. This doctrine is precisely the same in substance as the polytheistic notion which prevailed so extensively in Rome, Greece, Egypt, Africa, and Italy, and which ascribes a mystic, but real, virtue to the observance of religious rites, and is the germ of all idolatry and priestcraft.

---

## APPENDIX H.
### (p. 79.)

The first Christians held that the heart was purified by faith ; the accompanying symbol, water, became by degrees the instrument of purification in the " Catholic Church." Hence, holy baptism, as it was called, was at first preceded by a vow, in which the young convert expressed his consciousness of spiritual truth ; but when it became twisted into a false analogy with circumcision, the rite degenerated into a magical form, and the Augustinian notion of a curse inherited by infants, in consequence of original sin inherited from Adam, was developed in connection with it.

# NEW WORKS,
## RELATING TO THE SOCIETY OF FRIENDS.

Library Edition, with Portrait, 8vo, 2 vols., 14s.

## MEMOIRS OF STEPHEN GRELLET,

EDITED BY BENJAMIN SEEBOHM.

*Friends wishing to take a number of copies for distribution, will be treated with on liberal terms, on application to the Publisher.*

---

Fcap. 8vo, cloth 1s. 6d. ; paper cover 1s.

## MY MOTHERS' MEETINGS,

Being familiar conversations with my Cottage Neighbours.

### BY ELIZABETH BENNETT.

---

Demy 8vo, price 6d.

## QUAKERISM : CATHOLIC AND EVANGELICAL.

---

Fcap. 8vo, cloth, 2s.

## ADDRESSES AND PAPERS

ILLUSTRATIVE OF CHRISTIAN PRINCIPLE OR TESTIMONY,

Issued within the last fifty years, by or on behalf of the Yearly Meeting of the Religious Society of Friends.

EDITED BY JOSIAH FORSTER.

---

Crown 8vo, cloth, 5s.

## JOURNAL OF THE LIFE OF JOSEPH HOAG.

Containing his Remarkable Vision.

---

Demy 8vo, with Portrait, cloth, 10s.

## THE LIFE AND LABOURS OF GEORGE WASHINGTON WALKER.

(Of Hobart Town, Tasmania.)

BY JAMES BACKHOUSE, AND CHARLES TYLOR.

---

Third Edition, cloth, with Photographic Portrait, 1s. 6d. ; paper covers, 8d.

## THE SABBATH SCHOOL TEACHER.

A Memoir of RICHARD E. TATHAM.

BY JOHN FORD.

---

London :  ALFRED W. BENNETT, 5, Bishopsgate-street Without.